Marilyn Ellner lives in a three-hundred-year-old town in Southern Illinois with her husband, teenage son, and two college student daughters. She has two dogs, a Saint Bernard and a Pomeranian, as well as a kitten. She credits her writing ideas to being a salon stylist/owner for over 30 years. She loved listening to her clients and their crazy stories so much that she would put a 'what if' twist to the tales…which led to creating stories of her own.

Marilyn Ellner

ALI AND ABE

AUSTIN MACAULEY PUBLISHERS™

LONDON • CAMBRIDGE • NEW YORK • SHARJAH

Ordering Information
Quantity sales: Special discounts are available on quantity purchases by corporations, associations, and others. For details, contact the publisher at the address below.

Publisher's Cataloging-in-Publication data
Ellner, Marilyn
Ali and Abe

ISBN 9781643781457 (Paperback)
ISBN 9781641828291 (Hardback)
ISBN 9781643781570 (ePub e-book)

Library of Congress Control Number: 2020918564

www.austinmacauley.com/us

First Published (2021)
Austin Macauley Publishers LLC
40 Wall Street, 28th Floor
New York, NY 10005
USA

mail-usa@austinmacauley.com
+1 (646) 5125767

I wish to first and foremost thank God and my dad for giving me the strength to move forward. To my husband and babies for supporting me on this adventure. I would also like to thank Diane, Mary, Carrie, and Tina for the push. God bless you all!

Chapter One

How does one deal with an outspoken mother-in-law? Lana Mason has asked herself that question many times over the last few years. Today was no different. She shook her head calmly and shot the older lady a look that stated 'please…enough!' Unfortunately, Ellie didn't make eye contact with her daughter-in-law. She was too busy looking around the room trying to size up her next victim.

Lana wondered, for the hundredth time, why her salon clientele returned to her after the way Ellie verbally tossed her thoughts and words at many of them over the last few years. The elderly lady had definitely lost her filter as she aged. In a town of only a few thousand, Ellie has understandably earned the title of 'mean old lady' by many.

Lana would like to blame it on a medical condition that made Ellie lash out at people, but she knew it was just Ellie being rotten. To anyone meeting the lady for the first time, they saw a sweet little grandma with her frail frame and wrinkled face. Yet if one looked closely into her aging blue eyes, they would see a witty, almost devious glint, deep inside.

In the first ten minutes of sitting in Lana's chair for her Friday morning 'weekly do,' Ellie insulted one of the eight people patronizing the upscale *Mystique Salon*. After she finished the insult, she turned her maliciousness to one of Lana's employees…and it didn't stop there. Shortly after upsetting the stylist, she found a third party to embarrass!

Insulting only two of the eight clients probably didn't seem like a big deal in most towns. But it was if that town was as small as Ramona, Illinois! Ramona populated about three-thousand people and any negativity could spread like wildfire on a dry day. Losing just one client could cause a hit to your wallet and your reputation. Lana learned years ago that when a client was happy, they would spread good words about the establishment to a few people, but when they were unhappy, they loved to tell everyone who crossed their path!

Which is why there are rules at *Mystique*. Her biggest rule, if you don't have anything good to say then say nothing at all. This worked for her employees, but controlling the client's words, or in this case a witty mother-in-law, was always a different story. Ellie, in her elderly age, felt she had the privilege to speak her mind. If she didn't like someone, they usually knew it. Even the people she favored had to hear her opinion of what she felt were their flaws. Lana didn't think she purposely tried to hurt anyone, she just wanted them to point out their flaws so they would fix it. Ironically, she usually spoke what everyone else thought, but was too afraid to say because of hurt feelings. In some instances, when she didn't like a particular person, she laid it out with no filter.

As was the case with Jena Caine, the client in the chair next to Ellie. Lana guessed Jena didn't like the results of the bright red hair color she insisted her stylist put on her hair. Jena's eyes showed panic and anger. She was, in a loud but hushed tone, letting her stylist know she wanted her old color back. She was implying it wasn't at all what she asked for!

Of course, Ellie wasn't helping matters. Looking over at the younger woman she stated that the twenty-three-year-old was never going to find a man with that red hair...unless he was a fellow circus clown. Lana wasn't sure which was worse, pointing out that she looked like a clown or that she was in need of a man.

Lana silently agreed with Ellie that the color was not very flattering to Jena's pale skin and brown eyes. Her usual blonde highlights and caramel lowlights was much more flattering to her coloring than the red. It took a unique skin color to pull off red and Jena didn't have the correct coloring. Yet it was Jena who insisted on the color.

Lana knew Ellie's backhanded remark was out of complete dislike for Jena. Jena was notorious for being a spoiled brat and for saying and doing hurtful things to many people. Lana felt that Jena acted the way she did because she came from money and in her mind that made her more privileged than others.

Her family owned a chain of small banks throughout the Southern Illinois and Northern Kentucky area. Jena, the VP of loans at the Ramona Branch, felt the title gave her a license to treat everyone as if they were beneath her. It was sad that Jena was so malicious. Her personality made her a very unliked person around town.

To look at Jena for the first time, one would think she was attractive. Well, before the red hair anyway. Her normal blonde hair was full and mid-length. Her face was very pretty with big brown eyes and a full mouth. Her cheekbones were high and her face narrow. She was average in height and her body was slim and toned, due to the personal trainer she spent a fortune on every week.

Sadly, once a person got to know the VP, it didn't take them long to realize what kind of a person she was and that usually took away from anything attractive about her. Lana always believed that being kind made a person happy, while being nasty to others made their life full of anger and drama. Yet it seemed Jena was never going to understand that. She preyed on hurting people. Lana knew this firsthand by the way Jena treated Lana's daughter, Ali.

Lana looked back over to see Jena still glaring at her stylist. Regan looked back at Jena with frustration. It wasn't Regan's fault that Jena looked like Lucy. Jena had insisted on the color and Regan did what she could to discourage it, but Jena wasn't to be discouraged. She apparently read that Bright Fuschia Red was the 'in color' and because she was 'in' she had to have it. Now, realizing the look wasn't for her, she acted as if it were Regan's fault. Regan's day was going to be backed up because she was going to have to do what she could to make 'Miss High-Maintenance' look like she did before the red!

Lana sighed, then there was mother-in-law Ellie to deal with. Ellie just couldn't zip it. After her verbal attack on Jena, she turned to Regan and asked her what made her think a color like that would work on Jena. Implying that Regan wasn't a good colorist. So now because of Ellie's second insult, Regan became even more frustrated. Lana knew she had to take a hold of the situation before it got out of hand. Regan was her best colorist and the last thing she needed was Regan walking out on her, not that she thought she would, but you never know when someone has had enough.

Ellie justified her action because she made it no secret she thought Jena should frequent any other shop in town but *Mystique*. Ellie believed Jena only patronized the salon because she wanted to keep tabs on her granddaughter, Ali. Jena had a deep dislike for Ali. Ellie felt that out of all the stylists in Ramona, Jena patronized Ali's best friend, Regan, because she wanted to dig up dirt on Ali. Not that Regan ever gave Jena any dirt because she would never tell her friend's secrets. Plus Lana was pretty sure Ali didn't have any juicy secrets.

Ellie was only partially correct about Jena's intent. Jena came to her salon because it was the most elite in town. The clientele who frequented the salon had class and wanted to look their best and that was what you got when you came to *Mystique*.

Lana couldn't get Ellie's rollers in fast enough. Just when she thought Ellie was done with the insults, she made eye contact with a client across the room, Becky Black, and asked her when her baby was due because she looked like she was ready to pop! While that type of statement wouldn't insult the average pregnant woman…too much, it would if the woman had delivered her baby four months earlier. Which was the case with Becky! The distraught lady excused herself and ran into the bathroom.

Ellie smiled at Lana's mortified expression staring back at her in the mirror. Lana was sure Ellie knew Becky had her baby a few months ago because they talked about it last week. Ellie may be old, but she remembered everything.

Lana was sure Ellie felt Becky deserved that remark. Becky happened to be a bit malicious herself. She was the type that spread hurtful lies around the small town. She tried it several times in the salon. Her stylist, Dan, never fed into it. Yet sometimes the other clients did, which aggravated Lana to no end. Just because you heard it here didn't mean the employees were the ones spreading it. When the clients were seated in the waiting room or under the dryers, plenty of tales were being told.

Lana almost groaned out loud when she spotted Ellie's nemesis walk through the entry doors. Ugh, she thought, was today the day to be bombarded by the evil women of Ramona? Lana looked at the clock, wishing the day would fly instead of the slow ticking of the moving hands.

So now Madelyn Maple, Ellie's absolute least favorite person and the town gossip, struts into the salon area and plops down on the chair in front of Bobbi's station. It was to Lana's misfortune that Ramona's town gossip chose *Mystique* instead of one of the other five shops in town.

Madelyn was truly the biggest gossip in town. She lived to hear tales and spin them out of control. Tongues were going to be wagging once Madelyn hears from the other clients about Ellie's escapades today. Of course, only an exaggerated version was going to be spread around quicker than wildfire to anyone who listened. Not that Ellie's insults needed to be exaggerated.

Lana could give or take Madelyn. She and her family have been on the receiving end of Madelyn's gossip too many times to count. Which was why Ellie disliked the woman.

Madelyn's stylist, Bobbi Bates, owned the shop many years before selling it to Lana a few years back. Bobbi continues to do hair in the salon as an employee, so it wasn't really polite to ask Bobbi to ditch the lady. Especially when Lana had a 'No-Filter Ellie' as a client.

Lana didn't know what to do about her seventy-eight-year-old mother-in-law. She didn't want to hurt her feelings, but having her in the salon with other clients was going to hurt her business. Sadly, as Ellie aged, the sharper her barbs became.

Changing her appointment time to a quieter, less busy, time wasn't an option because Ellie insisted on the 10:00 AM Friday morning spot. Of course, she couldn't ask the other eight stylists to not make appointments during that popular time. Especially when it would be easier to just move Ellie. Besides, Ellie liked to drop in so there were never any guarantees as to who would be in the shop when she stopped in.

Demanding her mother-in-law to stop harassing the clientele wasn't an option either. Ellie always explained that if you can't be truthful to people then you aren't truthful to yourself. Lana wasn't really sure how being truthful had anything to do with being hurtful. Plus no one demanded anything of Ellie. In truth Lana didn't push the subject because she loved her as much as she loved her own mother. So she really didn't want to be at odds with the lady.

Lana was relieved that the only other person at the dryer area was Regan's other client, Sue. Ellie didn't know Sue, so the lady should be safe from Ellie's remarks. Or at least Lana hoped.

Looking around confirmed none of the other stylists had anyone ready for the dryers. It was just good business to isolate Ellie while she was in that area. She hoped it stayed that way until her hair was dry and ready to fix. Ellie tended to shout when she was talking to anyone while under the dryer because the dryer noise made her think no one could hear her.

Looking at the front door as the bells alerted, there was a customer walking in, Lana's frustration came to a halt when she spotted her beautiful daughter Ali stepping over the threshold. Ali had promised to stop in sometime today because her school had a holiday and there was no first-grade class for her to teach. Lana let out a sigh, this was just the distraction Ellie needed.

It was amazing to Lana, the transformation on Ellie's face, from spiteful old lady to sweet elderly grandmother as Ellie looked up and noticed her granddaughter's entrance. The bond between the grandmother and granddaughter was very special. Yet opposites they were. Her daughter had such a warm heart and a sweet demeanor...unlike her instigating grandmother who let everyone know what was on her mind.

"There's my Ali Cat!" Ellie shouted from under the noisy dryer. Ali Mason smiled and winked at her mother as she passed her to get to her grandmother.

"How's my sweet Granny Ellie?" she asked as she raised the dryer lid and kissed the elderly lady on her wrinkled cheek before lowering the lid.

"I'd be better if you'd come out to see me more than just for Sunday supper at your momma's house!" Ellie shouted.

"I know Gram, I've just had such a busy school year!" Ellie was leaning in toward her grandmother's ear so she wouldn't have to shout the way Ellie was. "There's so much going on with the year coming to the end in a few months. Plus I've been crazy getting everything ready for my trip to Nashville, next week, for the teaching workshops. But after that I promise we will get together and have a night on the town. Maybe dinner and a movie."

"Hell with that, I think we need a night of booze and hot men!" Ellie shouted. Ali threw back her head and laughed. So did most everyone in the shop. With the exception of Jena, who was being re-colored, and Becky, who finally returned from the bathroom and was getting her haircut with Angie. Of course, Madelyn rolled her eyes and stuck her nose in the air at the remark.

Ali loved her grandmother. She loved her spunk too. "Granny, I do believe you are correct. Us single girls are going to have to take an evening and kick up our heels, do some dancing, and pick up some hot guys!"

"Ali Lynn," her mother scolded from across the room. "Do not encourage her. She will hold you to it. And the Good Lord only knows what would happen if you and her hit the town."

Ali just laughed. She really should probably take her out on the town. She just wasn't sure she could keep up with her granny. There's been a few times she spotted the elderly lady tossing back a bottle or two. Granny liked to make what she called her 'Home Brew Wine.' Ali tended to believe it was more like a moonshine of sorts.

Ali walked away from her granny to give her mother a kiss on the cheek. "How are you, Momma?"

"Good, Baby Girl!" Lana said as she looked at her beautiful daughter with such pride in her eyes. Ali was the third of her six children. She was also the only daughter. Which, as far as mother/daughter relationships went, no two could be any closer.

Looking at her daughter was the same as looking into a mirror of her youth. She realized Ali resembled what she once looked like, only Lana refused to believe she was ever as beautiful as her Ali. Yet Ali believed she would never be as beautiful as her mother. When in reality, to most people, they were a stunning combination.

When Lana was younger, she was almost identical to what Ali looked like today. Ali's eyes were a dark green, and had a cat-eye slant to them. Her eyelashes were dark and long enough to be considered rare. Her face was flawless with her pert nose, full lips, with soft dimples when she smiled. Her cheekbones were high, yet soft, accentuating a light olive complexion that rarely used the slightest bit of makeup. Her eyebrows had the perfect shape with a little help from her momma and some hot wax.

Lana may be a bit biased but she thought her five-foot-eight-inch slender-built daughter was model perfect. Everything was well proportioned. Her breasts were full but not overly. Her waist was narrow, yet slid into a slight curve down toward her hips. She even had dainty feet for being a girl that tall.

Lana, being a stylist, loved her daughter's beautiful raven-colored hair that had a hint of red. It was long, but not overly long, as it fell several inches past her shoulders in big, soft waves. She had a slight swept bang with a soft angle around her face. Ali's hair color wasn't found in a bottle, it was all natural. Lana only trimmed it and the Good Lord blessed her with the rest.

Lana felt as most mothers felt, that her daughter was the most beautiful daughter in the world. Eyes turned when she strolled down the street. Men and boys of all ages took a second look when Ali was around. Almost every little boy in Ali's first grade classes have declared they were going to grow up and marry her one day.

What added to her appeal was that Ali didn't believe herself beautiful. She felt she was passably pretty, but never noticed when men gave her appreciated glances or truly ever believed when her friends commented on her appearance. When she looked in a mirror, she just saw Ali.

Lana had been the same way in her youth. She never realized her beauty and is very glad she didn't. Because Lana's grandma would always say 'You are only beautiful until you think you're beautiful...then you're just arrogant.' Thankfully arrogance didn't have room in her daughter's life...confident she was...arrogant she was not.

Ali did have an unlucky spot though, it was men. She was a good girl, and like most good girls she was looking for Mr. Perfect. To Lana's knowledge, Ali has had only two romantic relationships ever. High school sweetheart Todd Evans and college sweetheart Seth something-or-another. Both lasted a couple of years and Ali did the ending both times. Lana was glad her daughter was smart enough to take her time and have patience when it came to trying to find that special guy. There was no settling for Ali. She was holding out for that one to sweep her off her feet. She confided in her mother once that she'll know him when she meets him.

"Is Gram stressing you out today?" Ali asked with a sheepish grin on her face.

"You don't know the half of it!" Lana stated as they both snuck a peek at the older lady who was fast asleep under the dryer.

"What did she do now?"

Lana explained quietly what went on before her daughter walked in the door. Ali raised her eyes as she looked around the salon at Ellie's victims. Both ladies looked like they survived the beating...barely. It made her smile a little to hear about Jena, but was bummed for her friend, Regan, to have to deal with it. Ali looked at Jena's reflection in the mirror and thought about all the crap the other girl has put her through over the years. Ali never knew exactly what she did to warrant the anger. It started with dating a boy, but deep-down Ali felt like it was something more.

Ali tried to get along with Jena, but it didn't take long to see that there was a nasty streak in her. Jena had to be the leader of every situation. Had to be class president and date the most popular boys. She liked to spread lies about other people and get everyone to hate her victims. She was doing things with boys way before everyone else. Rumor had it her parents were friends with the school administration and they controlled who got cut from certain teams and who got the best roll in theatre. Jena had star positions in several theatre/sport teams she wasn't very good at. Many suspected it was because her parents called in favors to the administration. Jena was just mean and would go to any lengths to make life hell for anyone who crossed her.

It just so happened Sophomore year Ali became her next victim. Her problems with Jena began when she started dating Todd Evans. Todd was a sweet, handsome, popular, middle-class boy from Ramona. He wasn't a jock, but definitely a well-liked guy at Ramona High.

Jena decided she wanted Todd, aka Ali's boyfriend, and she was determined to have him. Ali always wondered if Jena truly liked Todd or did she just not want Ali to have him. The shrewd girl did everything to break them up. She snuck in his bedroom window to try and seduce him…only to find his grandmother was in town and was using his bedroom for the weekend. She started rumors that Ali was messing around with a senior. She tried to get the majority of the school to hate Ali. Fortunately, for Ali, most of their classmates were sick of Jena and her antics, to believe anything that came out of her mouth.

In the end, it didn't matter because by their senior year, Ali realized Todd wasn't going to be her forever. There was something missing. Something out there she didn't quite find with Todd. So they broke up. Todd was heartbroken but eventually forgave her before she left for Kentucky State University the following summer. Todd went away to school in Chicago to become a lawyer. Shaking her head to erase the memories, Ali looked away from Jena's profile before Jena could catch her staring.

Looking around, she smiled to herself. She always loved her mother's salon. When she was a young girl, she would hang out here as much as she was allowed. She was even a shampoo-girl in her early teen years.

The salon was a large open building. The receptionist's desk was the first thing you saw when you walked through the doors. The waiting room was off to the right of the entrance with a coffee machine and tons of magazines to be read by the waiting customers. Retail shelves sat to the left of the entrance.

Behind the receptionist, were nine stations. All occupied except for one. This station had a cute car-chair that was used for smaller children to make their haircuts fun.

The decor was done in mauves and yellows. The lighting was bright and clear to help all clients get a good look at their hair services. The salon offered facials in the rooms at the back of the building, and of course eye-waxing, pedicures, and manicures could be done at the salon as well!

Ali's favorite part about the salon was that not only did her mother own it, but her best friend, Regan, worked for her mom as a stylist. When Ali came to visit, she got to spend time with both. "You know, Mom, you can always ask Dad to have a talk with Granny?" Ali added, "She is his mother!"

"I know honey! I just don't want her upset with me. At her age, I don't want something bad to happen and bad feelings left in the air'"

Ali knew her mother loved her mother-in-law. Ali looked at her seventy-eight-year-old grandma and thought about what a lovely woman she was. She definitely aged well. Many older men in the small town always explained to her that Ellie was a hot dish in their day.

Her silver hair was once a beautiful natural blonde. Her eyes were still a stunning electric blue. She was wrinkled, but you could still see the beauty she had been at one time.

Ali also heard from the older men how Ali's grandpa, the late first Frank Mason, was a rogue before he met his Ellie. Yet Ellie had him on his knee begging for a wedding. Her grandparents had a beautiful life after that, raising two kids and many grandchildren. Frank passed away several years ago and Ali knew her grandmother missed him dearly.

"I can see where your hands are tied. I'm just glad she doesn't embarrass me. But then again, I don't embarrass easily. The best I can say is every time she speaks have someone run a loud dryer," Ali said with a laugh.

Lana sighed, "If only that would work."

Ali was still grinning as she walked over to Regan's station. Her friend was returning from placing Jena under a dryer and retrieving another client who's timer when off while in the dryer area. It was probably a good thing Lana decided Ellie's hair was dry enough and moved her back to her station, before Ellie could start back in on Jena, who was in the dryer next to hers.

"So you and granny drinking on the town?" Regan asked, with a raised eyebrow, as she started curling her client.

Ali grinned. "Yep, do you want to come?"

"Not on your life!" Regan grinned. "But then again...maybe." She grinned. "It might be fun just to watch you patch up every insult she spits out!"

Ali grinned. "I'm not finding that idea appealing! Sadly, she'd probably drink us under the table and have us married off before we were sober enough to know any better."

"This is true," Regan said laughing.

"Seriously, we need to get together as soon as I get back from Nashville."

"That sounds good. Even though I wish I were going to Nashville with you. When do you leave and come back?"

"I'll leave Monday morning, since it's only a two-hour drive. It runs through Thursday afternoon. Kris wants us to stay an extra night so we can do the whole music-row thing." Kris was the second-grade teacher at Peak's Landing Elementary School in Kentucky, where Ali taught first grade. "The workshops start early and runs most of the day. So no going out until Thursday afternoon. I think we are heading to Tootsie's that evening."

"Are you guys riding together?" Regan asked.

"No because her grandmother isn't doing well. So if she needs to leave at a minute's notice, she will be able to."

Regan, all five feet, two inches, reached up to give her best friend a hug. "Okay I know I won't get to see you before then, so have a great time and text daily."

Ali hugged her back and assured her she would. She really wished Regan could go with her to Nashville. They would have had a great time. Yet this was a work trip, not play, and Regan coming down for just a night wasn't really worth the time.

Ali went to say her goodbyes to her mother and grandmother. After hugs were being given and a promise to be early for their weekly Sunday supper, Ali headed for the door. Her grandmother stopped her by shouting her name as she approached the doorway. "Ali dear, what you need is just a good old-fashion tumble in the hay with some hot and handsome boy!"

Ali, along with everyone in the salon, looked at Ellie. After processing what her grandmother said, Ali's face turned red and she didn't know what to reply. Looking around she noticed many clients trying to hide their smiles and shocked expressions. Jena was openly smirking.

In all of her twenty-three years, she had never been more mortified. Which was her own fault, she thought, as she quickly made her exit, for boasting to her mother that her grandmother never embarrassed her!

Chapter Two

Who would believe shaving a face was the same as freedom? Abraham Parker…that's who! Abe smiled as he said goodbye to his personal barber at the front door of his apartment before going back to the bathroom. Abe looked again in the mirror and ran his hand over his soft, clean-shaven face and grinned. The short haircut looked good also.

It wasn't that he was being vain. Abe just needed a disguise and removing four inches of beard and six inches of hair was the way to do it. "Yep," he stated to the image looking back at him in the mirror. "Barber Dan was good at what he did."

Deep down he knew that soon it wouldn't matter that he shaved or cut his hair short. In time the disguise wasn't going to do the trick. Hell, for all he knew it may not work this time. That worried him because he needed to be 'normal' for a few weeks.

He felt freedom and peace of mind came less and less every day. When he signed up for this life, he truly had no idea how suffocating it could be with the paparazzi and fans. It worried him because he was starting to feel the burnout that came with the hoopla. He was second-guessing if going to the top was worth it in the end.

It was by his own doings that he was where he was, so he shouldn't complain. Ironically, he truly never believed that his voice would have him climbing the charts and making him one of the country's biggest rising stars. Sadly though, his real story was like that sappy country song that sold hits and paid the bills. Abe was blessed he did get a break and he is where he is today.

In hindsight he was glad he followed his agent's advice in the beginning and became "bad-ass scruffy," as per Max's words. Looking like a grade school boy at the age of twenty wasn't going to cut it. So while he was recording an album, month after month, he grew out the hair on his head and face, got some scruffy clothes, and looked the rough and tough part.

Unbelievably, it worked! Abe was climbing the charts while women threw themselves at him, and men thought he was as cool as hell. His music was upbeat, yet dug deep inside a person. He had a few hits climbing the charts.

One a ballad, the other a get up and move beat. It was the life many dreamed of.

He didn't dislike the lifestyle, he just wished it would slow down a bit. He needed to feel normal sometimes. A break from people asking if they could get him this or do that for him. He couldn't stand the hovering. He missed hanging out with his buddies and watching Sunday football. Or having a home cooked meal at his mom's, with his sister. He hated feeling like he has to give up one life to have the other.

Which is why when he got a two-month break from the business, all he had to do was shave his face, get a haircut, and no one was the wiser. Most fans and paparazzi didn't look for a clean-cut, boyish-looking Abe Parker.

Not that Abe planned to be anywhere near the paparazzi and fans during his break. Well, it wasn't really a break. He was going to be in the recording studio for most of that time. Then he planned to spend some time with his mother and little sister…some much-needed normal-family time. He and his friends planned to get together during the break. His buddies knew what it meant to him to have some norm in his life, so a BBQ at one of their houses was the plan.

First he had to test out his new face. After calling his driver, clean-cut Abe headed out the door leaving behind scruffy Abraham. There would be no testing the waters at his apartment complex. The security staff would never acknowledge anything. It was their job to see and hear nothing and to let no one in. Besides, they'd already observed the transformation over the few years Abe lived in the apartment.

His first test would be on his agent Max. Max has seen his shaved look the few times he went into disguise, but was always startled by the transformation. He was waiting for Abe at the dressing room he used the night before at The Grand Ole Opry Theatre.

As a rule, Abe would just jump in his pickup and head over to the theatre, but it was pre-arranged by Max to have a car and driver waiting to take Abe home after the performance. It was better to have his driver pick him up at the high security loading zone then to be confronted by screaming fans. Today, however, he had to head back to the lot to get his truck. It worked out because Max needed Abe's signature on a few papers and Abe had to get his keys from his dressing room.

After showing his pass to get through security, he found Max in the dressing room he used the night before. Abe watched for his friend's reaction to the cut and shave. Max did a quick double take then acted as if he wasn't surprised. Abe chuckled because he knew he fooled his friend.

"You had no idea!" he stated as he leaned against the doorframe.

"BS!" Max exclaimed. "I'm so used to you I would know if you dressed up drag."

Abe chuckled. "Right, admit I got you again?" His tone was in fun as he started signing the papers Max tossed his way.

"Hardly! I bet when you go out into the big bad world today everybody will see right through that pretty-boy look."

"I don't think so."

"They will! And do you want to know why?" Max questioned with a grin, "Because you, my friend, just scored another number one on the CMT charts this morning!"

Abe grinned. It was a good feeling to know the fans loved his songs. The song Max was referring to was a favorite of his. It was about things happening for a reason.

The song touched him in a personal way because he didn't always understand why things happened the way they did until the entire scene played itself out. He felt it all started when his father died in a car accident on his way home from work when Abe was sixteen and his sister was thirteen. His heartbroken mother had to pack up the small family ranch and sell it. She found a job and moved into the downtown Nashville area so she could clean hotel rooms while he tried to take care of his sister.

He believed, in his heart, that his father directed him in the direction he took. Abe's father loved to sing, not that he ever wanted to perform on the big stage. He just picked around on his guitar and had some sitting-around-the-house kind of guitar fun. He also taught his son to sing and play. Never once did he imply that Abe could be famous, but in death Abe wondered if he didn't guide him in that direction.

"My thanks goes to you, Max." Abe meant it. Max, like Abe's father, contributed to Abe's fame. Abe's father in the spiritual sense, while Max in the physical sense. If Max hadn't found him five years ago, he would never be where he was today.

Max was a great guy. At thirty, the tall, lanky, brown hair, clean cut, nice-looking, father of three, has accomplished more than most people Abe knew. He was also good at what he did…making people stars. Yet Max was more than an agent, he was a friend.

Tossing Abe the keys, Max grinned at his friend, "Don't forget the recording studio at 7AM sharp. And I hope your disguise works, buddy, because if not, you are going to have a plenty of screaming fans chasing you. Then you may have to dress drag!"

"I already have my phone alarm set. I'm making it an early night. For now, I think I'll stroll on down to the gift shop and see if I cause a stir or not." Abe stated as he followed his friend out the door.

"Good Luck. Pick me up a postcard while you're shopping!" Max chuckled as he turned to the employee parking lot in the back.

***

Ali was still simply amazed as she walked around the Gaylord Hotel in Nashville. Her fourth day here and she was still absolutely awed by its size. Never had she stayed in a hotel this large. As a rule, her parents took their family on vacation once a year when she was younger, but the hotels they stayed at were never anything as elaborate as the Gaylord.

Part of the hotel was under an atrium that housed thousands of plants and flowers. There were so many walkways it was easy to get turned around and even lost. Waterfalls were also throughout the walkways.

As crazy as it seemed, there was even a small boat ride that floated around in a small stream that ran through the atrium. Ali felt like she couldn't get enough pictures of the little hidden world under the atrium.

The one thing Ali promised her friend, Kris, was that she would get a picture of The Grand Ole Opry Theatre. Kris and Ali had a great time being roommates for four of the five days they were in Nashville. That was until late this morning when Kris got word that her grandmother's health took a turn for the worse. So she left immediately, while Ali finished up the finale of the workshop. She was glad it was done and over by lunch, but now she didn't know what to do with herself.

Ali decided to walk down to the theatre that sat next to the Gaylord. She hadn't decided if she should go home tonight or leave in the morning. The plan was for her and Kris to have a fun evening hanging out downtown before going home the following day. She was really looking forward to doing just that, but didn't wish to do it alone.

Ali was amazed at the beauty of the front of the theatre. Even though she wasn't a country music fan, she appreciated the style and charm of the building. She took the pics she promised Kris and checked out the gift shop inside the entrance. While there, she purchased a small replica of the building to pass on to her coworker since she didn't get to see the actual building.

Back outside, Ali decided to sit on a bench and enjoy the beautiful late March day. If there was one thing she loved, it was people watching. She figured it was from all the years of hanging out at the salon. As a child she would play a game with the stylist. She would try to guess everyone's story that patronized the business. She would then reveal her guess to their personal stylist and see if she was correct. Once in a while she hit the nail on the head other times she was so far off she made the stylist in the backroom laugh pretty hard.

The theatre was closed for the day with the exception of the gift shop. She figured that was why there weren't many people around on such a beautiful day. Mostly it was elderly sightseers occupying the gift shop and the benches sitting out front. She was sure the weekends had people crawling all over the place.

To her surprise she spotted a very handsome young man walking out of the gift shop alone. By the way he hesitated as he looked around, she assumed he was probably looking for his wife and kids or maybe a girlfriend. When he turned in her direction, Ali quickly looked away, not wanting to be caught staring. As she started scrolling through the pics on her phone, pretending to be busy, she wondered if he was as good-looking as he appeared at a distance.

Ali got her answer a few minutes later when she saw a set of cowboy boots appear in front of her. She jerked her head up to stare at the occupier of her thoughts and 'yes he was definitely good-looking!' Ali told herself to act calm…quickly. Taking a deep breath, she smiled, "Can I help you?"

Abe smiled. It didn't appear as if the stunning brunette sitting in front of him recognized him. If she did, wouldn't she be all star-struck? Or trying to snap a pic. Maybe even pulling out a pad of paper or asking him to sign her shoe?

She appeared to be the youngest person sitting outside, that was the reason he approached her. Everyone else at the gift shop was either blind or half senile so it was hard to know if they recognized him or not. If anyone was going to recognize him, he assumed it would be someone a little closer to his age. It didn't hurt that she was beautiful, so he didn't need much encouragement to approach her. He decided to test her further to see if she seriously didn't recognize him or if she was playing a game.

He started off with a big, flirty grin and some serious southern accent. "Hello pretty lady. Mind if I have a seat?" Ali wondered what sane girl would say 'yes she minded.' Mentally clearing her thoughts, Ali smiled and scooted over on the small bench to make room for him.

"So what's a beautiful girl like you sitting out here by yourself?" Abe asked with extra dimples and more sexiness to his southern drawl.

"Is that a pick-up line or are you just being polite?" she asked as she lifted an eyebrow a bit.

"Can it be both?" he asked. He was fairly certain she had no clue who he was, but just to make sure he continued with another question. "Are you hoping to catch a glimpse of some famous country singer and get their autograph?"

Ali smiled. "No, I'm not the country music type. I actually came here to take a picture of The Grand Ole Opry for my friend."

At his 'you have to be kidding' expression she continued with her hands up, "I know, I know, I'm probably the only girl in the Good Ole USA who isn't into country music. I think it's because I look at life in a happy way and I think country music is kind of depressing."

"Don't you think that's stereotyping a bit?"

"Maybe. I mean there are a few songs that I like if I hear them but for the most part I'm a pop kind of girl." Her smile turned into a thoughtful frown before she continued. "Actually the music my life refers to at this moment is Barney and Sesame Street." She chuckled.

Abe realized that she just implied she was a young mother. It shouldn't have bothered him after only just meeting her, but he found that it did. "A boy or a girl?"

Ali gave him a strange look before realizing what he was asking. She laughed and shook her head. "No, I don't have any children. I'm actually a first-grade teacher."

Abe felt his body relax and his disappointment instantly evaporate. Her laugh was sexy. Hell, she was sexy. Not the type that were always throwing themselves at him, but that 'I want to take you home and keep you' type. Wow, he wondered, where did that thought come from?

"Married?" he dared to ask.

She smiled and shook her head. "You?"

He shook his head as he became lost in her smile. She was absolutely beautiful. Just in the few minutes they conversed, he was mesmerized. It could be because he hasn't been able to sit around and have a conversation with a beautiful girl that he wasn't wondering if she liked him for him or just for his fame.

"Good, the name's Abe." He smiled as he offered her his hand.

She took his hand and looked in his soft, light green eyes and smiled. "Ali."

"Well Ali, so what's a pretty girl like you sitting out here by yourself?" he asked again with a grin.

"Well Abe, I was actually sitting here people watching."

"What are you watching...Cocoon." Referring to the 1980s movie where elderly people were trying to find the fountain of youth.

Ali nudged his shoulder with hers. "That's not very nice." Smiling she added, "I was thinking Golden Girls."

Ali's heart melted at his deep masculine laugh. What a funny guy. In the few minutes he was in her company, she picked up on his charming, witty personality, and realized she liked him. It didn't hurt that he was incredibly handsome.

His stance was exactly what she was attracted to. He had to be as least six feet tall, with slightly broad shoulders and a thin waist. It was easy to see, through the cut of his jeans and white T-shirt, his body was used to working out and exercise. His face had a nice brown color, not sunbaked, but just a nice natural tan look. His nose was long, narrow, and straight. She swore his lips were becking hers to taste them. They were the perfect kissable kind. His sandy-blonde hair was cut short and messy on top. She thought about how Regan would probably love to run her hands through that full head of hair. Not that Ali would let that happen. This man was everything a girl dreamed of and nothing she ever saw in real life. At least not in Ramona, Illinois.

"So what's a guy like you doing in a place like this?" she asked. "Are you hoping to run into Dolly?"

He chuckled, "So you do know some country?"

"Really…who doesn't know Dolly?"

Smiling, he replied to her earlier question. "I actually had to meet a friend that sometimes works here. I was just on my way out when I spotted a beautiful girl sitting by herself on a park bench. So I thought I would see if she was in need of any assistance."

"Oh darn, did she leave you?" she asked, looking around innocently, before nodding in the direction of an elderly lady sitting on a nearby bench. "Is that her?"

Looking in the direction she nodded, Abe started laughing. "Yep, she looks like she's in need of assistance, don't you agree?"

Ali giggled as just then an older gentleman sat next to the lady. "Darn, I think you missed your chance."

Abe looked her in the eyes and stated, "I hope not."

Ali actually blushed. She said the first thing that came to her mind to make the sexual tension go away. "So you said you met a friend that works here. Does that mean you are from Nashville?"

Abe quickly decided he needed to be vague with his answers. He didn't want her to know who he was yet. He loved the norm he was feeling. He loved that she wasn't star-struck by him. "I actually grew up outside of Nashville, but we moved to town when I was sixteen. We, as in my mom and sister also."

"What about your father?" At his sad look she touched his arm. "I'm sorry, you don't have to answer that. I was just curious when you didn't mention him."

23

Abe looked at her and realized that he wanted to tell her about his father. Oddly it was almost like he wanted to confide in her things he never shared with anyone. He also didn't want to dampen the mood so he gave her the basics. "My dad died in a terrible accident that involved the interstate, a semi-truck, and some black ice. That was nine years ago and the reason we moved away from the family farm and into town." To avoid discussing that dark time of his life, he asked her about her family.

She felt him withdraw a bit and could respect that. So instead of asking more questions she answered his question. "Well I was born, raised, and still living in a small town in Southern Illinois. I, like you, was raised on a farm." She looked into the distance and thought about the best way to describe her family. "My parents are in their fifties and they are still as crazy about each other as they were when they first met."

The love she felt for her parents was written across her face. Her smile was warm and her eyes sparkled when she talked about their love. He always held great memories of his parents so it spoke volumes about this beautiful girl's breeding. There was no pretense in that look. There was no resentment about what a poor childhood she had. There was just a happy kind of love look. Abe wanted to kiss her there and then.

To change the subject, he asked, "Siblings?"

Her whimsical smile immediately turned to a mischievous smile. "Five."

"Wow. So what number are you out of the six?"

"Third." Her grin grew before finishing. "And the only girl."

"That's cool," he stated, before it dawned on him what she said. "Really?" he asked, looking at her closely to see if she was teasing him.

"Yep...and all of them are about as tall as you."

Smiling at her he asked, "Are you trying to scare me away?"

"Maybe," she stated and she looked away. Wondering if she should lead him to believe she was interested or not. She was definitely attracted to him, but they lived two hours apart. Plus he never implied he was interested. Before she could chicken out, she turned her head back to him. "Or maybe not. I guess it would depend if you get scared easily or not."

Abe was enjoying the flirting. Over the next hour they laughed and shared stories about themselves. He really didn't want the afternoon to end. He didn't want to leave her just yet, but he found he was awkward when it came to asking her to dinner. Which was funny in itself due to the fact that he had thousands of women throwing themselves at him daily. Yet Ali seemed different. She seemed real.

"Did you drive here?" he asked as he nodded toward the parking lot.

"No, I actually walked over from checking out the Gaylord." She purposely led him to believe she was just visiting the Gaylord instead of informing him she was staying there. Something told her he was trustworthy, but common sense said always keep your guard up.

As they both stared ahead, there was a quiet calmness that settling over them. She found it awkward, he found it peaceful. Several minutes passed when Abe looked at his watch. "It's almost five," he stated.

Ali looked at him and said, "I'm sorry if I kept you away from something."

It was now or never for Abe. "Actually, I don't have plans for the evening and I'm sitting here trying to figure out a way to ask you to have dinner with me tonight."

Chapter Three

It was insane and so out of character for Ali to even think it was alright to go to dinner with a complete stranger, that she just briefly met, while visiting a strange town all by herself. To say yes was against every rule she was ever taught. This type of situation is what probably causes many girls to be abducted. Yet she felt safe with him.

Abe could see the hesitation in her eyes, which just confirmed what he believed earlier. She wasn't the fast type that was into hookups or one-night stands. He knew she was enjoying their time together as much as he did. He could tell she didn't want it to end, but she was hesitant about going off alone with a complete stranger. So to make it easy on her he suggested they walk back to the Gaylord and dine there. It was a safe bet for both. She wouldn't be getting into a car with him and the odds of being recognized at a hotel this large and busy was hopefully slim.

Ali agreed that dinner at the Gaylord was an excellent idea. She decided she wasn't going home tonight considering she had a dinner date. She was very reluctant to leave Abe's company anytime soon.

As they stood and made their way to the hotel, Ali asked, "Have you ever been to the Gaylord?"

"As crazy as it sounds, I can say that I have never been. I guess if you live here, you wouldn't have a reason to stay at a local hotel."

"Well, you are in for a treat. This place is magnificent."

"So what's your favorite part?"

She thought for a moment. "I think it's all the little bridges."

"Seriously, there are bridges in a hotel?"

She smiled. "Not like big bridges. They just have these cute little walkways...I'll just have to show you."

They walked through the parking lot of The Grand Ole Opry to the Gaylord. Ali had to jump to avoid a puddle of water. Abe reacted, when she slightly stumbled, by grabbing her hand to hold her steady. He took advantage of the situation and kept her hand in his.

Ali smiled inward as they walked through the entrance of the Gaylord. His hand was strong, slightly rough, and it sent tingles up her arm when he first grabbed it. Yes, she definitely liked holding it.

Abe admitted the Gaylord was a bit overwhelming, but definitely the place to be. The hotel was huge. People were all over the place following paths, walkways, and of course Ali's bridges. They were indeed bridges. They were all over the trails that led to so many different rooms. He was lost and decided it was just easier to let her lead and he follow.

The view was incredible as they walked through a doorway that led to a huge atrium. Flowers, trees, and plants were perfectly placed to give the look of a botanical garden. Walkways went in every direction. Waterfalls and benches were around every turn. He thought of his grandmother and how she would have loved the gardens. She had owned the title of horticulturist but she always said it was just a glamour word for playing in the dirt.

"Impressed?" Ali asked, smiling.

"Very much! I can't believe this was in my backyard and I never knew it. I was just thinking how much my grandma Ana would have loved this place." Ali could see the love he had for his grandmother in his smile. She too loved both her grandmothers. So it spoke volumes that he thought so much of his.

"Would have...as in she's gone?" Ali asked.

"Yes, she died a few years back. She was my mom's mom. She owned a nursery in a neighboring town outside of Nashville. After she passed, my mom didn't want to see it closed down so she sold it to Gram's right-hand worker. The nursery is still booming today."

"Then what does your mom do?"

"She owns a small boutique downtown. It's one of those places that sells girly things like jewelry, clothes and all that stuff you girls like." Abe was proud of his mother Sandy. When his father died nine years ago, she was heartbroken. Yet, she knew with two kids at home she couldn't wallow around in self-pity. She was also smart enough to realize she couldn't afford to stay on the sixty-acre ranch she and her husband shared. It wasn't a large farm, but enough farming for Abe's father Greg to get his farming fix in. He worked a forty-hour job during the days and did his farming on the evenings and weekends...and of course his son followed him around taking it all in.

Ali started to ask him the name of the boutique but Abe was tugging her hand when he spotted the Delta River Flatboats. Like a little child he grinned at her and walked over to the ticket window. He purchased two tickets and got in line. It was just their luck that they got a spot on the next boat going out. Once they settled into their seats, Ali felt Abe put his arm around her shoulder. She was so content right at this moment.

Abe was content also. More content than he had been in years. So far no one recognized him and he was hanging out with a beautiful, charming woman. It was nice that in the last few hours he hadn't thought about his tour, his recordings, his career life for that matter. With this girl, he thought a lot about his past.

Ali snuggled into the crook of his arm thinking about how just a few hours earlier she was sitting on a park bench contemplating going home. Now here she was taking a small boat ride that drifted along a makeshift river in the middle of a hotel, with an extremely handsome man that she was wildly attracted to. This was so out of character for her that she'd bet Regan was going to have a hard time believing her story.

Ali turned to look up at him just as he looked down at her. Their eyes met. Ali took a quiet deep breath because she knew he was going to kiss her when she noticed him looking at her mouth. Both leaning in, they knew they were going to finally taste what they wondered about only minutes after meeting. Each anticipating the wonder of their lips meeting.

Their answer came as their lips touched. Soft, lightly moist and yet electrifying. The tingling sensation went through both their bodies. It took their breaths away, making them want more. He used his tongue to nudge open her mouth. She gladly obliged him with wanting to feel him as well.

Abe only slid his tongue across hers before quickly pulling back ending the kiss. He stopped because it felt so good and they were in a public place and the extra attention was the last thing he needed.

Ali turned forward also realizing this was not the time or the place. Taking a deep breath, she was aware how her palms were damp and her body was shaken. She had never been affected so much by a kiss or by a man. She was afraid to feel. Could there be something here? Could he be what she was looking for? Hell, she knew nothing about him, only that he could seriously break her heart. Crazy considering they met only hours earlier. The Good Lord knew she was never this spontaneous.

Abe helped her out of the boat as the ride came to an end. He once again kept her hand in his as they walked along the paths of flowers and plants. Each smiling at a little girl with long curly dark hair, about four years old, bending over and smelling a flower. The little girl looked at her mother and said, "Yum…smell good!"

Ali and Abe made eye contact. "How adorable," Ali said.

"I know. I bet you looked like her when you were little." He ran his hand softly down her hair and stated breathlessly, "But now you are all woman, with hair still beautiful dark, curly, soft…just beautiful."

Ali's breath caught as his voice sounded so sexy and sensual. Shaking her head out of his trance she replied, "I was told I was a spitfire as a child."

"I can see that," he exclaimed.

"Do you like children?" Ali wanted to take the words back as soon as they came across her lips. He probably thought she was hinting at their children and already planning their wedding in her mind.

Abe's first thought was 'I'd like yours.' It scared him that his thoughts were spinning in that direction. He always felt he'd one day have a family, live on a ranch, just like the place he grew up. Sadly, in the last five years he thought less and less of that considering his occupation.

"I figure one day I'd have a few running around, wearing me out, worrying me to death that they'll grow up to be just like me. I could handle about four or five...how about you?" he asked with a grin.

She stopped in her tracks and looked at him with huge eyes. "Four or Five...are you kidding me?" she exclaimed.

He rolled his eyes before grinning. "I know! Some people are into the big families. I'd like to keep mine small and quaint. You know how it is coming from such a small family like yours," he teased.

Ali decided to play along with his game. "Well, I'm not sure that I can have your babies, Abe, if all you really want is four or five. I am into the big family tradition. Especially coming from a family of six children I have to admit that I think that should be a minimal."

Abe did give her pause to see if she was teasing or not. The glint in her eyes said she was. "Alright six it is," he exclaimed as he tugged her hand to start moving. "If I'm going to have to raise a brood full of hellions, I think I'm in need of some dinner to build up my strength. So let's find somewhere to eat, lady."

They came across a steakhouse and were seated toward a table in the back. They ordered dinner and a couple of beers. Over the next hour they shared funny stories of their childhood. She told him about life with five brothers getting into one mess after another. Usually with her right in the middle of it.

He spoke of life on the ranch. His childhood friends and a pesky little sister. His face spoke of love whenever he mentioned his parents. Ali felt it said a lot about a person when they had no fear of showing that kind of emotion.

Abe kept the table conversation to a safer time. If he brought up the present, he was afraid she would start asking questions. He could be evasive without really lying. He just wasn't ready for her to know the truth. He liked that she liked him for himself. He felt he was being the typical 'poor me' famous person. The kind that wants fame but then cries about not having a normal life. Sadly, you just can't have both.

It really wasn't that he wanted the fame. It all came to him being eighteen and working at a bar while going to college. He was paying his way through school and not wanting to burden his mom who was trying to get her boutique off the ground and providing for a teenage girl. So he worked at a popular local bar as a barback/busboy.

Abe had a habit of singing along to the bands while he worked. His boss and coworkers would praise him when they caught him singing along. One night he and his boss where cleaning up after a slow winter weekday night. The jukebox was still playing from the money dropped in earlier. Abe was singing a Toby song, not aware his boss, Dale, was watching him. Dale told him that he saw real talent in Abe and asked if he played an instrument and Abe stated he played guitar. Not much more was ever said after that. Until about four months later Dale had a solo artist cancel during one of the lunch crowds. He cornered Abe and asked if he felt he could sit in. Abe laughed and said there was no way in hell he could do it. Yet Dale was convincing and within one hour, Abe was facing a small crowd of about ten people.

Abe, probably due to the small crowd, found he was completely at ease on the stage. It didn't take him long to get into it. After two hours on stage, no breaks because he chose not to, he realized that he liked singing for people.

To this day Abe wondered if Dale didn't plan it all…down to having him do a solo act twice a week and a music scout stopping in to watch his performance a few months later.

The scout hooked him up with Max and helped him pick out his band. Abe's life went non-stop ever since. He had fame, women throwing themselves at him, a gold and hopefully soon a platinum album hanging on the wall. And the added bonus, more money than he ever dreamed of owning sitting in the bank.

Yet with all the fame came loneliness. Lately he was feeling as blue as a few of his songs. He had no idea why the empty spot in his heart was surfacing so much lately. He always knew it was back there…he just never allowed it to come forward. Yet, in the past few months he couldn't stop it from surfacing. He was blessed and he didn't feel right asking the Good Lord for more than what he was already given.

He had a great home, wonderful mother and sister, and a dream career. He didn't want to jinx it by asking for more. Hell, he wasn't sure if he was even in a good place to find love. Did he really have time to pursue a relationship? It would take a hell of a woman to put up with the time and the bullshit that came with being involved with an artist on the road. Dare he believe that God would let him find love also?

So for right now he just wanted to enjoy Ali with her catlike eyes. He smiled at her. "Has anyone ever told you that you have cat eyes?"

Slightly blushing she replied. "Actually, my Granny Ellie calls me Ali Cat."

"Well it's appropriate, you have the sexiest eyes I've ever looked into." He gave her a sideways grin causing his dimples to pop out on one side.

Ali's blush deepened as she thought about those dimples, then his mouth. She knew she was being bold. She could probably blame it on the two beers she had, but all the beer did was relax her. She knew her boldness came from how comfortable she was with him. They only spent a few hours together and she felt like they've known each other for years. On the other hand, she felt like she knew nothing about him. It was such a strange combination. Maybe the beer was getting to her more than she thought.

Abe was becoming extremely aroused as he watched her staring at his mouth with desire in her eyes. "Little girl, if you keep staring at me like that, I may just embarrass us both and pull you on my lap and taste that wonderful mouth of yours again!"

At her blush, he grinned. "Are you ready to get out of here?"

She nodded but was sad to think their evening may be coming to an end. Abe paid their tab and they walked out of the restaurant. Ali wondered what he planned next. Was their time together over…or was it just beginning? She wasn't sure he knew she had a room at the Gaylord. She just stated earlier that she was parked at the Gaylord, not that she had a room. Would he want to walk her to her car? Should she tell him her room is down the next corridor? Would she be bold enough to invite him in?

So many questions! She was never the spontaneous type to toss caution to the wind and do something as crazy as sleep with a man a few hours after she met him. Hell, she had only been intimate with two guys in her entire life. Both being long term relationships. Yet she was seriously thinking about being spontaneous now. She was almost in a panic of what to do next.

Abe took the panic away when he spotted a saloon entrance. Turning to look at her he said, "This place is like a world inside of the world. They even have a nightclub." He smiled as he listened to the band playing a popular country song. Peaking in the entrance he was glad to see it was fairly dark inside. He was pretty sure no one would recognize him in the establishment.

"I know you are a pop girl, but do you want to give it a shot?" he nodded inside.

Anything to prolong her time with him worked for her. She nodded and went inside. Abe chose a two-seat table toward the entrance, away from the stage. The seat gave them a great view of the semi-crowded room and the large stage where the band was playing.

After ordering a couple beers Ali looked out at all the line-dancers dancing on the floor. That was probably one of the reasons she wasn't a big country music lover...she disliked line dancing. She was a get-up-and-shake-your-bootie kind of girl. Not a 'do as everyone else' kind of dancer.

Abe interrupted her thoughts when he stated, "I take it you are not into dancing?"

Ali smiled and looked into his beautiful eyes. "Not that kind! I guess since you are a Nashville boy, you know all the steps to these dances?"

"I know a few basic ones. Dancing isn't really my thing."

"So are you or aren't you into country music?" She gave him a confused look.

"I didn't know there was anything other than country. Are you suggesting otherwise to this Nashville boy?" he asked, with a heavy southern drawl.

"I wouldn't dare!" she said sarcastically.

Abe almost panicked when the band started to play his song 'Now Is the Time.' A ballad about a man who stumbled across his true love when he wasn't even looking for her. He sat back and relaxed. He chuckled at how startled he got when he heard the band playing his song. For a second he thought his charade unfolded. It went with the whole disguise thing...paranoia. He was relieved to hear the band do well with his song. Of course, most bands in Nashville were great. They were here, playing for tips alone, just to get recognized.

Ali watched him, smiled, and asked him what he was grinning at?

He stood and offered her his hand. "Would you do me the honor of dancing with me? Slow dances are universal for all music types."

She smiled as she gave him her hand and let him lead her to the dance floor. She stepped into his arms and let the music sway them. Their bodies melted together as one. She couldn't help but feel they fit together perfectly.

Abe was feeling the same. He wondered what it was about her that made him feel so content. Never in all his life had he ever held someone he never wanted to let go. It was so bizarre, these feelings that were spinning in his head.

Sure, he's had a few relationships in the past. Never over a few months long. He has also had a few hookups, but never has he been this wildly attracted to someone both in a physical and mental sense. The problem was he didn't know what he was going to do about it.

Holding her close, he let the words of love circle around them, his words of love written in the song he created. The song he actually wrote himself.

Somehow the words seem to fit what was going on with himself and the beautiful schoolteacher whose cheek was pressed to his chest.

He didn't know how to go about seeing where this relationship could go. He was climbing to the top. A place most people couldn't handle. Hell, if truth be told, a place he wasn't sure he could handle. Could he put her through the torture of fame? She wouldn't have a normal life. There would be no more teaching because he was sure there would be no peace in her life as long as they were together. It wasn't like she was a groupie. She had no idea what she was getting into. She wasn't asking for a star. She was just hanging out with an illusion of a normal everyday boy.

Sadly, he was selfish enough to ask her to change her life for him. To give them a try. She was exactly what he was looking for, only he didn't know he was looking for her until he found her. Abe and Ali…they even sounded good together. For now, he wanted to be ordinary old Abe. He didn't want to scare her away. He didn't think she was the type to be star-struck and fall for some rising star. Plus, he loved being this normal guy. Soon he would have to tell her. Soon he would go back to that guy that was climbing the charts. He really hoped Ali would climb with him.

The song was ending, Abe pulled back causing Ali to look up at him. He stared in her eyes a brief second and they both met in the middle as their lips touched. He loved the taste of her. She caused tingling throughout his entire body. With a soft nudge of his tongue, she opened her mouth to him. Their kisses deepened and their tongues mated with each other. He pulled her tighter to him as he deepened the kiss. She ran her fingers through his hair while her other hand gripped his nape. She pressed her body as close as she could just to feel as much of him that she could.

Abe, remembering where they were, made himself pull away and end the kiss. He stared at her half-closed eyes and her full mouth. She looked dreamy and he felt dreamy. He turned and walked them back to the table. Before she could sit, he asked her if she wanted to stay or go. She chose the latter. Abe paid the tab and led Ali out the door.

"Now what?" he asked when they entered the walkway.

She shrugged. Abe looked around like he wasn't sure which direction to go in. He turned to Ali. "I never asked, where are you staying? You said your car was here but is your hotel nearby?"

Ali hesitated. She looked into his eyes before answering. "Actually, I'm staying here!"

Chapter Four

He didn't know what to do or to suggest at that moment. His mind was racing. She was staying here. Should he keep the night moving? Should he walk her to her room? Did he tell her the truth before he asked for her number?

Ali felt like she needed to break the silence. "Yes, I have one of the rooms we passed earlier. It has a balcony that overlooks the atrium." Without thinking she took his hand and led him in the direction of her room.

Abe followed her. He didn't want to hope she was leading him to a night in her arms. He knew she wasn't the one-night stand type. He wasn't either. He never hooked up with the girls at his concerts. He had a few relationships in the past. Mostly with women who he knew from the business end of his job. They always kept it casual because they knew the business and where he was headed and understood there was no place for them in that part of his life.

Abe followed her through the corridor maze. Maybe she just wanted to show him what the nice little cottage-like rooms looked like. He was relieved when they finally stopped at a door.

Ali pulled her key card out of her back pocket. "Wait until you see how cute these little rooms are."

He had to hide his disappointment that he was correct on why she was showing him the room. He was impressed at the quaint two-bed hotel room though. He followed her out onto the balcony and looked out at all the paths they took in the last few hours. He wondered how many people observed the two of them from their balconies. The atrium had a soft glow of the evening lights making it appear all the more romantic. There were families with small children playing in the walkways. Couples were holding hands as they pointed out the many different things going on around them. Teenage girls were taking selfies to show everyone on social media. It was such a perfect scene for such a perfect day.

He looked over at Ali as she smiled at the scene before her. He was awed by her natural beauty. If he ever wondered what a gypsy looked like, he was sure it was her.

Grabbing her hand, she turned to him. "Ali, I just have to say that I have had one of the best days of my life." As they looked into each other's eyes they shared a smile before he continued. "I know we have some distance between us, but I really want to see you again."

Ali took his hand again and walked back into the room and closed it behind them. She turned to him and put both hands on the sides of his face. "I want that too," was all she said as she kissed him.

She knew what she was feeling. She knew she wanted to touch and taste him. She slid her hands from his neck to his nape. As the kiss deepened, her hands explored him. She felt like she couldn't feel enough of him.

Abe was afraid that she was going to stop once she realized it was getting out of hand. After a few minutes he pulled away and looked at her. "I want you?" It was a statement and a question. He needed to hear that this was what she wanted also.

"I want you too. I don't think I have ever wanted anything more." She stopped him before he started to kiss her. "I want you to know that this is out of character for me. I have never slept with a man I just met. To be honest with you, I have only been with two guys and both were long-term boyfriends. I want you to know that I'm not sure I'm very good at this."

Abe looked at her as he has never looked at another woman. She was worried he'd think she was easy and then she worried she wasn't good. There definitely was a difference between the experienced groupies and the good girls. "Ali, I am shaken with wanting you. I feel like a teenager all over again when I'm with you. I am so afraid that I will disappoint you and you may never want to see me again. Let's just pretend for tonight that we are both new at this." At her smile, he kissed her. The kiss was tender and there was something warm and calm, filled with promises.

As the kiss ended, Ali stepped away from Abe. She reached up to pull her shirt over her head. His breath caught as he looked at her flawless skin. So perfect the way her collarbones' lines pushed through softly as her full breasts, hidden under a sexy bra, promised to be the perfect size for her small body. Her tiny waist, stopping at her jeans. He longed to taste her everywhere.

He stared through passion-filled eyes as she unzipped her jeans and pulled them off. Her hips curved perfect and led to the long journey of never-ending legs. Those thin, muscular legs were what every man dreamed to have wrapped around him.

Abe didn't trust his legs any longer. She made him weak. He took her hands and pulled her to him as he sat on the edge of the bed. He moved her to stand between his legs. He reached behind her and undid her bra. He stared at her full breasts before he took his hands and caressed them, continuously rubbing his thumbs over her nipples. He was so aroused as her nipples hardened under his caress. He took one in his mouth to taste her. She threw her head back and moaned as her hand caressed his head.

He stroked her breasts, one at a time, his tongue sucking and licking her as he massaged each nipple. As her knees started to buckle, he grabbed her and lifted her to wrap her legs around him. As he tasted and teased her breast, she slowly rubbed herself against his waist needing to satisfy the urge growing between her legs.

Abe stopped for a second and wrapped his arms around her to slow her movements. He had to calm them down before he disappointed her and embarrassed himself. He wasn't even into it a few minutes and he almost lost all control. That hasn't happened to him since he was a teenager.

Lifting Ali from his lap, he gently laid her on the bed. She watched him through half-closed eyes, as he removed his jeans and shirt. She was awed by his beautiful body. He had to be an athlete, she thought. How weird, she never asked him what he did for a living. It definitely had to do with sports because a person couldn't be built like that if you didn't train all the time.

She took a deep breath as he pulled protection out of his wallet. Laying down next to her in nothing but his boxers he whispered. "You drive me crazy. I am going to try to take it slowly so I don't embarrass myself, but you do make it hard."

He kissed her hard and long. His hands touched her everywhere. Her hands couldn't feel enough of him. Within minutes they both removed the rest of their clothing. When she pulled his boxers off and touched him, she was almost alarmed at the size of him. She wondered if he would hurt her. She smiled and thought she would love for him to hurt her. She stroked him long and hard. She loved the feel of him in her hand.

Abe's mouth once again found her breast. He was awed by how big and hard her nipples got when he touched her. His hands moved lower. He rubbed the outside of her thighs. His hand going up and down her legs as his mouth found hers again.

The kiss was long and fulfilling and his hands moved to the inside of her legs. They massaged and teased coming close to her warm moist spot…but not touching the heart of her passion. He wanted her to need it, to demand it.

She did need and demand it. The urge was so strong yet so far away because he wouldn't let her have a quick release. She was almost in tears with the wanting of his touch. Abe had other plans. He wasn't going to touch her, he wanted to taste her. He removed his lips from her mouth before trailing his tongue past her neck, over the top of her breast, through her belly button all the way down to that hot moist spot he craved. He moved her legs apart as his mouth came down on the one little area that drove her mad. She shook her head from side to side and dug her hands in his hair. She nearly came unglued as his tongue licked and sucked her special place.

Her breathing came hard and fast and the pressure built up. Just when she didn't think she could take it any longer her release settled over her in quivers…again and again. Not once did Abe stop until he knew she reached her point and came back down.

He was so hard with wanting her. After a quick stop to put his protection on, he kneeled above her and wrapped her legs around him as he entered her. She was so sweet, so tight. He almost lost it then and there. He paused and tried to count to ten, but by the time he got to seven she was pushing hard and fast against him. He reached her hips and started pulling her to him. She met him hard and fast. They went from wanting to needing. He could feel her pressure build. He thought to go easy but she was having none of that. She pushed harder and faster. He met her thrust for thrust, over and over until she tightened her legs around him and held on while her body gave into another release. He let his come as well. It exploded over and over. He was finally completely sated.

He fell to his side, bringing her with him so they could stay attached. Their breathing was harsh and fast. The pumping of the hearts was way above normal and they didn't care. Neither one had ever experienced such complete fulfillment.

When their breathing got back to normal, Abe kissed her long and hard. He got out of bed and strutted to the bathroom in the raw. Ali didn't mind. She loved looking at him. She smiled and was so glad she didn't feel any regrets. He wanted to see her again. Those words made her happy. She knew he was feeling this crazy attraction also. What was happening just wasn't normal. It was a roller coaster and she was ready for the ride.

Switching turns in the bathroom, Ali joined him in bed a few minutes later. She was a bit more shy than him and had put on a robe.

Looking at the clock, she was surprised it was after ten in the evening. She snuggled closer to him after disrobing. Pulling the sheet over them Abe was surprised to find he wanted her again. He tried to drive the urge down. He was only protected one more time, having only two condoms in his wallet. He wanted to make love to her in the morning, so he really needed to cool it bit.

Ali wanted his touch. He was going crazy with her touching him. He kissed her long and hard. His fingers made their way between her legs. Her breath caught in her throat as he slid his fingers inside her. He stroked her over and over until she was so hot and slick. He slid his hot wet fingers onto the outside of her and touched that spot that drove her crazy earlier. He stroked her again and again. She surprised him by gripping the hard length of him and stroked him as he stroked her. In no time they both found their release. They both shook from it.

They found sleep not long after. A few hours later Abe made love to her again. It was as if he couldn't get enough of her. Ali warned him she was a heavy sleeper, but she had no problem waking to his touch.

In the early hours of the morning Abe woke to Ali touching him. At first, he wasn't sure if she realized what she was doing but he loved the way her body was laying on his, rubbing and touching him everywhere. "Good Morning." He smiled into her eyes.

She smiled. "Good Morning. What time is it?"

Abe looked at the alarm clock next to the bed. "Five AM."

"Mmmm," was all she said as he rubbed her groin to his. Stroking harder and faster. "Ali, I don't have any more protection."

He could hear her disappointment when she stated, "It's okay, I just won't put you inside me." She sat on top of him and rubbed herself against the length of him.

After several long agonizing minutes, he couldn't take it. "Please?" he begged.

She lifted up and slid him inside and rode hard and fast. She was glorious as he watched her ride him over and over. He knew the point when she found her pleasure. She threw her head back and her body shook with it. It almost done him in as he pulled himself out and found his own release.

By the time Abe returned from the bathroom, Ali was down for the count. She didn't even wake when he moved her over so he could lay next to her. Looking down at her, his heart hurt…a good hurt. It was crazy, but he truly believed he may have just found the rest of his life. His last thought before drifting to sleep was that of his father. Weird, but maybe Dad was creating destiny again for him.

***

An hour later, Abe woke to the sound of his alarm. Jumping out of bed he turned to shut it off. The sound didn't budge Ali. He smiled and remembered she said she was a sound sleeper. Looking at the time he realized he had to get moving. When he set the timer, he had plenty of time to get ready and get to the recording studio from his apartment. Not from across town with a hike to his truck and a trip to his apartment.

He quickly got ready. After gathering his belongings, he tried to wake Ali. She really wasn't budging much. Abe decided to leave her a note telling her he'd be back this afternoon. He knew she was here for some teacher-thing. He assumed it started today because she had been free yesterday. When people came to Nashville it was always for the weekend happenings. He decided to leave his number with the note just in case.

Rushing out of the room, he thought to put out the Do Not Disturb sign. He was sure she wouldn't want a maid walking in on her. Within minutes he made it to his truck and was on his way. He barely made it to the recording studio in time. With him came the idea of a new song he wanted to write. 'My Little Ali Cat!'

***

Several hours later, Ali woke to a knocking on the door. It took her several minutes to become aware of her surroundings. Realizing she was naked, she smiled and thought of Abe. She figured it was Abe at the door. He must have stepped out for breakfast and didn't grab a key.

After putting on her robe, she opened the door to find the housekeeping attendant, not Abe, standing on the other side. The worker informed her that checkout was thirty minutes past and the lady needed to get her room clean for the next guest. Ali apologized and promised she would be out of the room in a few minutes. As she closed the door, she started rushing around the room quickly. Upon taking her robe off and tossing on the bed, she didn't see the paper falling from the table to the floor between the bed and table.

Still groggy, Ali was packed and ready in fifteen minutes. As she made her way to the front desk, she let herself think about Abe. Where was he? Why didn't he leave her a message? She was still confused as she made her way to the front desk to check out.

While checking out she was still dazed. She had to check out under Kris' name because that was whose name the room was in. She asked the lady at the front desk if there were any messages for her? The lady informed her there wasn't. Ali walked away in a daze. She walked over to the nearest bench and sat down. She grabbed her phone from her purse and checked to see if Abe left her a message.

She almost burst into tears when she realized she never gave him her phone number. She still scrolled through it to see if he grabbed her phone to leave her a message. No message from him. She did have texts from her mother, Regan, Kris, and the mother of one of her students, yet nothing from Abe.

Staring at her phone she wondered if the last twenty-four hours didn't exist? Had she dreamt all of it? Did she just meet the man of her dreams only to have him disappear? What is his last name? Where does he work? Who is he? Was she just duped?

Oh dear Lord, she had sex with a total stranger and she doesn't even know who he is. Was he just playing her? What if he was a thief?

Ali quickly looked in her wallet and found everything was in order. He apparently wasn't a thief. Had she been played? Did he just sweep a girl off her feet and then use her and leave her high and dry?

An hour later she was too confused to think. She stood up and walked toward the exit. She walked to her car feeling numb. After putting her suitcase in the trunk, she sat in the driver's seat. 'What next?' she wondered. Looking at the beautiful Gaylord building she felt her first tear fall. She really believed in him. She thought he was the one. What an idiot, she told herself. You sleep with a guy the first time you meet him and you think he's going to want to take you home to meet his momma? She knew better. It's just that it felt so right.

She tried to remember anything he said about himself that would help her identify him. She wasn't sure why she wanted to identify him. He was a user...wasn't he? She just needed to confront him. She needed to see if what she felt was real or was she being used. There were only two things that led to his identity, his mom owned a boutique and he had a friend at The Grand Ole Opry.

She decided to head over to The Grand Ole Opry first. After parking the car, she headed to the gift shop. She paused as she looked at the bench where it all started. She made herself move on before she burst into tears. Walking into the gift shop she asked the elderly lady, working the counter, if she knew of a nice-looking guy named Abe. The lady claimed she didn't and didn't think anyone else there did. Ali was under the impression they were very private about the staff or anyone connected with the staff.

Back in her car, Ali gave up. She thought about going to every boutique in Nashville...which according to google were many. Yet deep down she knew that was a dead end. She didn't have a clue on how to ask if the owner had a son by the name of Abe. It just wasn't possible.

So with a sadness she had never experienced before, Ali headed back to Ramona. Completely given up on ever seeing Abe again.

***

Abe wasn't giving up. He was in a hell of a mood. He stared at his phone willing it to ring. Why hasn't she called him? What if he never got to see her again?

He couldn't believe the turn of events. This morning he was at the studio on time and sang his heart out. Everyone had been impressed. Mac even stated that whatever happened since he saw him last needed to continue because Abe was like a new man. Of course, his fabulous morning turned to crap fast. Returning to the Gaylord he realized he couldn't find Ali's room. He didn't think to look at the room number when he left in such a hurry. He went to the front desk and asked if there were any messages left for him. After being told there wasn't, he had to do some sweet-talking to the lady behind the desk in order to get her to help him.

Abe even had to use his fame to get her to agree. Once he pointed out who he was and wrote down Max's number with the promise of autographed souvenirs and free concert tickets, she agreed to help him. He told her he was looking for the last name of a girl he met the night before. After explaining her name was Ali, but he didn't have a last name, he asked if she could find one for him. It took the lady quite a bit of time because there wasn't a room number. She informed him there was no room booked under an Ali, Allison, or anything similar to that. She also informed him that the teacher's convention ended the day before and almost all the teachers checked out yesterday or this morning.

After walking around a few hours, in hopes of spotting her, Abe gave up. He decided to call for backup. Max met him at the hotel and they tried bribing the staff for information but came up short. Max came up with the plan to see if he could find her name with the Illinois Department of Education. Abe prayed Max could come up with something.

Sitting in his apartment that Friday night he wondered where she was and what she was doing? Did she think he left her? Did she even want to be found? He had so many questions. How do you hang out for a day and not ask for a last name or what town she lived in? Better yet, how do you sleep with someone and not know their last name? He knew it was because he was trying to avoid any questions about the present. If he asked some, he would have to answer a few of his own. It was his fault for not being truthful from the beginning.

He hated that he felt so unsure. That was such a rare feeling for him. Yet how could he help it? He was so worried she thought he deserted her. He wondered if he was ever going to see her beautiful face again.

Chapter Five

As the end of May approached so did the end of another school year. Children were excited they had to only attend school one hour and they were done until the middle of August. Ali was the summer fun type, but had to admit she was sad to see her first year as a teacher come to an end. It was bittersweet, but much needed. She had too much on her mind and needed to think.

Sitting at *Bo's Eatery*, waiting for Regan to join her for lunch to celebrate summer, Ali was close to tears. The depression she was feeling was almost overwhelming. She, for the hundredth time, thought about the last two months. She thought about the incredible night she shared with Abe. Abe whatever his last name was. Abe who never came looking for her. Abe who probably just used her and led her to believe it was some kind of love at first sight.

She smirked at the last thought. She used to believe in love at first sight. She also used to believe that when you meet the one there would be fireworks. Yet she knew the truth. Just because there were fireworks didn't mean there was true love!

Ali truly thought he would try to find her. Maybe he did and just didn't have any leads. The same problem she had. She googled his name but found too many to filter through. Seriously, Abe...aka...Abraham, was all over the web. To begin with, everything Abraham Lincoln popped up first. Next there was hundreds of Abrahams' in Nashville. When that came up a dead end, she googled all the boutiques in the area, but nothing connected to an Abraham. She even looked at nurseries outside of Nashville...found nothing. She almost believed he didn't exist...if her heart didn't hurt so badly.

Now she felt it was the time to come clean with her best friend Regan. Regan knew something was up since she came home from Nashville, but Ali wasn't ready to pour her heart out. She had to work through the shame and embarrassment of what she felt. Plus she had to deal with the hows and whys of what she did.

It helped that she became extremely busy at school. The children had to be prepared with the end of the year state testing. There were the assemblies, plays and the school carnival she was in charge of. Plus there were kindergarten and eighth grade graduation, which all teachers had to be present for.

Thankfully, as of a few hours ago, school was officially over for the school year. Now she had time to think, time to cry, time to make decisions. She didn't know how to go on. She didn't know what she was supposed to feel or do.

Ali looked up as Regan slid into the seat across from her. The booth had high backs, giving the friends more privacy to talk. Ali looked at her beautiful friend and had to blink back the tears. She was so glad she had Regan in her life. The sister she never had.

Regan looked at her friend and immediately took her hands in hers. "Al, honey what's wrong?"

Ali blinked back the tears before grabbing a menu. "Let's order first...okay?"

"Sure." Regan looked hesitant at her friend before grabbing a menu.

The pair of girls were oblivious to the looks they received from many of the male patrons establishing the place. One tall, beautiful with dark hair and beautiful green eyes and the other a petite blue eyed, blonde hair...tipped with pink dye, and dimples that made most men do a double take.

Located in the heart of Ramona's business district, *Bo's* was a popular hangout for the businessmen and construction workers remodeling the historical courthouse on the town square. Ali didn't necessarily want to meet in such a busy place, but Regan had about an hour for lunch and since the *Mystique* was within walking distance, *Bo's* was the place to go.

After giving the waitress their orders, Regan turned to her best friend. "What's wrong?"

"Well I've decided to come clean about what happened in Nashville." As she spoke, she blinked back any tears and decided she would save the tears for when she was alone.

"Good, you've put me off for two months telling me you would talk about it when you were ready. You have no idea what has all gone through my head." The worst thought that kept recurring was that her friend had been violated of some type. Regan knew that Ali was smart enough to go to the authorities if that happened. Which in this case would have been Nashville. She figured that Ali didn't want anyone here to know what she went through. Which they wouldn't considering Tennessee was two states away.

"I know and I am sorry. I just wasn't ready to talk about it. I had to work some things through." Taking a deep breath and exhaling, "But I'm ready now. I have to be!"

"Al, I'm warning you now, if someone hurt you or violated you in any way, I can't promise that I won't find the SOB and do him some bodily harm." Ali smiled at the five foot two inches of tiny and thought she was as good as her word. She could be a hellcat when provoked.

The two girls have been best friends since kindergarten. They sat next to each other at the same table. From the moment the teacher placed two boys at their table they had a mutual goal. They were controlling those boys…and they did. They showed girl dominance. The two boys never stood a chance. The girls have been best friends ever since.

"I wish you could help me find someone, but not for the reasons you think. I'm sorry if you were led to believe something terrible happened to me. I actually never thought for a second you'd think that or I would have reassured you that wasn't it."

"I probably should have confronted you, but I really did want to give you your space on this. So quit keeping me guessing…what happened?"

Ali's tears filled her eyes again. "I fell in love. Only I think I was played for a fool."

Regan took her hand and gently squeezed it. "What happened?"

Ali was so glad to finally be able to speak of it. She shared with her friend every detail, thought, and feeling she could remember about the day spent with Abe. She dabbed at her tears a few times but was glad they went away.

Neither paid much attention when the waitress sat their plates in front of them. Ali did pause in her story until the waitress left. Regan never asked a question until she was all done. She was actually stunned. To the best of her knowledge, her friend has never acted so impulsively.

"So he wasn't there when you woke up? Are you sure he didn't just run out for coffee?" When Ali shook her head and said she waited around for a long while and he never showed back up, Regan asked, "Was there not a message on your phone or a note anywhere? No last name given from either one of you?" Ali shook her head again. "That's crazy Al. We have to find him. He was probably trying to find you as much as you tried to find him."

Ali looked at her friend. She was so blessed to have Regan in her life. Her sweet friend didn't judge her. She actually was trying to turn this into a love story. Only after two months of hearing nothing, Ali was afraid it was more of a heartbreaking romance where the guy was a jerk. Even though deep down she didn't believe Abe was a jerk. She truly believed he felt what she had…but she would never know.

"Regan, I hate to break it to you but this story will have to have a different happy ending. There is no way I am ever going to see Abe again. I've given up. It's never going to happen because he disappeared into thin air." Looking off she sighed. "But I will say that it was the happiest day of my life. I never knew it could feel so beautiful between a man and a woman. I'm not just talking about the making love, but the hours before that. The getting to know one another." She smiled at the memory.

"Al, there has to be some way to find him, to make him a part of your life."

Ali looked at her long and steady. "I will have him always a part of my life and I don't just mean his memory."

Regan leaned forward in the booth and gave her friend a confused look. "Then How?"

Ali took a deep breath and let it out. "I'm pregnant."

Ali watched the shock register on her friend's face as she sat back in the booth. Regan was stunned. Ali knew everything was spinning around in her head because she too had that same reaction when she left the doctor's office before coming to the diner.

Regan smiled while tears filled her eye. "Al...you're going to be a mommy!" she whispered.

Ali, crying...whispered back, "I know!" Grabbing Regan's hand, she squeezed it.

"Now what?"

"I don't know. I just found out an hour ago. I suspected a few weeks ago but decided to put it in the back of my head so I wouldn't have to deal with anything until school was out. Last week when I was starting to panic, I made an appointment. I picked today, our annual 'Summer's here' lunch, because I wanted to tell you everything, including if I was or not. So now I guess I am going to have a baby!"

"What do you think your family is going to say?"

"I have no clue. I guess I will tell them at Sunday supper." Telling her family was what worried her the most. Her parents were wonderful and understanding people. She knew even if they were disappointed, they would be understanding. It was the five brother's she worried about.

"Al, can I make a suggestion?" At Ali's nod she continued. "I believe what you shared with this guy was something special. I'm not judging you, but you know this town can be tough. Your mom and I hear BS all the time at the salon. While it's a fact that we will show the door to anyone who has a bad word to say about you, I suggest to fabricate the story a bit. Only because you freak out whenever there is any gossip going around about you...hence why you always stay above the radar."

"What are you suggesting?" Ali was feeling more terrible by the second. She wanted to be the I-don't-care type, but Regan was correct. She hated knowing rumors would be flying around about her. Yet she was the idiot that hooked up with a stranger the first night she met him. So now she would have to live with her mistakes. Yet strangely having Abe's baby didn't feel like a mistake. She put her hand to her stomach and knew what she felt was happiness inside her…not a mistake.

"Okay so hear me out. Can we tweak your story a bit?"

Ali wasn't comfortable with lying. As a child, anytime she told a lie she would usually rat herself out. She wasn't good with living with the guilt of a lie.

"Go on." She was willing to hear her out.

"So instead of saying you just met the guy and…well…things happened, why not say you spent the entire time with him while you were in Nashville?"

"But Kris would know better. She was there the first three days."

Regan met Ali's coworker, Kris, a few times. She lived in Kentucky in the town of Peak's Landing where both Kris and Ali worked at the elementary school. Regan always like Kris. "Can Kris be trusted to keep a secret?"

"Yes, but I'm not sure I can keep up a charade," Ali said uneasy.

"It's really not a lie hurting anyone. It's just a lie helping you to not look like you sleep around." At her friends injured look, Regan continued. "I don't think you do but you know how this town is. Can't you see Jena Caine having a field day about this?" Regan went on at Ali's dreadful look. "So I think we should say that you have been seeing Abe for months. You met him online."

"Ugh…this is getting worse and worse." Ali moaned.

"I know, but we don't live in a big city where no one knows you or cares what you do. Ramona is notorious for gossip. So we have to have a plan. And I say you met him on the internet. He's from Nashville. When you went for that long week you got to know him. You both were crazy for each other. Say it went on for the next few months. Yet over time you realized a long-distance relationship wasn't going to work. He travels for his job too much and you never get to see each other. So then the two of you decided to take a break and shortly after you found out you are pregnant. Then explain that you guys are going to try one more time to make it work for the baby's sake."

"And when he never shows up…?"

"That's where it's no one's business. I can act like I've met him. That he comes here once a month. Then as your time comes near, he is just too busy because his job makes him travel a ton. Then we will say the two of you had a fight and you sent him on his way."

Ali thought about what her friend was saying. It did seem like a good plan. She just wasn't sure she could pull it off. She had so many thoughts running through her head she just couldn't make any decisions yet. "So do you think I should tell this fabrication to my parents and brothers?"

"If you want my opinion I'd tell Lana the truth, who in turn will tell your dad, but I'd let the boys think you and Abe have been together for a while and you just didn't tell them about him because they get all protective whenever you talk or date a new guy."

"I'll think about what you said. I just can't believe I am in this situation."

She noticed Regan looking at her watch. "Hey listen I know you have to get back to work." She grabbed her hand and squeezed it. "Thank You for always being my best friend. I'll call you tonight!"

They slid from the booth and Regan gave her a big hug. "I'm here a thousand times over. Love you and I'm buying lunch!" she said as she snagged the bill. "It's not every day I get to hear I'm going to be an aunt," she whispered with a grin.

"Thank you and love you too!"

Ali followed her friend out and got into her car. She put her head on the steering wheel and sighed…what was she going to do?

***

The following day Ali was waiting at the shop for her mother to get done with her final Saturday appointment. According to Regan, Lana was the last stylist working that day. Ali was glad because it gave her time to talk to her mother. Lana gave her daughter a hug after locking up and flipping the close sign.

"I'm so happy to see you. Give me a minute to clean up. Do you want to grab a coffee when I'm done?" This was Lana's routine for a Saturday. If there was time at the end of her day, she walked over to *The Coffee House*.

Ali nodded. She was nervous. That surprised her because her momma was her backbone. She was the mother that wiped her tears and would verbally shred anyone who tried to hurt her family. Ali just hoped she wouldn't see disappointment in her mother's eyes when she spilled the beans.

Lana could sense something was wrong with her baby girl. She knew something was up ever since she came home from her five-day trip to Nashville. Lana didn't want to pry. She knew Ali would confide in her when she was ready. She was glad the time was here. Lana didn't know how much more time she was going to give her daughter until she got to the bottom of what was eating her up.

After the station was swept, the hair utensils sterilized and put away, Lana grabbed her handbag and keys and followed Ali out the door. 'The Coffee Shop' was next door to the salon. As they walked in, Rita started making Lana's usual. Ali ordered a hot chocolate, knowing she was supposed to stay away from caffeine.

The warm spring day was so beautiful, mother and daughter decided to sit at one of the tables that lined the front sidewalk. To Ali's relief, it was after lunch so the place was empty. After taking a sip she looked at her mother and once again the tears started falling. She was aware that her hormones were out of whack and she resented the tears that kept falling because of them.

Ali looked into her mother's eyes and spilled everything about meeting Abe. When she got to the part about their night together, she kept looking at her hands because she was too ashamed to look into her mother's eyes. She looked up into her mother's eyes and told her about the creation she and Abe made.

Explaining about the baby was hard, but Ali wasn't ashamed she and Abe made a baby. She was surprised that she no longer felt shame about her child. She also realized she felt like smiling not crying when she thought about her baby. She was elated to see her mother smile and tears falling down her face.

"Are you saying I get to be a grandma?" Lana asked with such excitement Ali felt the tears fill up her eyes again. She nodded her head.

Lana stood and pulled her daughter to her and hugged her with all the love a mother could hug a daughter with.

Ali was so relieved. Her mother didn't judge…she just loved. Sitting back down she told her mother she was due at the end of December. She also told her the plan Regan suggested and she decided to use. Her mother agreed if it was going to help her save face then she needed to do what she needed to do. That putting stress on herself was adding stress to the baby which was never good. Plus people could be cruel to children about their heritage.

Lana was going to tell Frank, Ali's Father, the truth. She agreed that the boys were better off believing the fabricated version. She knew Ali didn't want her brothers to judge her. Even though Lana believed the boys never would. In the end it was Ali's choice and if it made Ali feel better, then that was what needed to be done.

Chapter Six

The summer months came and went and Ali was back in school in no time. Christmas Eve brought on the winter break she so needed. Standing in her kitchen she absently rubbed her round baby-bump. She couldn't believe how fast time went when one was pregnant. She was grateful she was one of those women who loved being pregnant.

She felt like it was only yesterday she found out she was pregnant. Looking back, she couldn't fathom changing anything about that beautiful night she and Abe met and created this wonder growing inside of her. Her only regret was not ever finding him.

She was thankful for the support of her family. Her father was excited to be a grandfather. Her oldest brother, Frank Jr., didn't say much because that's how he was. If anything, he was probably upset that he wasn't there to protect her from the man who got her pregnant.

Jake was her second oldest brother and probably her favorite. He was her hero brother. He always came to the rescue. Ironically, he was also FBI. Jake right away asked when he was going to meet the guy and what was his name so he could 'run him through.' This made her panic until she said she wasn't going to have him interrogate the baby's father and quickly changed the subject. She wasn't sure her ploy worked, but her mother reassured her that Jake would leave it alone for the time being because he had a lot going on. He apparently just finished a big case and the only details she had was a suicide and a big sex-trafficking bust involved.

Ali knew his job was stressful and she worried all the time he'd get hurt in the line of duty. Once when she voiced her concerns, he stated, "Al, if I make a difference and save just one person then I feel I was here for a reason. Yet if I save more than one, I believe I was put here for a purpose. So quit worrying and know that if anything ever happens to me…I left knowing it was my time and my purpose was finished." He grinned and added, "But feel free to say a prayer or three for me." Ali respected his words and prayed a lot for him.

Her three younger brothers were too busy finishing school and chasing girls to give it more than a passing thought. They were going to be her baby's spoilers. The ones to play and laugh and buy her baby everything. They didn't care if they met the dad or not and believed he was in the picture because she said he was.

Granny just grinned and said, "So you followed your granny's advice huh? Well I didn't mean for you to get knocked-up, but what's done is done. I almost gave up on ever getting to hold a great. Should've known you'd be the one to come through for me. Unlike the useless men in this family. Should have given birth to a female instead of a male. They drag their damn feet too much!" Everyone was trying not to laugh at her outburst.

Her father was happy. Not just happy, but ecstatic. She was sure her mother had something to do with the very tall, broad, burly man's thought process. Her mother was good at that. He told her he couldn't wait to be grandpa.

Ali did worry what would happen at Peak's Landing Elementary when they got wind of it. According to Kris, since it wasn't a parochial school, they couldn't do anything to her. It would be discrimination. Besides, there were two unwed mothers teaching at the school. Plus the janitor had a baby out of wedlock while he was in wedlock.

She found that Kris was right about the staff at PLE. Everyone was excited about Ali having a baby and even threw her a little shower at school. Ali cried through most of it. She knew Kris was behind it and was also a great friend who kept her secret and even acted like she met Ali's boyfriend on several occasions. Now she just had the town to deal with,

Chapter Seven

The town bought the story pretty good as well. Regan and her mother were asked here and there about the father and they were very convincing about meeting the baby-daddy and thinking he was great. Ali hated all the lies, but in the end, she had to protect her baby.

Of course, Madelyn Maple stuck her nose in the air a few times when passing Ali or Lana on the streets or in a shop. Mother or daughter didn't care, they were too busy planning for baby. Ali stated she didn't want a shower because that would make things awkward when the father didn't show up for it. Lana agreed but insisted on going crazy when it came to spoiling her first grandbaby.

Jena was going berserk trying to figure out who the baby's daddy was. Regan was spinning all these great tales about meeting Ali's man and hanging out with the happy couple. Even went as far as saying she and Ali were going to his hometown one weekend. When in fact the two girls were going to Chicago for some more baby shopping on the Miracle Mile. Jena repeatedly asked for the father's name and Regan always blew her off by saying, "He's not from here. So you wouldn't know him." Then quickly changed the subject.

Regan didn't feel like she was really lying because it was Jena she was spinning the tales to. Jena just wanted to take the information Regan gave her and use it against Ali. To her dismay, Regan never gave her any dirt! Of course, the shrewd woman took Regan's tales and twisted them to make Ali look badly. Regan confided the twisted tales to her friend because she didn't want her to hear Jena's words from others. Ali acted as if she didn't care but she knew she wasn't fooling Regan. To Ali's credit, since being pregnant, she learned to toughen up when it came to the small minds of the small town. Regan always had her back and made sure she reassured everyone that Jena was full of it and reminded them that Jena has always had issues with Ali.

As a rule, Regan would have kicked the spoiled diva to the curve as a client if she and Ali didn't agree that the whole 'friends close enemies closer' expression worked for them when dealing with Jena. So she just continued to pump Jena's head with BS about Ali and her baby's father.

Ali sighed as she looked out at the morning snow falling over her back yard. She was so excited to have found the perfect house and moved in months before the baby arrived. The stone brick and gray-sided cottage was on the outskirts of town. She had two full acres that sat back from the main road but close enough to walk to a neighbor's house if she needed something. Her favorite part of the house was the backyard. It was surrounded by a tall white-picket fence and came with a swing set from the previous family.

Inside was cozy yet fairly large. She had four bedrooms, two baths upstairs. The lower level has the dining and living room open together while the kitchen was separated. Her two-car garage was small but okay for her because it fit her small SUV well.

She was glad the basement was finished. One of the two rooms was set up with cabinets used for storage, the other was once a game room. She loved that it was a walkout because the outside light provided plenty of light to the room.

Noticing the snow was getting heavier, Ali wondered if she should leave for the farm sooner than the afternoon. She didn't want to be snowed in at home on Christmas. With baby expected any day she didn't think it was wise to be stranded between home and the five miles to her parents' home.

Her appointment with her doctor, yesterday, showed the baby was doing fine but in no hurry to meet mommy. Doc explained the baby was happy inside and didn't seem in any hurry to come out. He promised if the baby wasn't here by the New Year, he would induce her.

As the snow fell harder, she decided to grab her overnight bag and gifts and leave for the farm. Turning toward the stairs she felt a 'pop' near her lower stomach and panicked at the puddle of water landing on the floor between her feet. Taking a deep breath, she smiled and relaxed a moment and rubbed her stomach thinking this year she was going to receive the best Christmas present ever.

***

Christmas Eve brought one of the biggest snowstorms Nashville had seen in years. For a city that averaged about six inches of snow a winter, there was panic in the air. All the grocery stores sold out of milk, eggs, and bread before the first snowflake fell. Salt trucks were laying liquid salt on the roads and most everyone was tucked in for the next few days.

Abe was no different. He didn't have any desire to fight the weather. He was content being snowed in at his favorite place. His home! He smiled as he looked around the two-story log cabin he built on the small ranch he grew up on. He was so excited when the farm came up for sale several months ago. Of course, he jumped all over owning it. The old farmhouse he grew up in wasn't livable. Having it torn down was a bit emotional but he knew modernization was important so he built a beautiful log cabin in its place.

The house was him. It was everything he pictured himself living in. The rugged look of wilderness. The huge fireplace. A kitchen any chef would feel proud to call his own. The loft that was outside the four bedrooms on the upper level had a view of a beautiful lake…his lake. It surprised him how content he was staying put. Not touring for a few months sounded perfect to him. He hoped the snow didn't last long because he was excited about getting the antique John Deere tractor out of the shed so he could plow the road.

After bidding goodnight to his visiting mother and sister as the clock chimed Christmas, he stared out into the night for a long while. Oddly, a strange feeling gave him pause. Not sure what it was he turned and walked to the big picture window and stared out into the night. She snuck into his thoughts again. His Ali-cat. He didn't know why but the last few days she had been in his head much more than normal.

He would always wonder what happened to her. Why she took off. He knew she felt what he felt. He could read it in her eyes. He knew he'd always wonder why she took off before he returned. Why not call him? These were questions he never found answers for.

He wondered if they just got separated by circumstances. Maybe she did look for him. He wondered if she spent months looking just as he did. He took everything she said to him and picked it apart to try and find any clue to her whereabouts. He knew she was a schoolteacher and lived in Southern Illinois. He had Max check out every Ali, or any name close to that, working as a teacher in Illinois. Once Max got the names, they sent them to a private investigation firm who matched the names to pictures from social media. Of course, none of the pics were his Ali. The PI even tried looking up the public census that had six children…it's amazing how many six children families lived in Illinois. After months of looking he finally gave up. Finding a needle in the haystack would have been easier.

So here he was thinking of her again. He figured it was because of the holidays. Or the fact that he has had no desire to meet other women. At every concert, since meeting her, he looked into the crowd to see if she was in the audience. He even went as far as going back to the Gaylord and walking around just to feel close to the memory.

He questioned his sanity and decided there was something wrong with him. This obsession he had with her made no sense. There were billions of women out there, he didn't understand why he couldn't get this one out of his head. If she was what some called a 'soul mate,' then wouldn't they be together? Wouldn't it have worked out for them?

He wondered if she really would fit into his lifestyle. Was it fair to even throw her into the middle of the chaos he was living? Recording, tours, dinners, parties and meet and greets. Hell, he was rarely home. He toured six months out of the year. The other six he was writing and recording. He wasn't sure he had time for a girlfriend. He didn't know if she was up to the hoopla. In the last six months he climbed to the top. His song, the song they danced to, 'Now Is the Time,' hit number one for months this summer. The album went platinum because every song on it was a big hit.

He knew he needed to stay focused. Many have made it this far and could climb no higher. He didn't want that. He did want to make it to the top. Mostly because he didn't know what else he would do with himself. His only other dream was to turn the ranch into a cattle farm. And that involved money, lots of money. Touring and recording was the only way he knew to earn the money to get the farm moving. So if putting a few more years into his career was what he needed to do then that was what he was going to do.

Watching the snowfall, he decided he was spending too much time thinking about a lost love. He decided his New Year resolution was to move on. He hoped it was a possible task. He didn't want to waste his life pining away for someone he may never find again.

Moving away from the window he headed to his bedroom. Climbing the steps his thoughts were on his New Year's resolution coming in a week. The point in his life when he was going to let her go completely. Until then he had seven days to think and dream about her.

***

A few hours away, another looked out a window into the snowy Christmas Eve night. She was angry. Her first year without the one person she could always count on. The one person she always followed. Her leader of sorts…her family.

It was all because of him that she hurt so badly from the lost. He killed her and now he would pay. He took from her and she planned to take from him.

***

Two hours north in a Paducah Kentucky hospital, Ali laid on a bed with the back propped up. In her arms snuggled the baby girl she delivered an hour earlier. She looked at her dark-haired beautiful baby with tears rolling down her cheeks. Her little girl was born on Christmas day by a few minutes. Ali vowed she would always have a birthday party separate from Christmas. She never wanted her baby to feel neglected. Looking at her little girl she silently made several vows to her. Promises of happiness and always being a loving mother.

She looked up as Regan walked back into the room. Her friend, along with her entire family, had been by her side all evening. Regan was returning from walking her family out. The family needed to get home before the snowstorm got any worse. Regan stated she was staying the night at the hospital.

Ali was glad for the company. She knew she wasn't keeping her friend from anything. Regan's only living relative was her father, Dan, and he was working the night at the casino across town. He was head of security. He chose to work so the other employees with small children could have Christmas off. Regan never minded because she always spent Christmas with Ali and her family.

"How is she doing?" Regan whispered.

Looking up at her friend, Ali replied, "Isn't she wonderful, Regan?"

"She's so beautiful Al…and tiny."

"I know."

It was a blessing that of the two wonderful nurses on duty for the night shift, one was Regan's client. Ali didn't know her, but she figured that because she knew Regan, the lady went above and beyond to make her comfortable. Ali guessed Sue to be in her late thirties. She was an attractive lady, with bobbish hair and a pretty face. She seemed fatigued but Ali figured working the night shift did that to a person.

The other nurse, Nancy, was an older lady with a genuine smile and a kind heart. Ali sensed both ladies worked hard and seemed to be tired around the eyes. But they showed only affection and support to the new mommy and baby, which only proved to Ali that there was so many good people in the world and nurses were at the top of the list.

Sue explained that they would be taking care of Ali and the baby throughout the night. She promised Regan a cot would be brought into the private room so Regan had a comfortable place to sleep. Regan thanked her. After checking the IV and seeing to Ali's comfort, Sue left the room.

Regan asked Ali if she minded her turning on the television. Ali reassured her she didn't mind even though Regan knew Ali never watched TV. She rarely ever had it on while she was home. Tonight, she was just content staring at the beautiful baby she held in her arms.

It was a bit of a bumpy road these last few months. There were times she didn't think she could make it through alone. She knew she was never really alone. She had her family and her friends, but she longed to have the baby's father next to her.

She was so honored to have such wonderful parents and family. She was sure her brothers were a bit disappointed in her…especially her older brother Jake. He didn't say he was disappointed, but she seen it in his eyes. She did use the fabricated story Regan came up with about the breakup. She told the boys she wanted to end it because her boyfriend was too busy and she needed to move forward. The boys weren't happy to hear this and wanted to have a 'talk' with him. At their request, Ali wouldn't give up his name because she wasn't sure what they were capable of. Thank goodness her mother made them move away from the subject by explaining Ali was hormonal and to let her emotions do their thing and how it will all work out in the end.

So here she was months after hopping through all the obstacles that leaped in front of her, looking at the precious little baby in her arms and knew she'd do it all over again in a minute! Her baby was flawless. Well, with the exception of the half dollar size birthmark on her left shoulder blade. It was jagged on the edges and reminded Ali of the shape of Texas. Ali, already acting like the protected mother, believed it would only add to her baby's charm.

Ali glanced up as Regan flipped through the channels. She was so glad her friend was here. She was glad for the company at this time of the night. She was too excited to sleep and too emotional to be alone.

"So what have you decided for a name?" Regan asked as she looked over at Ali before going back to channel surfing.

"I don't know. I keep coming up with Ana. I love the…oh my God Regan flip back!" Ali shouted.

Regan jumped and looked at her friend. "What…what is it?"

Ali quieted a bit so she didn't startle the baby. "Go back to the previous channel," she stated.

Regan turned the channel back. "Here?"

"No go one more."

Her friend did as she asked.

"Stop, right there…turn it up." She nearly jumped out of the bed. Not a good thing for a girl who just went through twelve hours of labor and was stitched from end to end of her bottom.

They both listened as the lady on the TV interviewed the scruffy, bearded man. "So the next album will be released this spring…correct?"

"I hope so!"

"I also hear you are now barking on a new adventure. Ranching?"

The bearded man nodded his head. "Yep, I've recently bought a small place outside of Nashville. I even have my own tractor," he smirked.

Ali stared at the television. She couldn't believe it...there was Abe as big as day talking with the host. The disguise was good, but even in a flash of channel surfing she could tell it was her Abe. She couldn't believe what she was seeing. Her Abe was a country star? Could it be real? It made sense. Didn't it? She didn't know what to think.

"Ali, what is it?"

"That's him, Regan!" she nodded to the television. "That's Abe."

Regan's mouth dropped open. She looked from the screen to her friend then back to the screen. Her eyes looked like they were going to pop out of her head when she watched the interviewer turn to the camera and say, "Well folks, that's it for our show. I'd like to thank Abraham Parker for coming by and talking to us. If you haven't got it, you need to get his newest album 'Time Machine.' This is one great album."

As the show went to commercial, Regan flipped the television off. She turned to Ali. "Oh My Gosh!"

Ali was crying as she looked back at her friend. "I never had a clue. He was completely clean-shaven. His hair was cut short. No one approached us. How?"

"I don't know, but what a great disguise. Everyone puts stuff on their person so they can hide. He does the opposite." She shook her head at Ali and started pacing. "I love the guy. I mean I love his music. He's sexy with the beard, ball cap, and sunglasses. I even have all his music downloaded to my phone. I just can't believe it's the same guy. I mean I can...the interviewer called him Abraham...he must go by his full name as his stage name." She stopped pacing and looked at her friend. "I'm sorry. I'm rambling. I'm just shocked." She plopped down at the edge of the bed. "What are you going to do?"

"I have no idea. If anything, knowing Ana's father is a famous country singer star makes the situation so much harder to deal with."

"So you've decided on Ana as her name?"

"Yes, I think it always was going to be. I was just too emotional about giving her his grandmother's name." Ali looked at the sleeping baby in her arms. "But now that I found out who he is, I believe in my heart I should name her Ana."

"I love the name." Regan paused to sit on the edge of Ali's bed. "So now that you know who he is how are you going to get in touch with him?"

Ali was saved from replying when Sue entered the room with another older, attractive lady. The nurse introduced the lady as Anita and stated she was there to help Ali to fill out the personal information on the birth certificate? Ali nodded and Regan proclaimed that now was a perfect time to hold her

Godchild. Taking the baby in her arms she walked over to the window and was quietly explaining to her all the mysteries of the world.

Scooting up in her bed Ali went to work reading all the medical information listed for Ana. She smiled as she put down Ana's name. When it came to the father's name, she looked up at Anita with a confused look.

Anita asked her if everything was fine. Ali shook her head. "I don't know if I should give her the father's last name or not?" she whispered with tears in her eyes.

Anita patted her hand and asked if he was in the picture? When Ali shook her head, she asked if there was a chance he could be. Ali hesitated before nodding. Anita asked one final question…was he a good guy? Ali nodded as Anita suggested she hyphenate the baby's last name.

Ali smiled because that was the perfect solution. She thanked the older lady for the suggestion and put Parker-Mason as Ana's last name. Minutes later, Sue came back in to check Al's vitals and was happy at how well she and baby were doing.

Regan repeated her question as soon as they were alone again. Ali stared at her baby for a long minute before answering her. "I would never want to keep him from his child, but now that I know who he is…I realize I have no idea who he is. So I think I am going to give it some time and see how it plays out. I don't want to take the chance of having to leave her with a stranger every other weekend. Or worse yet, he may decide he wants to keep her. And let me tell you he probably has a ton more money than me, so if he fought me, he could win." Tears welled up in her eyes. "Then there's the question of why did he leave me that morning? Obviously, I was just a one-nighter to him!"

Regan placed Ana in her mother's arms. "Ali, let's not jump to conclusions. If you talk to him you will have your answers as to why he left."

At Ali's worried look Regan continued, "Plus I think the law is only if he had just cause to take her away from you would you lose custody."

"Are you one hundred percent positive?" Regan shook her head at Ali's question.

"Then I can't take that chance. Besides, how does someone find someone like him?"

"Your brother is FBI…he could figure it out!"

Chapter Eight

Thanksgiving was fast approaching in the town of Ramona. The leaves were turning quickly and winter was right around the corner. Ali looked down at her almost four-year-old, taking a nap on the floor with her butt in the air. When Ana was tired...she was tired! The little girl could sleep anywhere. Ali scooped her up and carried her to her bedroom. Pulling the blanket back, she tucked her in nice and tight.

She couldn't believe how lucky she was. This little girl stole her heart. She was a sweet, affectionate, loving little girl. She was helpful and polite. She could be sassy at times, but it was so cute when she was it was hard to discipline her for it.

Ali knew she did well in raising her daughter. Maybe she was arrogant for thinking so, but everything she did was to ensure this little girl had a wonderful life. She never wanted to look back with regrets when it came to the upbringing of her child.

Her only guilt was not letting Ana's father know about her as soon as Ali realized who he was. It was fear that prevented her from getting in touch with Abe. Now so much time has passed that Ali was afraid he would retaliate and take her daughter from her. She felt it was too late to do anything about it.

For months after figuring out who he was she researched everything she could on him. Of course, she found everything about him as a star but nothing about the boy she met. The one who was an ordinary guy. She wondered if the stories he told her about his childhood were true. After finding his father's obituary she decided maybe he was truthful about that time in his life.

She and Regan did try to figure out different ways for her to get in touch with him. It was impossible. Big stars kept their private life top secret. It wasn't that she was going to contact him...she just wanted the info in case she decided it was time.

The only solution that was a for sure way to get the information was her brother Jake. Jake was FBI and she was sure he could use his influences with the FBI to get to Abe. The problem was Ali was afraid to confide in Jake. She lied to her brothers and she was too prideful to tell them the truth. She didn't want them to look at her or Ana differently.

It wasn't easy getting over Abe. The first six months she wondered what it would be like to see him again. Would he be happy to see her? Would he want to marry her and make it right? Then after she saw several photos matching him up with a popular actress, she became heartbroken. It was the first time she has seen him for what he was…a star. Someone who lived in a completely different world.

Eventually she came to the decision they were destined to be apart and took that for what it was. There was just too much time gone and at this point she was sure he'd resent her for interrupting his famous life. So she breezed through the next few years doing what she loved most…raising her beautiful daughter.

Looking down at the sleeping baby in the huge bed she knew, without a doubt, she would never let anyone take her away. She wanted Ana to know her father, but she didn't know the father well enough to trust him not to hold it against her that she kept this from him.

In the past four years Ali continued to read everything she could find on the internet about Abe. She came to understand why he wasn't recognizable to anyone that night in Nashville. Not only did he have a good disguise but when she first met him, he was just becoming a rising star. In the four years since she last saw him, he made it to the top and was still going strong.

She knew she would one day tell her daughter who her father was. But she felt it was going to be when her daughter got older. She really did believe she was doing the best for everyone involved. Abe was at the top of his game and she didn't think he'd appreciate the wrench she would throw in his lifestyle.

Ali walked into the kitchen when she heard her phone. Looking at it she was surprised to see it was a text from Todd Evans, the boy she dated ten years ago in high school. He was asking when would be a good time to call because he had a question for her.

She leaned back against the counter and smiled at the text. She was sure he was probably going to ask her out. She has been expecting it since she heard he and his girlfriend broke off their three-year relationship a few months ago and he moved back to Ramona to set up his family law practice.

She only expected it because she caught him staring at her every time they were at the same place. She would catch his eyes and he would wave and she would wave back. Funny, but he would never approach her.

Then last week they ran into each other at the grocery store and he got up the nerve to talk to her. They spoke for twenty minutes in the produce line. At the end of the conversation he asked if he could call her. Ali didn't have the heart to decline his request so she gave him her number.

Of course, if she dated him, Jena would probably flip. Ali heard through the small-town gossip mill that Jena was planning to snare the young lawyer. Ali couldn't imagine the fury Jena would lash out if she knew Ali and Todd were talking again.

She really wished she knew what Jena's beef was with her. She never gave up. She spread all kinds of rumors about Ali and Ana. Speculating who the father was. Regan heard the tales but could never prove they were from Jena…but they knew. The girl really needed to realize that she was never going to have true friends or someone love her unless she stopped her selfish malicious ways.

Sighing, she looked again at the text. What to do? She knew she was going to have to let Abe go. She hasn't touched another man since him. And it was starting to get to her a bit. She really did miss companionship. Plus Todd was a great-looking guy with dark hair and brown eyes. He was tall and nicely built. His smile was killer and he had a sweet personality. She realized there was not a lot of chemistry in high school but now that they were older maybe there could be something there. Plus she was sure she could trust him around Ana. Not as a father figure by any means. Ana had enough of those with Ali's father and brothers. Yet it might be good to show Ana that it was okay to share her mother. She didn't want Ana to have issues later on seeing her mother with someone.

Ali decided it was time to move on. Before she could chicken out, she texted him that he could call now and the phone rang a few minutes later. She smiled when she heard his voice.

"Hi Ali, how have you been?"

"Good! And you?"

"I'm good." He explained how he was settling in since moving back home. He recently passed his bar while living in Chicago. He went on to say he missed home and was back here for good. He added that his mom was keeping him up on all the town gossip. Ali was sure he was letting her know he knew about her being a single mom and was okay with it.

Ali and Todd talked for about a half hour before Ana walked into the kitchen and hugged her momma's legs. Ali patted her head and told Todd she was glad he called and they got to catch up. She was surprised to feel bummed they couldn't talk any longer.

Todd must have felt the same way because he asked if she and Ana were free the following day for the Sunday Matinee. He said the new Disney Pixar film was coming out and he was dying to see it.

She laughed and was flattered that he was making a point to include Ana. Even to go as far as having researched what movies would accommodate a three-year-old. She happily agreed to the movie and assured him her daughter would love to go as well. Lately she has been thinking Ana was old enough to go to a movie theatre but they just never got around to going to one. So it was decided he would pick them up for lunch and a movie at eleven the following day.

When Ali got off the phone, she picked up her daughter. Turning around she placed her on the island. "So how did my little princess like her nap?"

"I was tired," Ana said in her cute little voice. "But I's not tired no more."

Her momma ran her hands over the unruly mess of beautiful dark curls. Everyone said she favored Ali, but Ali believed she had her father's dimples and smile. No one, but Regan, knew who her father was so they had nothing to compare her to. She never confided in anyone else about the identity of Ana's father. After her baby was six months old, she started the rumors that she and Ana's father were separating for good because he was moving too far away. To her surprise most everyone left it at that.

"So my pretty girl, tomorrow we are going to have an adventure?"

"Yippee!" she shouted as she kicked her feet out on each side of her momma's waist. "What is it…What is it?"

"Well, Mommy has an old friend. His name is Todd, and he wants to take us to lunch and then we are going to go to a place where there is a big television. We will get to sit in a chair, eat popcorn and watch a cartoon. Doesn't that sound like fun?"

Her daughter gave her a silly excited look and her little mouth rolled into a goofy expression where her mouth formed an *O*! "Wow!" she exclaimed before her little face turned serious. "Who's Todd?"

Ali should have known her inquisitive daughter would start asking questions. "He's a friend of mine. He just moved back here and he wants to meet you."

"Is he my daddy?"

Ali was completely taken back by her daughter's question. Ana had never asked anything about her father. She, on a few occasions, called Ali's dad…dad, but Ali nipped that in the bud right away.

Since enrolling Ana in preschool at Peak's Landing two months earlier, Ana has been much more aware of her surroundings. She guessed since most kids had a mommy and a daddy Ana was now curious about her own dad.

"No sweetie he isn't your daddy. Why would you wonder that?"

"Henry asked me who my daddy was. I's told him I don't have one. He says everybody has one."

Ali panicked. Why didn't she think that her little girl would start asking questions when she started school? "Ana-ba-nana," using her nickname to make the subject less painful, "Everybody does have a daddy. You have a great daddy and one day you will meet your daddy. But right now, your daddy is busy working all over the world."

Ana's eyes got large and she stretched her arms wide. "Like he's working this much everywhere?"

Ali smile and hugged her little girl. "Yep that much." She decided to change the subject. "So are you excited about the big movie tomorrow?"

"Oh Yes!" She put her hands to her cheeks. Then another frown came across her forehead. "Is the boy your boyfriend?"

"Ana Grace Parker-Mason…" Ali using her daughter's birth name. "What do you know about having a boyfriend?" her mother teased.

"Henry says he's my boyfriend. That's when a boy and girl hold hands and kiss."

Oh Dear Lord, her three-year-old is telling her about the birds and bees. Maybe she shouldn't have enrolled her in preschool at such an early age. Even though she was glad she did. Ana was advanced for her age. Nothing genius-like, but very smart in all areas. What shocked Ali the most was how much her daughter loved to sing.

Ana would go about her day singing everywhere she went. She loved music, but most especially country. Ali had to admit that might be because ever since she realized who Abe really was, she started listening to his music. She found she liked singing along to his words…most especially to the song they shared the night they danced. 'Now Is the Time' was her absolute favorite song. Sadly, it usually brought tears to her eyes.

At first his music was the only country music she listened to. Then over time she started putting it on in her car. She was still a pop girl, but she did have a new love for country music. Plus she wanted to keep updated on his life by seeing if there was any mention of him.

Putting Ana on the ground and patting her butt telling her to go play, Ali smiled. It was cute the way Ana sang her daddy's songs. She felt she owed it to Abe to have his little girl know his music. She wondered if music was a talent passed from generation to generation.

**

The woman's hands were shaking. She needed her fix. It seemed like the rush was harder and harder to come by. Stealing pills wasn't enough anymore.

Shooting needles into her thighs wasn't enough to make it go away anymore. It just gave her passion for her revenge stronger.

She let a few years go by and now she was ready to avenge her sister. He made her die and now he was going to pay. That pretty little school teacher and her brat were going to pay. Literally and figuratively. She planned to line her pockets and seek her revenge. Then her life would be complete.

No one in this cruddy town knew she had a problem. Who would have thought that she'd have to move to BFE to seek revenge? Her nerves were shot because she couldn't stand living here any longer.

When she was at work no one suspected she had a problem. She knew how to keep it under control. Yet the juice was more expensive and they needed money to buy it. And her job paid crap.

There was nowhere left to steal from. They had every clinic in the area on lockdown. Plus if there was any more stealing done, all fingers would be pointed at her lover if anyone caught wind he was an ex-con. He already served one prison term for theft and she didn't need him getting caught again. He was her gopher and she needed him. Plus she had a plan. A great plan. She was going to have him do a little kidnapping. It would be perfect because she knew of the perfect kidnapping that would lead to her revenge. Perfect little teacher gets knocked up by famous Daddy who's rich and famous. How perfect that she stumbled onto that juicy bit of info. She was sure her sister saw to her finding out that tidbit of gossip.

She's just relieved she had been sober enough to make the decision to not end their lives, but to wait and reap from the benefits first. The world didn't know about his kid so she was sure they would keep the kidnapping as private as they could. Plus the slut lived in this Godforsaken small town so the kid would be easy pickings.

***

Ali and Ana were both sitting under dryers at the *Mystique Salon*. Of course, they were playing pretend because neither one needed the dryer. Ali was waiting on her mother to finish her client so she could give her an updo for her work Christmas party. Ali busted out laughing as she watched her daughter cross her legs and pretend to be interested in the 'People' magazine.

"Excuse me ma'am," Ana said to her mother in a snotty voice, "but can youz get me a cup of tea please?"

Ali, and most everyone in the shop, started laughing. "I'm sorry my lady, but I am a queen and I do not do such trivial work. I am to be waited on hand and foot just like yourself!"

"Well I never. This peasant needs to be whipped!"

"I do agree! It's hard to find good peasants these days!"

"Oh look...here comes peasant Regan now!" Ana exclaimed with a giggle. Regan went over and tickled the little girl's ribs. "I'll show you a peasant." Ali watched as her daughter squealed. Her little girl was something else.

As Regan finished and started walking away, Ana shouted, "Well I never!" Then recrossed her legs and held the magazine back up to look like she was reading it.

Ali almost choked. It just dawned on her that Ana was mimicking Madelyn Maple the town gossip. To make matters worse Bobbi had Madelyn's chair turned toward the dryers as she was finishing the teasing to the back of her hair. From the look on Madelyn's face she knew Ana was making fun of her.

Turning to her daughter she gave her the 'shh' sound with her finger to her lips. Ana smiled, nodded and gave her mother back the 'shh' sound and continued looking at the magazine.

Lana, having seen the entire display was bursting with love for her daughter and granddaughter. What a sight they were. Both so beautiful with the dark, curly, raven black hair and catlike green eyes. It reminded her of when Ali was little and she would play with her at the salon.

Looking at Ali, she was glad to see there was a small gleam in her eyes again. She guessed it was because she was dating Todd Evans. Lana always wondered if they would end up together. She liked Todd. He was always kind and attentive to her daughter. Yet Lana worried that her daughter was just settling. That was something she hoped none of her children ever did.

She could see how it could happen with her daughter. Being a single mother was tough and could be very lonely. She probably felt she had to find a father for Ana. Lana prayed that wasn't her interest in Todd. No one should ever settle. There was true love out there. She knew this because she found it with Ali's father.

She was sure her daughter's time for love would come one day. Ali was a sweet, thoughtful and loving person. She was everything a man could want. She was still very slender after having Ana, but a little curvier...making her look more woman than a child. In Lana's opinion who ever caught Ali's eye was destined for a great and happy life.

As she motioned for the girls to come over for their updos, she chuckled because Ana sat down first letting her grandmother know she was getting a makeover as well. Lana went to work making her girls even more beautiful than normal. She herself was excited because while Ali was at her Christmas party in Peak's Landing, Miss Ana was staying the night with her and Frank. That was a rare occasion because Ali rarely shared her nights with Ana.

Lana knew Ali and Todd were staying in a hotel instead of driving the forty minutes it took to get back home. They were being cautious because they planned to have a few drinks and didn't want the risk hurting themselves or anyone else. Lana wondered if tonight would be the leap her daughter would take to get over Ana's father.

***

Several hours later, on their way back to the hotel, Ali was wondering the same thing. Was she ready to take her relationship with Todd another step? Did she wish to become sexually involved with someone?

Looking at him as he pulled into a parking space at the hotel, Ali believed she could. It wasn't like they have never been intimate. They were each other's first everything. First kiss, first boyfriend/girlfriend, and first sexual partner. She remembered it had always been nice when she was with him. Not like the intensity she had with Abe…but nice.

Mad at herself for letting Abe slip into her thoughts, she turned to Todd before he got out to open her door and put her hands on both sides of his face and pulled him to her for a kiss that was full of passion. Todd was happy to oblige.

Ali was excited she felt something close to passion when she pulled away. She smiled and got out of the car, letting him hold her hand as she followed him into the hotel. She was nervous, but he seemed just as nervous so that made her feel better.

Stepping into their hotel room Ali walked into Todd's arms. He stood there hugging her and rubbing her back. Looking into her face he lifted her chin with his finger and kissed her long, slow and sweet. It was such a gentle kiss. His kindness was in the kiss, but Ali knew she wasn't ready. After dating him for the past two months she still wasn't ready.

Looking around the room she remembered another time and another hotel room. She was expecting the magic to be here like it had been there. What her and Abe shared was a different kind of magic. She told herself that was over…now was her and Todd's time.

"Ali, I don't think you are ready for what's next." His words had her looking at him. "But I believe there is something here between us. I am more than willing to wait until you are ready. I would just be content holding you all night long."

His words were so sweet. He was so sweet. The last thing she wanted to do was hurt him again. "Todd," she reached up and put her arms around him. "You're wrong…I am ready." She kissed him long and hot.

Chapter Nine

The next day Ali was sitting on her couch thinking about the night before. She smiled as she thought about her night with Todd. She could tell he had some practice since high school. Even though his lovemaking was the slow and steady kind, he brought her some much-needed release. She decided she could be happy with the nice and safe love Todd offered her.

She relaxed as she waited for her parents to drop off Ana after church. She and her little girl were going to do some Christmas shopping together since the holiday was only two weeks away. Most moms usually didn't like shopping with a child Ana's age, but Ali loved it. They had so much fun together.

Besides, Ana wanted to pick out her own gifts for her grandparents and Uncles. Which Ali knew they would love more than any other gifts they would receive. Her brothers simply doted on their niece.

After her parents left, mother and daughter headed out the door and made their way to a department store. Ana found all of the five uncle gifts immediately...including Grandpa Frank. What she wanted to purchase for them made her giggle so much Ali noticed they were drawing a crowd. Her laugh was contagious. Especially when Ana held up the long red underwear she wanted for the men. The kind you would see on an old western show where the material was one piece from head to feet and the backside was closed off with just a couple of buttons.

The little girl had everyone around them pitching in comments like 'I bet those would keep your uncle's warm' and 'why do you think there's a button in the back.' She shook her head as she realized her daughter was a natural entertainer. She had no problem charming these people.

After several minutes of choosing the right sizes for the men, Ali found Ana at the jewelry counter. She thought Ana was trying to find something for her grandmother, Granny Ellie, and Regan. Glancing where her daughter was looking, she was surprised to see it was a section of pocket watches. Just as Ali started to explain that she found all the correct sizes for the men she noticed the sad look on her daughter's face.

Ali bent down to be eye level with her little girl. "What's wrong, Baby Girl?"

After a moment, Ana turned to her mother. "Mommy, can I's buy Daddy a watch like this one?" she asked as she pointed to the watch that had a crucifix on it. "I know I won't get to sees him, but one day when I do, I can give it to him and I's tell him that Jesus will always lookout for him since he moves 'round lots."

Ali didn't know how she kept her composure and the tears back. She nodded to her daughter, whose little face lit up. Motioning for the sales clerk, Ali could barely talk as she indicated to the watch, asking if they could purchase it.

The rest of the shopping trip went by in a haze for Ali. She didn't know what to do about Ana and Abe. She felt like she was hurting her little girl by not giving her the chance to get to know her father.

She decided that as soon as Christmas and Ana's birthday was over, while she was on break, she was going to try to reach Abe. She would wait until then because she didn't want any disappointment for her daughter during her Christmas and birthday. She was going to have to confide in Jake and see if he could help.

***

The last day before winter break was chaos at Peak's Landing Elementary School. Ali couldn't contain the excitement the kids were having during their classroom party. Presents being open from the gift exchange were scattered everywhere. Parents were in attendance to join the festivities. Food was passed, spilled, stepped on while the kids ate in their circle on the floor. Ali couldn't wait until the bell rang and she could go into the pre-k room and grab Ana.

She was overwhelmed at all the gifts her first graders gave her. She received gift cards, candy, flowers, mugs, and ornaments. She was touched that so many parents were so thoughtful.

Not wanting to stay at the school any longer than needed, Ali asked her aide to keep an eye on the class as she took a bundle of the gifts out to her car. The PLE staff parked in the back. Ali, not taking the time for her jacket, rushed through the lunch area, and past the cafeteria window. She paused only long enough to kick out the doorstop so she didn't lock herself out. Hurrying to her car at the end of the lot, she was startled to be stopped by a deliveryman asking for directions to the cafeteria. She pointed him in the direction of the door she exited.

Putting everything in her trunk took seconds and she decided to keep it unlocked for a quick second trip. Within a few minutes she was back in her classroom where Hope, her aide, was cleaning up and waving to several of the kids and their parents. Five minutes to go and Ali was relieved to see the parents starting to leave with their children before the bell rang. Once one left the others seemed to follow suit leaving only three kids left to ride the bus home.

Rearranging the chairs and picking up didn't take the two girls long. As Hope led the three kids out to the bus stop, Ali grabbed the rest of her gifts and everything else she needed to have home for the two and a half weeks the kids were on winter break. Making one last trip to her car she quickly put everything in the trunk and upon closing the hatch an eerie feeling of being watched snuck up on her. Deciding to lock the car she headed back to the cafeteria doors. She noticed the delivery truck was still parked in the back and thought it was odd that a food truck would be delivering food to a school that would be closed for a few weeks. She looked up and spotted a lady, with a scarf around her head and big sunglasses on, sitting in the driver seat. The woman sat back as if she didn't want Ali seeing her.

Ali got a weird feeling in her stomach. She decided she should probably stop by and talk to the lunch lady and inquire about the truck. Entering the building she ducked into the cafeteria looking for Mrs. Lauer. She couldn't find her and wondered if the lady left for the day? And where was the driver she spoke to earlier? Heading back through where the kids ate their lunch, she decided to see if he was in the school office.

Ali came up short when she came face to face with the man. He was rushing through the empty lunchroom with her daughter in his hands. His hand was covering her mouth and she was kicking at him over and over. His arm had her arms pinned.

With no time to think Ali screamed and leaped for her daughter, kicking and throwing jabs at the man's face. The intruder was trying to hold onto the child and ward off the half-crazed mother. Realizing, after several moments of abuse, the mother wasn't going to quit, the abductor had no choice but to let the little girl go.

After Ana's release he quickly headed through the door into the back-parking lot. Ali made no move to follow him. She just kept hugging her little girl and rubbing her hands up and down her asking if she was hurt. Ana was crying and kept saying she was scared. Ali couldn't let her little girl go.

Hearing the commotion, most of the staff ran into the lunchroom. Not letting her daughter out of her sight, Ali explained what happened. As questions were going back and forth the Principle, Mr. Spring, took charge. He asked his staff to see to the safety of all the children first. Thankfully there wasn't any in attendance since the bell rang right after the commotion. He quieted everyone and asked Ali if she and Ana wanted to come into his office until everything calmed down. Ali agreed. She knew it was protocol to contact the authorities. She also knew she was calling her brother Jake first. Seeing Hope, she asked her if she could grab her handbag from her desk and meet her in the office.

Inside the main office Ali asked the secretaries Bonnie and Evelyn to look after Ana while she was in the principal's personal office. She didn't want her out of her sight but she didn't want to scare her with details. She thanked them and immediately pulled out her phone. She told the principal she needed to make a phone call before they got down to what happened.

Jake answered on the second ring. "Hi Ali Cat or is this my Ana Girl?"

Ali almost smiled. Ana liked to call her brothers from Ali's phone. It was cute because they never knew who was calling. Yet instead of smiling she burst out into tears. "Jake someone just tried kidnapping Ana!"

Jake, who was sitting at his desk doing paperwork, leaped to his feet. "What?"

"Yes, someone tried to take her." She was hysterical. "I had to physically pull her off him."

"Al, calm down and tell me where you and Ana are?" Jake knew he had to be calm because his sister wasn't.

"I'm at school and Ana is with me."

"Okay. Have you called the authorities yet?"

"No, I called you first," she said in a calmer voice.

He was relieved that she knew to call him first. "Alright, I'll take care of the authorities, but you are going to have to stay put until I get there. It's about three and a half hours from Memphis to you. So I'll see you in about two and a half." Indicating he wasn't going to abide in any speed limits. He would have a siren on the entire time. "Ali, is anyone with you?"

"Yes, Mr. Spring, my Principle."

"Okay, put him on the phone."

"Okay, and Jake…I love you and hurry…oh and don't get yourself killed rushing here…you'll be of no use to me then. I love you!" She handed the phone to Mr. Spring and told him her brother wanted to talk to him.

After looking into the main office, she was relieved to see the secretaries playing with her daughter. Turning back, she was watching Mr. Spring's head bobbing up and down agreeing with whatever Jake was saying. When he said his goodbyes, he handed her the phone.

"You have quite an impressive brother there. FBI...I can't believe I didn't know that. It's good to know this case will be dealt with by real professionals. Nothing against PLPD, but I doubt they have ever handled a kidnapping attempt."

They talked a few minutes trying to figure out if it was a random kidnapping or if Ana was the actual target. Ali excused herself and went in the other room and sat with Ana. She was sick to her stomach and didn't want to discuss it. In the back of her head she replayed the scene. For some reason she felt like the kidnappers knew who she was. It might have been the way the driver looked shocked when she walked out of the building. Of course, she didn't think nothing of it at the time.

Thinking back, she remembered the lady in the front seat was trying to hide herself. Of course, that could be because they didn't want anyone to be able to identify them. Oddly, she had an odd feeling she has seen these people before.

The PLPD was at the school minutes later. There were two officers. They identified themselves as Officer Dinges and Officer MacGrey. They told her they were just gathering the basics on the case for their records. But an attempted kidnapping of a minor was a federal case and the FBI would be here soon to take over. He explained that the kidnappers could still be in the area and he was quickly gathering information so they could call in an all-points bulletin. She couldn't tell if they were annoyed that the case was out of their hands or relieved. But she didn't care. She wanted her brother handling it.

Officer Dinges asked her to give an account of everything she could remembered. She told him about going back and forth to her car and about the deliveryman and woman. She went on to tell him about confronting the man and how he took off.

The officer asked her to give as much detail as she could about the van and the two people driving it. She listed everything she remember. Her description of the driver was vague, but she found she gave a fairly good one of the men who grabbed her daughter.

Ali didn't say much more to the officer and didn't explain to him her brother was FBI. She knew things could be touchy between local police departments and FBI and she decided to let Jake handle that area. Officer Dinges looked content with her description and moved on to speak with Mr. Spring, leaving her alone for the most part.

Relief flooded through her as she spotted her parents walking through the office door a half hour later. Ali rushed over to hug her mom and burst into tears. Frank gathered up his granddaughter and gave her a big hug. Ana was going about a mile a minute telling her grandpa about the mean man who tried to take her...until her mommy beat him up and got her back. Ali almost cried when she saw the worry in her father's eyes as he hugged his granddaughter tight.

Ali asked her mom how she knew to come. She replied that Jake called them and asked them to be with her until he arrived. She was so relieved to have her parents with her. Her mother told her she had the receptionist cancel her day by telling her clients she wasn't feeling well. Jake advised her to keep a low profile until they got to the bottom of the situation.

Mr. Spring offered Ali his office so she could talk to her parents in private. She immediately went into detail about what happened. She lost all composure by the time she was finished. Her mother had tears streaming down her face as well. All she kept thinking was what if the kidnapper succeeded? What if her little girl was gone from her forever?

Her father stood and walked over to her and pulled her in his arms and hugged her tight. "It's okay little girl. The Good Lord kept her safe! She needs you to stay strong. We will get to the bottom of this."

An hour later Ali was relieved to see Jake and his partner Will walk through the school office door. Before she could greet him, Ana flew out of her lap and leaped into his arms. "Uncle Jake the Snake," she screeched.

Giving her a big hug, he replied, "My Ana Piranha."

She giggles at his nickname for her. Ali smiled at her brother and daughter. It was such a fabulous thing to have the love and protection of five brothers. What was even better was that they loved her little girl as much as they loved her.

Jake's presence dominated the room. The gun attached to him was intimidating to everyone, but his family, who was used to it. Out of all five brothers she looked like him the most. He was tall, a few inches over six feet. His hair was long and shaggy…she figured it was because he was undercover. His face was tanned under the scruffy beard. His eyes were a beautiful shade of green. Ali knew he was considered handsome because many women made fools out of themselves over him…including her almost four-year-old daughter.

Ana wouldn't let him put her down. He kept her in his arms and he bent to give his mother a kiss and hug his dad. Lana and Frank were happy to see their son. Thanksgiving, a few weeks earlier, was the last time they all hung out. Living a few hours away in Memphis made it hard to get back and forth every weekend.

Ali was relieved that her mother was able to bribe Ana out of Jake's arms by offering to help her color a picture for her uncle Jake. Ali motioned for her brother and Will to talk in the principal's office.

Inside the office, Ali gave the rundown on all the events that occurred from the time she went to her car the first time until the confrontation. The men asked her so many endless questions she thought her head was spinning. No she hasn't felt like someone was following her lately. No she hasn't had any confrontations with anyone. No…No…No…she didn't have any idea who the kidnappers were.

"Jake," Ali looked at her brother, "do you think the kidnappers were after any child or do you think they were after Ana?"

"Well there is only one way to find out. Are you okay with me talking to her?"

Ali would love to not scare her daughter any more than she already was. She knew that in order to find out who and why this occurred she had to trust Jake. She nodded her okay and watched Jake walk out the door to retrieve her daughter.

Ana was glad to have her uncle's attention. She smiled at him as he sat her on the edge of the desk. Sitting in front of her he had her undivided attention.

"So Jelly Bean, do you think you could answer me a few questions?"

"Uh huh." She nodded her head at her uncle. "Did you know some bad guy wants to take me?"

"I did hear that baby girl. Can you tell me what happened?"

"Yep." She looked at her uncle waiting for him to talk.

"Okay, so when did you first see the mean guy?"

"I's went to the hallway to get my's coat."

"Were you by yourself?" Jake asked.

"No, Hailey was with me," she stated.

"Was Hailey there when the mean guy came?"

"Yep, we were going back to our room, but the mean guy stopped me and said momma needed me."

"Think real hard princess. What exactly did he say?"

"He says…Ana, hey your momma wanted me to come and get you."

"Are you sure he said your name?"

"I'm sure." Her eyes started filling with tears. "I'm sorry Uncle Jake. I shouldn't believes the mean man, but he was at school."

He hugged her to him. "You didn't do anything wrong baby girl. Can you tell me what happened after he talked to you?"

"Hailey left me and the man grabs me. He hold me tight and put his hand on my mouth. I tried to scream but can't. I kicked him but he was running with me. Then I see mommy and she grabs me back." Ana smiled at her mother…who felt like throwing up after hearing her daughter explain what she went through.

73

"Okay baby girl, can you go finish your coloring for me?" She nodded to her uncle and climbed down from the desk and made her exit.

Will, saying nothing up to this point, looked at Ali and stated, "You realize they were after your daughter in particular?"

Ali nodded. He was being direct. She knew they were letting her know the seriousness of the situation. Will was like family to the Masons. He was a soft-spoken, good-looking guy in his early thirties. He and Jake have been partners for several years. He fit in with the rowdiness of their family gatherings. So she was comfortable with his bluntness.

The men talked for several minutes before they exited the room. Ali was surprised to see several more agents inside the main office when she vacated Mr. Spring's office. Jake was talking to the two local policemen. Will was directing agents to the crime scene so they could take prints. He pointed out to Ali that the odds were not in their favor when it came to prints. There were too many people in and out of the school.

Jake made his way to Mr. Spring. He informed him that the school was going to be on lockdown for as long as the kidnappers are at large. He went on to explain that the next two weeks the school was going to go through a complete transformation. There were going to be security cameras everywhere and a buzzing system that monitors all people coming into the place. Plus there was going to be a security guard on the staff every day there were students on the premises.

He informed him that there were plenty of grants available to pay for the security guard and the permanent security cameras he wanted to install before school was back in session. He, himself, would sit down with spring and help him write the grants. He also explained to the older man that he needed to call an emergency board meeting tomorrow for six in the evening. He explained that he would also personally go in front of the board to discuss the changes. The last instruction was to try and keep the kidnapping as quiet as possible since it was considered a target on one particular child and not a perp out looking for any random child…even though it will be treated as so. Not only for the safety of the children but for the school reputation as well. The last thing he, his family or the school needed was media swarming everywhere.

Ali watched her brother in awe. He just took complete control of her school. Funny but Jake made her boss think he was the one in control. Mr. Spring was suddenly feeling very useful. Never seeing Jake at work, Ali was impressed.

Ana was yawning. Ali was exhausted. Jake must have sensed it also because he made a call outside and was given the okay to leave in her car because they checked it over for any prints or explosives that may have been planted there.

Jake tossed his keys to Will and explained to his sister that he was taking on her case and Will was finishing up the paperwork on the case they have been undercover on for the last three months. The case was cracked a few days ago and as soon as Will finished, he was heading to Ramona to help out on her kidnapping case. Ali thought it felt odd that she was a "case!"

Jake held his hand out for Ali's keys. After Will promised to walk his parents out, Jake and the girls hugged Lana and Frank goodbye with a promise to be in touch in the morning. He reminded Mr. Spring that he would be there by three the following afternoon to work on the grants and to join in at the six o'clock meeting. Picking up his tired niece he followed his sister out the door. By the time they got Ana in her seat she was out like a light.

Ali was exhausted by the time she climbed in the passenger seat and decided to reply to Todd's text asking how her day was when she glanced over at her brother getting in on the driver's side of the car. Ali noticed a white envelope with the name Miss Mason sitting on the dash. "Where did that come from?" she asked out loud.

Chapter Ten

Jake looked up at the envelope sitting in front of him and stopped Ali's hand from grabbing it. "You don't know where that came from?" he asked nodding to the envelope.

"No…I've never seen that before," she stated.

"Was your car door unlocked?"

"I always lock my…oh my gosh!" She felt suddenly sick. "Jake, remember I came out here a few minutes before that man grabbed Ana, to put some presents from my class into the car. I didn't lock it because I knew I was coming back out. When I came back out, I noticed the lady in the truck looked suspicious so I locked it back up and was heading inside to see why there was a delivery truck outside when school wasn't going to be in session for a few weeks."

"Well if I had to go with my gut on this, I'd say someone dropped you a little present and then when the kidnapping failed, they couldn't retrieve it because you locked them out." He called over to one of the detectives fingerprinting the crime scene. The man explained he was instructed to only investigate the outside of the car because it was locked and they assumed the kidnappers wouldn't have been inside of the car because it was locked. Jake repeated what his sister told him about the locked door. Jake nodded to the driver window. "I'm hoping it's a present from our kidnappers."

Ali watched as the crime scene investigators dusted and analyzed the envelope before Jake opened it with gloves on. He pulled out his phone and took a pic of the letter before the investigators put it in a Ziplock bag. It took investigators a little time to check out the inside and brush for prints. It wasn't long after that they were on their way.

Her curiosity was getting to the best of her. She waited until Jake was on the interstate before she asked him to tell her what was in the letter. He handed her his phone and told her to look at the pic.

Ali swore her heart stopped beating when she read the contents of the printed letter.

Dear Miss Mason,
Your kid will be fine
as long as you cooperate.
I am in need of some cash
so get the wealthy, famous
baby daddy to pass us the funds.
You will be given further details
on where you can send the money!

Jake watched her turn white as a ghost. "Ali," her brother grabbed and held her shaking hand. "Honey, I need you to breathe." He started worrying as her breathing turned hard and fast. He knew she was hyperventilating and possibly going into shock. He pulled the car over at the first exit he came to and quickly walked around the car. Opening the door he unbuckled her and pulled her into the cooler air.

He gave her a hug and soothed her by rubbing his hand up and down her back. "Come on sis…I can't have you crack on me…Ana needs you sis!" He softly shook her until she looked at him. Her tears were almost his undoing. "Ali, it's going to be okay!" Then watched as her tears fell.

Ali cried for a few minutes and then shuttered from the cold. She reassured her brother she was alright. Once they were back on the road Ali decided to come clean with her brother.

Jake spoke first. "So apparently the kidnappers put the letter in your car before they kidnapped her. If I had to guess I'd say we were dealing with amateurs. Which should make for an easy arrest."

Ali knew he was trying not to ask about the contents of the letter. "I'm worried that he isn't finished with me because now I can identify him."

"That is why I plan to move in your place for a few weeks…months…years. I'm not letting you and Ana go unprotected until I find the bastard who tried hurting my niece."

Ali was relieved he wasn't leaving her alone. She was spooked. So having Jake around made her feel better about the situation. She knew she needed to be open about the contents in the letter.

"I have a question Jake." She paused before continuing. "Have you ever heard of a country singer name Abraham Parker?" She knew he listened to all kinds of music so she wasn't surprised when he replied.

"Sure, who hasn't?" As it dawned on him what his sister said, he looked at her with both eyebrows raised. "Are you saying…?"

Ali nodded. "Yes, he is Ana's father."

Jake had to run it all through his head. Ali goes to Nashville for a week. Says she met the guy online and they share a romantic week together. She gets pregnant but doesn't really want to be with the father. The father moves around a lot. Father doesn't really have a relationship with Ana. Visits once in a while…or that's what Jake had been told. Jake wouldn't know if he did or didn't because he wasn't home enough to meet the guy.

"Are you telling me you met Abraham Parker on an online dating site?"

"No. I'm sorry Jake. I did fabricate the story a bit because I didn't want my brothers to be ashamed of me."

"Ali, we'd only be ashamed if you felt the need to lie to us." He let that sink in before he continued. "Why don't you start from the beginning?"

It took the entire forty-minute drive to explain to her brother everything that happened from the park bench at The Grand Ole Opry to present day.

Pulling into the driveway Jake looked at her and said, "That is one hell of a story!"

"Try living it!"

"So are you saying when you googled his first name, it never showed Abraham Parker anywhere?"

"No. Abraham Lincoln, Abraham Vigoda, Abraham Alvarez. The list went on. If I put in Nashville, well then I had a list of every person in Nashville with the name Abraham. Plus you have to remember, four years ago Abraham Parker wasn't that big of a star yet. He was climbing to the top but not quite there!"

Her brother carried his niece to her bedroom upstairs. She was probably out for the night. Ali made coffee and sandwiches for the two of them downstairs. When Jake joined her, he told her what needed to be done.

"You are going to have to come clean to Parker…for many reasons."

"Actually, a few days ago I decided to do just that right after her birthday. I was going to ask you if you knew how I could get in to see him."

"I'm sure I can use my badge since he is officially involved in the case."

"Can it wait until after her birthday?"

"Al, you have already deprived him of three birthdays, do you really think it's fair to exclude him from her fourth?"

She could see the logic in what her brother was saying. She knew she was just using any excuse to prolong the confrontation ahead of her. She decided to give her brother the okay to meet with Abe as soon as possible.

"There's one more thing you should be aware of, Ali." He was looking for his sister's reaction to his news. "If the tabloids are to be believed, Abe was engaged on Thanksgiving."

She tried to hide the hurt, but Jake saw it. He was afraid that she thought herself in love with the man. Maybe she was. That could be why, until recently, she never became involved with anyone. One of the brothers recently informed him her old boyfriend was back in town and they were a couple again. Things were going to get heated for his little sister and because her heart was involved, he wasn't sure he could fix the situation.

***

With shaking hands, the woman shot the needle in her vein. She needed to forget about the botched-up job they performed earlier in the day. She knew they should have hired professionals. But he thought he was just as good as any professional.

Now the slut could identify him. He was pacing back and forth in the living room of their shack. He was mumbling about not going back to prison. He was confused as to why she put the envelope in the car before he even had the kid. She didn't feel like she owed him an explanation but she did justify her actions by explaining she was worried he'd rushed out with the kid in his arms there wouldn't be time to drop the envelope. Plus the door was left unlocked so it was better to put it inside than on the windshield. Of course, in hindsight she didn't think about the bitch coming to her car a second time. Thankfully she only got into her trunk and not the front seat where the envelope was. If that was the case, she'd just run the little mommy over and be done with it.

What did she care if he was mad about the note? She was the one pissed because he botched up the kidnapping part. Seriously how hard could it be to snag a kid from a scrawny girl? He was twice the size of the slut. He could have just shoved her and kept running. What kind of dumbass lets a small woman and little kid beat the shit out of him?

She was shocked when he tore out of the building running like the devil himself was on his tail and didn't have the kid in his arms. The next thing she knew was he was yelling drive, drive, drive. She took off like a bat out of hell! It was a good thing no one followed. After deserting the van where she kept her car hidden in the woods, they drove straight to the shack making sure no one followed.

Now they were going to have to figure out a new plan and he was really going to have to stay hidden. The bitch could identify him. With him having a record, it could take no time for her to pick him out of a crowd in this puny little town.

She wanted the satisfaction of killing the bitch. It was her revenge she was seeking. She felt satisfied when she thought about blowing the bitch's brains out. If her kid was near, she'd put a bullet between her eyes as well.

The thought of Ali Mason sprawled out in a coffin made her smile. Sitting back, she was starting to feel good. She was suddenly oblivious to him and his pacing and mumblings. She just wanted to float away to her happy place...visions of the dead bitch and her kid lying next to her floated around her head.

***

Pulling into the parking garage in downtown Nashville, Jake was a bundle of confidence...Ali was not! Jake came through on finding Abe. He used his connections and got in touch with Abe's agent. The meeting was set up in the agent's offices two days after the attempted kidnapping.

She was nervous about leaving her daughter for a few hours, but Will arrived at the ranch yesterday and had the job of babysitter today. She knew her parents and Will would keep her little girl safe. So that did cushion the worry a bit.

Ali panicked as they stepped onto the eleventh floor inside the tall high rise and walked into the office. Jake told her he didn't give the music agent, Max Dobson, any details, just that he needed to question Mr. Parker about an FBI investigation.

Max assured the agent that Abe was in town and they could meet as soon as possible. Max didn't want any bad publicity so he was willing to cooperate in any way he could. Plus he was very curious what Abe would have to do with an FBI investigation? Over the last several years he and Abe have become as tight as brothers. Abe was his friend first and client second. As far as Max knew, Abe shared pretty much everything going on with him, from how the pressure of the industry was getting to him, to how he wasn't sure if his fiancé was his forever.

Jake would have made the appointment for the previous day, but had a day full of submitting the necessary grants and convincing the schoolboard that the school needed an updating on their security. He even hinted that there would be no lawsuits from his sister as long and the necessary changes were made. The board readily agreed.

The secretary walked Ali and Jake into the conference room where Mr. Dobson was waiting. He shook hands with both and asked them to call him Max. Offering them a seat at the long table, he explained that Abe would be there shortly. Ali, too nervous to sit stayed standing next to her brother.

As both men talked about the upcoming NFL games Ali turned to the sound of the door opening. There in the doorway stood the center of her thoughts for the last few years. She couldn't take her eyes off him. He wasn't quite the scruffy musician she first saw on the television the night she gave birth to Ana, but he wasn't the clean-cut Abe she met four years ago. Not that it mattered either way, she still thought he was incredibly handsome. Not wanting to be caught gawking and feeling very insecure, she quickly looked down at her clenched hands. So many thoughts going through her head. She was afraid he wouldn't remember her. Afraid, after today he would hate her.

Abe, with his hand still on the doorknob, spotted her while she quickly looked away. He wondered if he was dreaming. He recognized that face as the one that still haunted him years later. Was he really looking at his Ali Cat? How did she find him? Why was she here? God she was as beautiful as ever! So much was running through his head as well.

Max needed him here because he was being questioned in an FBI investigation. So why was Ali here? Who was the man with her? Her husband or boyfriend? He didn't know where to go from here. He wanted to grab Ali and swing her around.

"Abe, good you're here." Max took control of the situation. "Come in and meet Detective Jake Mason and his sister Ali."

Stepping in the room he closed the door behind him. Did Max just say sister? He was positive he did! He looked at Ali and grinned. Walking over to Jake he shook his hand before turning to Ali and smiling. "How have you been Ali Cat?"

Ali was relieved to see he remembered her. She smiled into his handsome face and replied. "Good." That was all she could say, not trusting herself to say anything more.

She was almost glad he wasn't the clean-cut Abe she first met. That Abe could melt her with just a smile. This one could melt her as well but the camouflage did rough him up a bit. His beard was cut short, shorter than he wore it in his early career days. The last few years he took on the more reserved scruffy look with the shadow effect more than the long-bearded look he wore in the early days of his career. She noticed he aged a bit in the last few years but only for the good. His hair was the messy trend that was the style these days. His skin was a nice tan and his mouth was as beautiful as her haunting memories often teased her about.

Jake watched the two of them completely absorbed into each other. He was glad Parker remembered his sister. He was also happy to see that Parker was looking at her with something close to adoration. He didn't want to see his sister hurt. But if he had money riding on it, he'd bet Parker wasn't going to be happy when he found out Ali kept him from his daughter for the last four years. He had a feeling it was going to be a while before the man looked at her with anything but contempt.

Even though, Parker better not treat his sister with anything but respect. Ali had her reasons for doing what she did. As her brother, he stood by her decisions. Maybe not agree…but he still stood by her.

Max was confused by the pair staring at each other. Who was this girl and how did Abe know her? It took him a minute before it dawned on him. This was the girl Abe searched for high and low for months. Max had felt terrible for his friend during those months when Abe never saw her again. As far as Max knew, to this day Abe never acted like that over a girl!

Jake broke the ice. "Parker…" he addressed Abe but looked at Ali to make sure she was up to the confrontation. At her nod he continued. "I'm going to leave you alone with my sister so she can explain what this is all about. I want you to know that I do need to speak with you before you take off…is that clear?"

Abe gave him a confused nod and Max reassured the detective Abe wasn't going anywhere. Jake and Max left the room leaving Ali and Abe alone.

Abe stared at Ali until she made eye contact. He still couldn't believe she was standing in front of him. She looked the same only different…more mature. Her hair was slightly shorter but still the beautiful raven color he loved. Her face was slightly more mature looking, yet she still looked very young…and innocent. The body he fantasized about for many months was still slender…yet curvier in all the right places. Abe mentally shook himself to stop his mind from drifting off to the night they spent together.

When she finally looked at him, he walked over to her, reached for her hand and led her over to the table and pulled out a chair for her as he sat across the corner from her to easily face her only a foot away. Neither commented about the shock that pulsed through them when he took her hand a moment before.

"How long has it been, Ali?" he asked, still surprised and happy she was there.

She knew what he was asking. How long has it been since the night they spent together? She really didn't want to think about that night. She was having a hard-enough time absorbing how handsome he was. Then he insinuates about 'the night' and flashbacks start coming into play. "It will be five years this spring," she stated shyly.

"Why didn't you call me?" he asked.

"How could I call you; I didn't have your number. I didn't even have your name. Why did you take off?" She tried to not sound defensive and accusing but her emotions were getting in the way.

"Ali, I left my number on a piece of paper from the hotel notepad that was on the table next to the bed. I had a seven o'clock appointment at the recording studio that I couldn't miss. I tried waking you but you were out like a light."

She read the truth in his eyes and the way they pleaded with her to understand. She also realized that before she had Ana, she was a hard sleeper. "I'm sorry Abe," she whispered. "I never saw the note. I thought you walked out on me," she said looking him in the eyes.

Abe took her hands in his. "Ali, I searched months for you. I even had Max looking. It was like you fell off the face of the Earth." He gave her a lopsided grin. "Are you really a teacher and what is your real name?"

She looked at him with a confused expression. "Yes, I'm a teacher and my name is Ali Mason. Why do you think I'd fabricate that?"

"Well none of the rooms at the hotel were booked to an Ali, Alice, Allison, or anything close to that and I couldn't find a registered teacher with the Illinois State Board of Education named Al of any kind that looked anything like you when googled or on social media."

Several things crossed her mind, first…anyone can find out anything, anytime on the internet unless they truly want to find someone as in her and Abe's case. Second…he did try to find her. Third…he went to a lot of trouble to try and find her. Fourth…she still was infatuated with him.

"Kris, my coworker staying with me at the Gaylord, put the room in her name. She left the day before because she had a sick grandmother and was needed home. Sadly, her grandmother passed away that weekend. Anyway, I stayed to finish the workshop the day I met you. Kris and I kept the room until that Friday because we planned to have one evening hanging out in Nashville. As for am I a teacher? I teach in Kentucky, which is almost my back door. I received my degree at KSU. I applied for my license in Kentucky because I had a job offer there before I graduated, so at that point there was no reason to get an Illinois license."

That explained a lot to Abe. So she wasn't in town for the weekend. He pretty much assumed that when the lady at the desk told him the reservations for most of the teachers ended that day. "So what about the note?"

She shook her head. "I didn't see a note." Looking sheepish she continued. "But that could be because as you are well aware I was a hard sleeper. Housekeeping woke me around eleven-thirty. Check out was at eleven. So needless to say, I was in a hurry to get out of the room."

So many hurdles had blocked them from being together. Four years had changed so much for him and probably her, he thought. He suddenly remembered he had a fiancé. A good girl that wouldn't probably like that he was sitting at a table reminiscing about the most incredible night he ever experienced.

Yet for some reason he needed the closure with Ali. He couldn't let her walk out of his life without knowing if there was something between the two of them. "So, when did you realize I was who I was?"

Ali stood and walked over to the window. Looking out she saw nothing. She turned to find him staring at her. "Why didn't you tell me who you were?" she asked.

Abe knew the answer because it was what made him fall for her. He walked over to her and took her hands in his. "You were the first person to make me feel like a normal, everyday man. You looked at me as a woman should look at a man. Not some starstruck groupie."

Ali's eyes filled with tears. Abe mistook the tears for lost time. He nudged her chin to look in his eye. "I've thought of you every day since the first time I met you Ali Cat," he said softly.

Ali dropped her hands and turned away to try and stop the tears. Abe gave her a minute to clear her thoughts and recompose herself. Taking a deep breath Ali dried her eyes and turned back to him. Moving toward the table she put her hands on the edge as if to support herself.

"Abe, you asked me when did I realize who you were." At his nod, she continued. "It was the following Christmas morning…when I was in the hospital giving birth to our daughter."

Ali watched as a large display of emotions swept across his face. He looked at her long and hard. "Is this some kind of a joke?"

Ali, wiping at her tears from across the table, shook her head. "No. Abe I had no idea how to get ahold of you. I did my own investigating but came up with nothing." She gave a watery chuckle. "You would think there wouldn't be that many Abes or Abrahams in the Nashville area but there is. Of course, ninety percent are over sixty, so that narrowed it down. I guess there's a reason you aren't listed in the white pages. I'm guessing famous people have unlisted numbers."

"But you forget, we had protection!" he sounded angry.

God, this wasn't going how she planned. She looked him in the eyes and said, "Not the last time."

His mind flashed back to her and her beautiful body riding him long and hard. He had to shift the thought from his head because he was starting to get aroused with the memory. Now definitely wasn't the time to be thinking about that.

"So you're telling me you had no idea who I was until you had the baby. So why come clean now? What do you want? Do you need money?" He was getting angry. His perfect dream girl wasn't seeming so perfect now.

She was hurt and on the verge of becoming angry. "I can afford to take care of my child. That's not why I'm here."

"Then what is? I really can't believe this." He started pacing and was running his fingers through his hair. "I thought you were different. And now you are telling me I have a child." Then, as if realizing what he said he stopped and turned to her. "What's her name? What's she like? Why isn't she here?"

Looking in his eyes she replied. "Her name is Ana."

Abe looked at her with a startled expression. That had been his grandmother's name. Did Ali know that and if so, then how. Suddenly he had a flashback about telling her of his grandmother. He couldn't remember if he told her the name.

As if reading his thoughts Ali said, "You talked about your grandmother and her love for flowers. I remembered seeing the love in your eyes when you spoke of her. So I named Ana after her."

Abe looked at her for several minutes. The anger he felt right now wasn't going to go away for a while. Was she telling the truth? If so, who was she to take the first four years of his daughter's life from him?

Turning to her he asked, "How did you find out who I was when she was born?"

"There was a blizzard coming through that Christmas. My friend Regan decided to stay snowed in at the hospital with me in case I needed anything. She was channel surfing when I glanced up and you were on the television. Needless to say, I was a little shocked." More like flabbergasted but he didn't need to know that.

"Okay, I can give you that, but what about the next four years?"

Ali walked back to the window, put her back to the frame and looked at him long and hard. "I guess I have many excuses…and that's what they are…excuses."

He took his hands out of his pockets and she could see him fisting and unfisting them. She knew he was angry but was trying to keep his composure.

"Try me," was all he said.

Taking a deep breath. "Okay, let's start that I had just had a baby. I'm hormonal, I feel large and gross. No way I could let you see me after all that time looking like that. Call it vanity." He looked her up and down letting her know he didn't see how that was possible.

Ali blushed at his appraisal. "Then I had to deal with living in a small town. Rumors were already spreading like wildflowers. My best friend, Regan…the one with me in the hospital, came up with a fabrication." She took a deep breath. "You see…where I live people judge. I'm a schoolteacher. I'm a role model, not an unwed mother."

"So what was the fabrication?"

"I told everyone I had been talking to a man from Nashville for several months. We met online. He and I got together the week I was in Nashville. When I got home, I found I was pregnant. So the father and I were trying to make a go of it with a long-distance relationship."

"So what happened when the father never showed up?"

"That's the plus with having a mother and best friend as witnesses to meeting the father and verifying he was a nice guy and a good father. Sadly, the father and I weren't suited so our relationship never worked."

"Wow, you thought it all out." He looked at her with amazement and distrust. "You are really good at lying. So why should I believe the child is even mine?"

She couldn't believe what she was hearing. That statement finally pushed her to her breaking point. She was giving him the greatest gift one human could give another and he was throwing it back in her face.

If he wanted to hurt her, he found the correct button to push. He was angry that she was one of the few people he ever trusted and in the end, she was like the others. He pushed her and didn't care. She was up to something and he was going to get to the bottom of it.

Before he could speak, she went at him verbally. "I don't care what you believe. I don't give a fig if you do or don't want any part of our daughter. Because you see she's my daughter. No one but mine. I didn't plan for it to happen but it did." She glared at him with those intense catlike eyes he was once crazy over. "You donated a necessary part but I'm the one who carried her for nine months," her voice hit a higher pitch as she continued her rant. "I'm the one who had to be ridiculed by close-minded people. I'm the one who held her when she had a boo-boo. I'm the one who sat up every night she had a fever praying to the Good Lord she would be okay." She took a deep breath to try and calm down.

Abe looked at her coldly. "You know something else you did Ali…you took all that away from me. If she's mine…and yes, I will have it tested…why didn't you give me the chance to hold her through the nights when she was sick? To wipe her cuts and scrapes? What did you think I was going to do today when you threw this at me, jump for joy and make us a big happy family?" His anger got to the best of him as he looked and her and fairly shouted, "You basically stole a daughter from me!"

Chapter Eleven

Jake, sitting outside the door making small chitchat, heard the shouting. He was unable to make out the words but knew it was getting heated. Deciding it was time to intervene, he stood and headed for the door.

"I'm going to break this up. I'm not sure if your client wants you in there or not?"

Rising, Max stated, "I'm pretty sure I have an idea of what's going on. I'm thinking your sister is the same Ali that Abe searched months for a few years back."

Nodding, Jake was happy by the other man's words. He liked hearing that the guy cared enough about Ali to search for her. Standing back he followed Max in.

Max was taken back by the anger on both faces. "Are you guys okay if we come in?"

Ali turned back to look out the window as Abe motioned them in. Jake walked over and put his arms around his sister's shoulder.

She wiped her eyes and whispered to her brother, "I can't do this anymore today. I got as far as telling him he has a daughter but I can't go any farther. Can you please give me the keys and I'll wait in the car for you?"

Nodding, he handed her the keys. She reached in her handbag and pulled out a small photo album and handed it to him. As she hugged him, she asked him to see that Abe got the album. He watched her walk out the door before turning and placing the book on the window ledge.

Abe was too distracted watching Ali's retreat to notice the book. He wanted to stop her but his feet and mouth wouldn't cooperate. He had so many mixed up emotions going through his head.

Jake could see the anger, hurt, and confusion going on in the guy's head. Hell, he'd be angry too if someone dropped a bomb on him like his sister just did to the poor guy. Yet he believed Ali's intentions were honorable and he was going to see that Abe knew it too.

He drew both men's attention when he leaned against the window frame and said, "I need to know if you have any intentions of getting to know my niece or not?"

Abe took a moment to realize the man was referring to his child. He was also aware that even though Ali's brother seemed calm, there was an underlined anger behind those eyes and he was sure it was because of him.

When Abe didn't reply, Max looked at him and asked, "Is he implying what I think he's implying?"

Abe looked at his long-time friend and nodded. "Yes, Ali had my child four years ago. She just got around to telling me."

Jake noted Abe was trying to keep calm. He was glad to hear him say 'his' daughter. Deep down whether the poor guy admitted it or not, he knew Ali wasn't lying about the baby being his. As all big brothers are known to do, he decided to defend his sister.

"Here's the deal Parker. I don't give a rat's ass if you want to be a part of my niece's life. She has five uncles that fill the role of father." He almost felt sorry for the guy when he saw the anger reach his face at the thought of someone else playing daddy to his kid. "But I'm going to explain a few things first." He paused, making sure he chose his words carefully. He didn't want to make the matter worse for his sister or his niece but he had to make sure Abe knew he wasn't going to put up with any bullshit.

"Five years ago, my sister comes home from Nashville pregnant and scared. To avoid being ridiculed and having her baby thought of as a bastard she fabricated a love story that would hush some of the gossip in a small town. After the baby was born, she finds out that the father is some big star amongst a bunch of hoopla. She's hormonal and not feeling like she could possibly compete with all the groupies he has hanging onto his every word." Jake watched Abe wince at the description of his life.

He continued. "Then when the guilt gets to her, after the baby is a few months old, she has no idea how to even approach you. She doesn't want me or her other brothers to know that she lied to us. Because you see…Ali isn't a good liar and it made her sick to know she lied to us. So she chickens out again."

Seeing that he still had Abe's attention he went on. "There were many thoughts going through her head by this time. One, you were touring all over the world…how could you make time for a baby. Two, what if you decided you wanted to take Ana from her…remember you left her in that hotel room without a 'hi, bye, kiss-my-ass, or anything.'"

Abe interrupted. "I left her a note," he stated. When Jake gave him a look of doubt by lifting his eyebrows, Abe continued. "I did! Ali and I just discussed this. She admitted the maids woke her up and she rushed to get packed and could have easily overlooked the note."

Jake was relieved that the guy didn't just up and leave his sister. Yet he still wasn't finished with Abe.

"So where was I? Yep two, taking Ana away from her." Jake put his hands on the table and leaned toward Abe. "But we both know that wouldn't happen. You know why you can't try to take Ana from Ali?" Before he could answer, Jack continued in a calm and deadly voice. "Because you'd have to go through me to get to her. And I can promise you, you don't want to do that!"

Abe looked at Jake with disgust and stood up and leaned forward to get a good look in Jake's eyes. "You're right I don't want to do that, but not because of your threats…but because I would never keep a child from a parent…unlike your sister!"

Both men stood staring at each other. Jake was the first to back down but only because he truly believed that Abe got the raw end of the deal. He really should have been made a part of Ana's life as soon as Ali knew who he was. Jake still had to let the guy know he wasn't going to pull any bullshit as far as his sister and niece were concerned.

"Touché Parker, you made your point. We both know where the other stands." Taking a seat, he motioned that Abe should do the same. After Abe sat, he continued. "We have bigger fish to fry."

"You are right. When do I get to meet my daughter? Did you bring her to Nashville?"

Jake was glad to see that Abe truly wanted to meet Ana. He smiled at the thought of how much Abe was going to be pleasantly surprised by his charming niece. "No, but we will set something up whenever you are ready. Ali doesn't want to keep you away from her anymore. You may not believe this but she has always had the intention to find you and let you know about Ana."

Looking at Jake, Abe asked, "What fish?"

Jake decided he needed to fill him in on the rest of the tale. "I want you to know first that Ana has started asking questions about you since she started pre-k this fall. Enough that Ali decided she needed to tell you about Ana soon. It's your choice if you want to be in her life and my sister doesn't want anything from you. If you chose to be in her life Ali will not stop you. She will even try to accommodate you as much as possible. Though you need to remember your lifestyle…now put a four-year-old into the middle of it." Jake wanted Abe to know they truly wanted nothing from him.

Jake and Abe looked to be in a staring competition, Abe's expression giving him nothing. "She was going to have me find a way to get in touch with you after the holiday and Ana's birthday." When Abe asked why then, Jake shrugged and said Ali would have to explain her reasoning. "I do know the reason why it's now instead of then."

"Why?" Abe asked.

Jake looked at Abe intently. "Someone tried to kidnap Ana from her Preschool class two days ago!"

Abe and Max both sat up in their seats and stared at Jake.

"What?" Abe almost shouted. "What the hell is going on? This is like some crazy dream I haven't woke up from!"

Jake preceded to tell the two men about the incident at school and about how Ali stopped the man from grabbing her daughter. Both men didn't say anything for several minutes because they were trying to process Jake's words.

Abe was the first to speak. "Have they been caught?"

When Jake shook his head, Max spoke for the first time. "Any leads?"

"No, but we think we have a motive."

Both men waited for Jake to continue. When he didn't say anything, Abe started to feel his temper flair. "What's the motive?"

Jake looked back and forth between the two men then his eyes settled on Abe. "Someone knows she's your daughter!"

"Oh my God!" Was all Abe could say.

Max, being an agent and always handling PR, looked at Jake and asked him why he thought that. Jake pulled out his phone and showed the men the pic of the letter.

Jake addressed both men. "Because there is a child involved, we get to take the case. With that being said you have the best on the case."

Abe dared to ask, "Are you implying you're the best?"

Jake shook his head. "In my line of work there are hundreds of the best. When you put them together, they can do incredible things and have some serious power. So when it comes to my niece…only the best of the best will be on the case!"

"Who all knew Abe fathered a child?" Max asked.

"As far as Ali knows it is just her and her best friend Regan." He held up his hand to stop Abe from asking the obvious. "No Regan would never rat out Ali. She is like family to us. But I need to make sure she didn't accidentally let it slip to someone. That is my plan for this evening."

Looking at his watch, Jake felt he left Ali in the car long enough. It was time to get moving. He gave Abe a lot to think about. Standing, he looked at Abe and said, "Now what?"

Abe stood and said, "When can I meet my daughter?"

"As soon as you want?"

"Tomorrow!"

Max decided now was the time to chime in. "Abe, I'm thinking you need to go to her and not have her in Nashville. It sounds as if she doesn't need to be in the public eye so it would probably work out if you go to…?" He looked at Jake for the name of the town.

"Ramona, Illinois. It's about two hours north of here. I'll write down the address."

Watching Jake take out his card and jotting down Ali's address, Abe asked if the town had a hotel. Jake replied there were two decent ones.

Max interrupted. "Abe, I think it's best if you have a more private setting. I'm hoping no one recognizes you as it is. Yet staying in a hotel could cause quite a stir. How will you get to know your daughter that way?"

Jake and Abe knew Max had a point. "Ali can put you up." Jake stated.

Abe chuckled. "I think your sister would like to stay as far away from me as she can."

"I'll handle Ali. Besides, she has a four-bedroom cottage and I'm staying there until the kidnapping is resolved. Plus it will give you time to get to know Ana!" Jake stood to let them know it was a done deal. "What time can we expect you?"

Abe looked at Jake and said noon. He didn't know what to think about Ali's brother. One minute he was in Abe's face, the next he acted like he wanted him in Ali and Ana's life. Jake shook Abe's hand with a grin on his lips. That grin only made him nervous. It was then that Abe realized he didn't have a choice but to trust him. Besides Ali, who took off because she couldn't stand to be in the same room as him, Jake was the only connection he had to his daughter.

Jake looked at Abe and read his thoughts. He really did feel badly for the poor guy. He also realized this man hurt his sister. Maybe not intentional, but then again maybe he did…Jake couldn't be sure. His instincts said Abe was a good guy. Yet he couldn't bet on instincts alone when it came to his sister and niece. The only thing he knew, from the story she told him about meeting Abe and the way she couldn't handle being in the room with Abe, his sister was in love with the guy.

Jake walked over to the window ledge and grabbed the album Ali handed him to give to Abe. Turning to the two men he said, "My number is on the card. I know there is going to be some PR and paparazzi issues that are going to arise. So call me as soon as you decide on what story you come up with." He turned to Abe. "Did Ali explain what she told the town about the pregnancy?" When he nodded Jake turned to Max. "Use what she said…tweak it if you have to, then let me know so the family is on the same page."

Max nodded. Jake walked over to Abe. "I want you to know, until very recently Ali hasn't shown an interest in anyone since you. I'm telling you to not play with her heart. If it's there it's there…if it's not then don't lead her down a dark path. I'm not sure she could handle losing you again!" He placed the book in front of Abe and walked out the door saying nothing.

Abe was surprised to see it was a photo album Jake put in front of him. He put his hands on the cover not ready to open it. Max's words jerked him out of his thoughts.

"So I guess congratulations are in order?" Max asked hesitantly.

Abe gave his friend a strange look. "I guess."

He wanted to get excited, Hell, he always wanted kids. Yet what if this was some bullshit being pulled over his eyes. It wouldn't be the first time. Over the years he's had women try all kinds of ploys to get their hands into his fame. Which was why he didn't date much. Then when he met Shea, he didn't have to worry about it. She was also a country singer fighting her way to the top.

She knew what it was like. She lived the life he did. That was why they got along so well. Before he met her, he was ready to call it all quits. He was tired of the traveling and the hoopla, but she pumped him back up again. She made him see that life would be boring and lonely if he gave it up. She made him second-guess his dream of living the normal life.

He wondered how she was going to react to his news that he had a little girl. It was odd, but he didn't know if his petite, brunette, country girl even liked kids. Well she would have to because he had one and he planned to be a part of his daughter's life.

Looking at Max, he asked, "So what do we tell the fans?"

"What story did she use in her town?" Max asked.

Abe explained the fabricated story Ali told her family and friends. Max said to go with it if word gets out. Only they were going to tweak it that they met through a friend and had shared a romantic week together. They were going to let everyone believe he has always been a part of the baby's life but kept it low profile to protect his daughter. As far as he and Ali…they decided they didn't suit and remained friends because there was no love interest there.

Abe grabbed his book and thanked Max for clearing his schedule until well after the New Year. As Max walked him out, he promised to keep in touch. Abe left quickly, wanting to get home so he could collect his thoughts and look at the album in his hand.

***

Ali had a million questions to ask Jake when he got into the car. Instead she let him weasel his way through the downtown traffic and jump on the interstate before she bombarded him.

"So, what did he say about the attempted abduction?" she asked him.

"There wasn't much he could say. I think he felt like shit knowing Ana was probably kidnapped because of his fame."

"Well that isn't his fault." Ali stated.

Abe looked at her and then back to the road. He shook his head. She was so angry with the man one minute, defending him the next…'Women!' he thought.

Jake explained almost everything that happened in the meeting. He left out how he and Abe almost came to blows because Abe was pissed he didn't get to be a part of his daughter's first four years. He did reassure her that Abe had no intention of taking her daughter away.

"You don't know how relieved I am to hear that. It was my biggest fear all along," she stated.

"Also, Ana's going to have company tomorrow," he stated as if no big deal.

"What?" she almost shouted. "Tomorrow? Are you kidding? That's four days before Christmas. I can't be ready for him by then. Why tomorrow?"

Jake looked at his sister for a second before turning back to the road. "Because he's missed out on the last four years and he doesn't want to miss another day."

He knew his statement hurt her and that wasn't his intention. She has to understand Parker's point of view. "Al," he grabbed her hand and gave it a squeeze. "I don't mean to hurt you but you have to see where he's coming from. Also, you are going to have to try sharing Ana with her dad…you owe it to both of them," he said gently.

Ali stared out the car window and collected her thoughts for a few minutes. He was right. It was just going to be hard letting someone in her and Ana's perfect life. She had a nagging question in the back of her head asking herself how did she think Todd was ever going to fit into her and her baby's lifestyle. That was a thought she pushed away because it was the last thing she could deal with now.

She was sure that Abe wouldn't be staying around long. She'd bet it would take a week or so before he'd run off and play country star. Obviously, he was living the dream. So being stuck in Smalltown USA wasn't going to appeal to him. Which was just fine with her because her life would go back to normal. At least that's what she planned to tell herself over and over.

"By the way," Jake interrupted her thoughts, "Abe will be staying at your house!"

Ali looked at him incredulous. Was he kidding? Of course he was? Abe didn't want to stay at her house any more than she wanted him there. There was no longer anything between them so there was no reason he couldn't stay at a hotel. "Funny Jake!"

"I'm not kidding Al!"

"Then please tell me why Abe is staying with me? Ramona has two perfectly good hotels, even though I'm sure Mr. Country Star is too good for them!"

"That's exactly why he has to stay with you. He's too well known to be hanging out in a small-town hotel. Right now, we have to think about Ana's safety!"

Ali knew he was right. She needed to quit acting like a selfish brat. This wasn't about her but about her daughter. Ana came first…always.

"While we are on the subject, I need to know who all knew Abe was Ana's father."

"It was just Regan and myself. I didn't even tell Mom because I wanted to let sleeping dogs lie."

"Is there anyway Regan could have accidentally let it slip. Like maybe to one of her clients?"

"No, if that happened, she would have told me." At his doubtful look she stated, "You can ask her yourself. She's coming to dinner tonight at the farm. I need to fill her in on what transpired today and let the fam in on the reason we think Ana was almost kidnapped. And don't give me hell about letting Regan in on what's going on. She has a right to know. She's been with me since day one…besides it's a girl thing. You wouldn't understand!"

Chapter Twelve

That evening Abe was trying to make his fiancé understand what transpired earlier in the day. Shea was angry. Abe had never seen her so angry. To anyone else she looked perfect with her petite, little body and her long dark hair framing the flawless skin that graced the cover of magazines everywhere as the upcoming hottest new country star. Abe could see the anger flaring in her dark brown eyes.

"Abe, I can't imagine why you wouldn't tell me about having a kid when we first hooked up?"

Abe hated lying to his fiancé, but something in the back of his head was telling him that the less she knew the better. The more she ranted and raved the more he was glad he gave her the same fabricated story they were going to give the rest of the world when the story got out.

"Shea, I told you, I haven't seen my daughter in a while. Her mother and I had a bit of a fight the last time I visited. Then I went on tour and you know how it is." God it made him sick to be acting like a Jackass for a father. Lying wasn't his thing but he wasn't sure he could completely trust her and that was something that bothered him. Ironically it was in that moment he realized his feelings for Shea couldn't be deep if he couldn't completely trust her with something as important as the birth of his daughter. Maybe he was jumping into this marriage for all the wrong reasons.

"Why not tell me before now?"

"It is for the protection of my daughter that we keep a low profile on her. You know how some idiots are out there. We've always been afraid someone would try to hurt her if they knew she was my daughter. So it just wasn't something I ever thought to bring up since meeting you this spring!" There was that Jackass feeling again.

"So how long are you going to be at this hillbilly town of Romeo?" Not correcting her on the town's real name he just shrugged. He wanted to be gone as long as it took to get to know Ana.

"Well I have some time off…maybe I'll come stay a few days as well!" She wasn't happy with him spending time with his child's mother. He obviously cared about the woman at one time.

Abe didn't know how to break it to her that he was staying at Ali's house. So he let it go at that. He didn't think she would take the time to go to the 'hillbilly town' so he wasn't too worried about that.

"Also, I won't be home for Christmas. Ana's birthday is Christmas day so I'm going to spend it with her."

"Ugh. What's the point in having you as a fiancé if you don't want to spend time with me!" Walking over to the kitchen table she tossed her handbag over her shoulder. Turning to Abe she shouted. "I don't think I can handle much more of this." She flared her arms up dramatically. "I'm not going to let a kid be number one in your life. You and I are the next upcoming Faith and Tim. Don't throw it away because you knocked up some bimbo and now you're trying to be a do gooder!"

Her words made her ugly and Abe had enough. She obviously didn't really care about him. She was just trying to be the next big country duo. After seeing Ali today, he wondered what he ever saw in Shea. Her words showed her real character and it wasn't a pretty picture. She only just found out he had a daughter and she's already making demands and feeling threatened by a mire four-year old. Looking at her he saw the shallow and vain person she really was and he wasn't impressed. Actually he was disgusted.

Quietly he spoke. "I'm telling you now, you don't have a shot in hell coming close to the love I feel for my child. Your first mistake was thinking you did." What a shock to know his words were true even though he hadn't met his daughter yet. Just knowing about her for a few hours took hold of his heart and bonded him with a connection. He wasn't going to touch on the part of him that was asking if the connection had anything to do with the buried feeling he had for her mother.

He nodded to the door. "I think you need to head to the door and drop the ring on the table."

Shea panicked. She saw the anger in his eyes too late. She needed Abe in her life. They worked good together, sang good together, made love good together, and the world loved them together.

She walked over to him and ran her hands up his chest. "Baby I'm sorry. I was just shocked and hurt that you never told me you had a baby." She cooed.

Abe pulled her hands away and turned her toward the door. "Sorry Shea, I don't think it's going to work!" He wondered what he ever saw in her in the first place. Sure she was pretty on the outside, but there was something cold on the inside. How did he ever let himself get involved with someone he didn't love…much let get engaged? He realized he was just settling for the marriage and family part of it.

He knew he picked Shea because she showed him they were reaching for the same thing…fame. Yet in reality he realized she was no different than a groupie. She didn't want him, she just wanted a piece of what he was. Honestly, she didn't really ever hide what she wanted…fame, money, stardom. Deep down he knew she was just using him to get to the top but he didn't care because he was tired of being alone.

Shea started to worry at the look of disgust on Abe's face as he stared at her. She was nobody's fool and realized in that instant she had to do damage control. There was no way she was going to let a little brat disrupt what she worked so hard for these last few months. Trying again she gave him a sultry look and slid her hands up his arms and around his neck. "Let's not fight Baby!" she softly cooed. "We can get through this." She leaned in to pull his mouth to hers.

Abe wanted no part of her. Reaching up he pulled her arms from his neck. Stepping back, he stated, "I think you need to leave!"

Shea panicked and pleaded one last time. "Don't do nothing rash. Give it some time and we can talk about this when you get back!"

"Goodbye Shea."

Steaming, she turned and pulled open the door. "We aren't through Abe. When you get time to cool down you know where to find me. I'm not giving you the ring back until we talk again." She rushed out the door before he could stop her. He had no intentions of stopping her. It was just a ring. He didn't care if she kept the damn thing or not. He had bigger worries than Shea and a ring. Like who was trying to kidnap his daughter? A daughter he never met.

Abe ran his hand through his hair and felt like a tornado came rushing into his life today. Seeing an old love, finding out he had a daughter, and breaking up with a fiancé was a lot for one day. What he wanted most to do was look at the pictures in the album Jake gave him.

He didn't open it yet because when he arrived at his house, Shea was waiting for him. He pretty much forgot about her when he made plans to leave town. After seeing the way she reacted to him having a daughter, he was relieved she was gone. Maybe he wasn't being fair to Shea because many feelings surfaced after seeing Ali today. Those old feelings made him realize that he and Shea never had anything as close to what he felt in one night with Ali. So it was probably for the best he and Shea move apart.

Shaking his thoughts away from Ali and Shea, Abe wanted to focus on his daughter. First he needed to share his news with his mother and sister. Shooting them a group text, he asked if they were free for the evening. His mom lived down the lane from him and his sister took up residence in his old apartment downtown. Odds were his mom was free but he doubted if his social butterfly sister was. She was always busy with whatever it was a single twenty-six-year-old female did.

Like he expected, his mom could make it but his sister wanted to know if it was worth breaking her plans for? Abe assured her it was. His mom offered to toss together some supper for them and bring it over. Abe readily agreed and didn't mention he didn't think he had the stomach to eat tonight.

Sitting down on the couch, Abe looked at the small album. It was a small scrapbook type that held three or four pics per page. The cover said 'Daddy's Little Princess.'

Opening to the first page, Abe looked at the sonogram picture of what he guessed was Ana in her mother's stomach. On the left side of the book were lines used to describe the picture on the following page. On it Ali wrote…'My Dearest Abe, I found out today we are going to have a baby girl. I'm so excited, yet so scared. I know what we felt when we made her was too early to be called love, but it's the closest I've ever come to the feeling. I wish you were here with me. I'm so scared taking this journey alone. Yet I have to be strong for her. I just hope one day you and I will meet again and you will get to meet your daughter. Love Ali.'

The next page had the same layout as before. Abe realized the book was more of a diary than a scrapbook. The picture was of Ana. He slid his finger down the pic as if wanting to touch her, wanting to be there when she was born. It must have been taken with an instant camera, minutes after she came into the world. The left side read…'My Dearest Abe, you are a father. We share a beautiful baby girl. She was born Christmas morning at 12:06 am. She is beautiful. I feel I am already in love with this perfect creation we made together. I am too tired to write much more. I just wanted to share with you this experience minutes after having her. Love Ali.'

Abe looked up and blinked back the tears. He remembered that Christmas well. That was his first Christmas here at the ranch. He remembered Ali was on his mind heavily that night. Was God trying to tell him something then? What he wouldn't give to have been there. What poor Ali went through by herself. She said she had friends and family there…but she was still by herself.

The third page was a picture, taken with an instant camera, of Ana dressed with a cute little pink dress and a headband surrounding a flock of dark curls. To the left he read Ali's entry…'Abraham Parker. Wow I can't believe I just found out who you are. It's a bit of a shock. I have so many questions to ask. I'm so afraid you left me that morning because of who you are. I'm trying not to feel used. Dear God please don't let me be just someone you played. I'm sorry I'm putting this in here. I just have some serious emotions going on. In my heart I believe you felt something for me. Because of that belief, I am naming our daughter after your grandmother Ana! She looks like an Ana, Abe. So Ana Grace Parker-Mason it is. Ali, Ana, and Abe…it even sounds cute together. – Ali.'

Abe noticed she no longer ended with 'Love Ali' or started with 'My Dearest Abe' on the following picture. It was labeled 'Three Month Pictures.' Ana was laying back on a pillow in a pretty yellow dress and a big flower headband covering her forehead. He grinned when he noticed her curly hair sticking out in every direction.

Ali wrote…'Abe, as you can see, I think our little girl has my hair. Wow Abe, she's getting so big. I admit I don't see a lot of you in her. That's probably good for me…I don't know if I could handle that. I think about you too much as it is. I don't know what to do as far as contacting you. I wouldn't really even know where to begin. I admit I have read up on your bio. You really are becoming the next big thing. I'm just worried there isn't any room in your life for a child. I know that shouldn't be my choice to make. Yet how can it not when I live, breathe, sleep, and eat for our child. There's just so much to think about. – Ali.'

Ana's six-month-old pic had her sitting up. She was holding a rag doll in her hand and her thumb was in her mouth. Abe thought she was the most beautiful thing ever.

Ali wrote…'Abe our little girl is sitting up, she coos and says mama and dada. She loves to be played with and she just popped through her first tooth. I want you to know I didn't contact you because I don't want you to blame me for ruining your life…not that I believe having Ana would ruin your life…but you might! – Ali.'

Abe sat back and tried to think about what he would have done if Ali came forward and said he was her baby's dad. He truly didn't how he would have reacted. One thing that was for sure was he never would have turned his daughter away. Hell he was half in love with Ali then. He would have probably married her on the spot and settled down in the cabin. Yet would he have been happy? Now at this place in his life he would be, but back then he was climbing. Would he have appreciated the interruption or wonder what might have been if he didn't reach the top at some point? He would never know.

The next several pics and messages were every three months and were studio pics. Ali never got personal again. Just explained where Ana was in the growing stage and would relate a cute funny story here and there. But nothing personal until the last pic and entry dated a few weeks ago. It looked like a school picture of Ana dressed like a little fairy with her long curly hair and her little round cheeks. His daughter was absolutely beautiful and looked just like her mother.

Ali wrote…'Abe, can you believe what a beautiful little girl we have. Oh Abe, she's so funny and witty. She has everyone wrapped around her finger. Also, wait until you hear her sing. Which I am hoping it will be sooner than later. Abe, she's been asking about you. I think it's time. I cannot keep you apart any longer. I just hope you are as proud of her as I am. Ali.'

Abe wiped his eyes. He was surprised to see himself crying. The last time he cried was when his father died and he was alone in his bedroom. These tears were not of sadness but more of tears of awe. He was so confused. He wanted to be mad at Ali, but deep down he understood why she did what she did!

The knock at the door interrupted his thoughts. Wiping any proof of tears off his face he placed the album on the fireplace mantle. He realized it was later than he thought. Letting the ladies in, he hugged them both and sniffed the air. "Mom, thanks for bringing dinner it smells wonderful!" It did smell delicious, maybe he was hungry after all.

"That would be soup, salad, and warm bread." Sandy stated. Abe looked at his mother with love. She was the perfect mom. Always understanding, never judging, and forever there! She was still beautiful at fifty-three. She stood about five-seven and was slender. Her hair was highlighted with soft browns and blondes. The only wrinkles were laugh lines around her light green eyes that matched Abes.

His sister Amanda was what all his friends called the 'knock-out.' He would have taken offense to it but considering she has graced the front covers of several magazines over the years he took it all in stride. She was about five-ten with long blonde hair, olive complexion, with those same light green eyes. If he wondered what Barbie looked like in real life, he'd guess it would be his sister. She turned heads everywhere she went.

Plopping down at the table Amanda stated, "Let's eat!"

The next half hour the threesome talked about their week. Abe was glad they were here with him tonight. They shared a special bond. If he had to guess he believed most families were not as blessed as their family! Yes, they lost his father years ago. Yet they kept it together all these years later.

Last year he was elated when his mother sold half of her business to a coworker. She was now a silent partner at the 'Booming Boutique,' and had more free time than ever. The first thing he did was talk her into buying the small homestead next door to him. She was excited to fix the little cottage up and was ecstatic to be next to her son.

As they sat in the kitchen, Abe kept the small talk light. He wanted everyone to finish their meal before he broke the news to them. As soon as they finished, he asked them to come into the living room. After the girls took a seat, he started pacing.

"What is it honey? Is it about Shea and the wedding?" his mother asked.

Shoot, he didn't even think about explaining he and Shea's breakup to them. "Well actually, that's one of the things I have to tell you. I broke it off with Shea earlier today," he stated.

"Thank the Good Lord!" his sister exclaimed.

Her mother shushed her. Turning back to her son she asked, "Are you okay?"

Abe reassured her he was fine and it was his decision. It was funny to realize that his mother didn't seem overly upset by the news. He knew his sister didn't like Shea, but he wondered if his mother ever did? Hell, part of the reason he proposed was because his mother kept dropping hints that he wasn't getting any younger since he turned thirty a few months ago.

"Actually, that's not even why I asked you here. I have something else to tell you." He quit pacing and rubbed his hands down the sides of his jeans. He didn't know what he was so nervous about. He knew his family would be happy about Ana. Taking a deep breath, he turned to them. "Do you remember a few years ago I spoke of a girl I met? She was staying at the Gaylord and we hung out." He let that sink in before he continued. "I told you guys that I liked her a lot but we got lost from each other?" It took them no time to remember who he was talking about. It was the only time they had ever seen him act so heartbroken over a girl.

"Yes, I remember her," Sandy stated as she looked at her daughter to see if she remembered. Amanda nodded.

"Well it seems as if I finally found her," pausing briefly, he continued, "well, in truth, she actually found me!"

Sandy looked at her son. She wondered why he didn't seem happy. Was it because he was with Shea or had been? He said that was over so why the lack of emotion? "Isn't that a good thing dear?" she asked.

Abe started pacing. "I don't know. I didn't really give you both all the details about how we met. I think I just told you a real short version." He stopped pacing and looked at them. "I met Ali in front of The Grand Ole Opry." He paused and turned to them and smiled. "She was sitting outside people watching. I was testing out my clean-shaven face and haircut." He chuckled, "I was happy she didn't recognize me. But the truth was she wasn't into country music so she had no clue who I was." He started pacing again. "We talked and hung out all afternoon into the evening." He paused and looked out the window in deep thought. "We really got to know so much about each other that afternoon, but never any facts about each other." He turned to them. "That was mostly my fault, I didn't want to be recognized and I will admit I liked being a normal person, so every time the conversation got close to our personal lives, I would change the subject."

Amanda looked confused. "But you told Ali who you were right?" She remembers thinking the girl knew but didn't want to be found.

Her brother shook his head. "Actually I didn't. I liked that she liked me for me. Plus she isn't a country music fan so she wouldn't recognize me. And back then, with a clean face, I wasn't very recognizable."

"So how did you get split up?" his mother asked.

Abe became uncomfortable, he knew he had to come clean. His mom was going to put two and two together. "Well the thing is…Ali and I…well we felt something. Something I didn't know existed. So things happened."

Sandy decided to let him off the hook. "So what you are saying is two consenting adults spent the night together? It's okay, Abe, I know what S.E.X. is. I've done it at least twice in my life."

"Yuck, Mom…that was a little TMI," Amanda stated.

Abe laughed. Glad some of the tension left. "Okay, moving on. So Ali and I had a special night together. Well the next morning I had to be at the recording studio early. So I left her a note with my number and asked her to call me so we could meet up later. Well, she slept in and was late for check out. Needless to say she rushed around and never saw the note."

"Wow, that sucks," Amanda stated.

"But now she found you? I'm surprised it took her so long. You've become a household name. Surely she recognized you," her mom stated.

"Well that's why I asked you both here. There's more to tell you…or show you." He walked over to the mantle and grabbed the Album. "I'm going to clean up in the kitchen while you take a look at this." He set the book on the table in front of them and walked into the kitchen.

Cleaning up, he wondered how they would feel about Ali. Would they resent her for keeping the news of Ana from them? He couldn't blame them. Yet since she wasn't here to defend herself, he felt it was only right that they read her words. Those words helped him to understand some of her motive.

He looked up as his mom and sister walked in the kitchen about a half hour later. Their faces were streaked with tears. Without saying a word he opened his arms and they both walked into them. He held them close for several minutes before anyone spoke. Finally his mother said, "I'm a grandma."

Abe nodded, not trusting himself to speak.

"When do we get to meet her?" Amanda asked.

"Well she lives about two hours north of here and I'm going there tomorrow to stay for a few days. I'm hoping you both will come up for Christmas and her Birthday."

"What's the name of the town?" his mother asked.

Abe pulled the card out Jake gave him earlier. He copied the information to pass on to his mother. "Ramona, Illinois. I looked it up on my maps earlier and it's a little under two hours from here…two from Nashville. It's a small town but Ali's brother assured me there's a couple decent hotels there."

"What hotel are we staying at?" Amanda asked, assuming they'd be staying at the same hotel as him.

"I'm actually going to be staying at Ali's house. Or at least I think I am. Her brother Jake and Max figured it would be less public." The next part Abe hated to have to tell them. "Which brings me to the next thing. This isn't as good as the last…actually it's the opposite."

Abe took a deep breath and told his mother and sister about the attempted kidnapping of Ana. Both women were deeply disturbed. After answering about a dozen questions, most he didn't have answers for, he warned them. "I think from here on out we need to start looking over our shoulders and not take chances." He looked at this sister as he spoke.

Amanda was beautiful, a bit wild, and took risks. His fame never seemed to roll over to her and cause her problems. Possibly because she had her own fame to identify her. She was a professional model…or was a professional until she 'retired' last year at the ripe old age of twenty-six. According to her, she wanted to retire while on top. Even though she still posed for plenty of local shoots for extra cash.

"Are you implying I take risks?" She glared at her brother.

"Are you implying you don't?" he shot back.

"I'll have you know—" She didn't get to finish because her mother interrupted.

Sandy held her hands up to stop the argument. She knew nothing bad would come out of the banter but now wasn't the time. "You two enough. So basically, we need to watch our backs because who ever tried to take my grandbaby may try for one of us?"

Nodding, Abe smiled. So grandma was already calling Ana her grandbaby. It made him happy that she was excited about his daughter.

Hell, he thought a little later as he ushered them out the door with the promise to see them Christmas Eve, he was no different. He was adjusting well to the idea of having a little girl.

First things first, he needed to give his buddy Daniel McCullens a call and see if he would make a house call early in the morning. He wanted to be clean-shaven and hair clean cut for his reunion with his daughter tomorrow. Yep it was for his daughter…he told himself. It had nothing to do with the little girl's mother.

Chapter Thirteen

Abe wasn't the only one thinking about cleaning up, Ali smiled when Jake walked in all trimmed up and looking ruggedly handsome. He kept a shadow on his face but most of the wild mop on his head was now only a few inches long.

The Mason family farm was unusually crowded for a Wednesday evening. Everyone who gathered thought they were there because Jake was in town. The guest list consisted of Frank and Lana, all five Mason boys, Granny Ellie, Ana & Ali, her best friend Regan, and Jake's partner Will.

Jake and his parents felt it was better to tell everyone at once about the kidnapping. Regan was invited because Ali wanted her there and Jake wanted to ask her about Abe. No one thought anything odd that she was at the ranch, to everyone she and her father were a part of their family.

The plan for the evening worked great, after supper Ali laid down with Ana in Ali's old bedroom until Ana was asleep. Ana was going to spend the night with her grandparents because Ali was meeting Todd later so she could fill him in on everything. Ali was good with this because Will was also camping out in one of the spare rooms until the kidnapping case was solved.

Upon entering the living room Ali made her way to Jake. He knew what was going on so she stood by him for support. She had always hated the lie she told her family and was glad to get it out in the open. She just dreaded doing it.

"Hey everyone," she shouted over their talking. When they turned to her, she continued. "So the reason you were all asked to come here was not only because Jake is in town but because of why Jake is in town."

No one said a word which only made it worse for her. "So I've asked you all here because I'm in a bit of a situation." Ali took a deep breath and her hands started wringing. "When I found out I was pregnant with Ana I lied to you all." Taking a deep breath she continued. "I actually had a one-night thing with a man I just met in Nashville!" She paused. She was too embarrassed to look anyone in the eyes.

Granny Ellie shouted, "Well, it was about time. If you ask me every girl should rock the boat a time or two. Why in my day I—" Several people shouted "Mom" and "Granny" to stop her from going on.

"What? It is what it is. It's not like all of you are perfect and haven't done a thing or two that wasn't inappropriate!" she exclaimed.

"Okay, Mom," Frank Sr. stated to his mother. "We get it. Now let Ali finish." He looked back at his daughter and nodded for her to finish.

Granny took some of the edge off the situation for Ali. She was so thankful for her. Ellie wanted everyone to know they made mistakes. It was almost if her granny knew it was a lie from the beginning. "Anyhow, I met a man while in Nashville. We hit it off. Without going into details, I think it was kind of love at first sight for me and I thought or think for him also." Taking another deep breath, she continued. "So one thing led to another and well...things happened."

"Okay, we get it," her youngest brother Adam stated, not wanting to think about his sister and things 'happening.'

"So the next morning Abe, the guy, left me a note to call him. Only I never saw the note. I was late checking out, housekeeping was at my door, and I guess I just didn't see it." She paused briefly wondering how different it would have been had she seen the note. "I waited around for a while hoping he would come back...but he never did. So I headed home, pretty bummed and a bit heartbroken."

Looking around the room she could see they weren't angry, just intrigued by the story. Her oldest brother Frank was looking at her with confusion. He was the quietest of the brothers. Growing up he was the brother who always tried to protect and shield her from anything bad. "About two months later I found out I was pregnant. Yes, I'm a big girl and should have known better but things happen. Anyway the story gets crazy...actually surreal." She made eye contact with her mother. "A few hours after I had Ana and you all left the hospital right after you saw her..." She looked at Regan, then back to her family. "Regan stayed with me at the hospital. She happened to be flipping through the channels and as I looked up, I spotted Ana's father on the television. He was being interviewed."

She looked into eight startled faces. Her brother Frank Jr. was the first to speak. "Dear Lord, please don't tell me he's a serial killer or something?"

Ali smiled and shook her head. "Thank the Good Lord no. Actually, I'm thinking you all will recognize his name."

"Who?" asked Jon, her second to last brother.

"Abraham Parker!" she stated. She almost laughed at their shocked faces.

"No way!" Adam sat up in the chair. "That guy is famous. He's probably had more women…" He paused and cleared his throat. "I mean cars than he knows what to do with." Embarrassed about what he implied after his sister just admitted she was one of those women, Adam sat back and shut up.

"Who in the hell thinks they are Abraham Lincoln? He's been dead for some time!" Granny shouted.

Everyone chuckled. Regan, sitting next to granny, patted her hand and explained that they were talking about Ana's father, Abraham Parker, and how he is a famous country singer.

"Well, if he's my great-grandbaby's daddy, I'll be wanting some front row tickets to see Kenny Rogers when he comes to town," Granny exclaimed.

Ali laughed at her granny. "I'm not sure about Kenny tickets but maybe you can see Abe perform sometime."

Everyone started talking at once. Jake whistles to get everyone's attention. "She's not done yet. There's more," he stated.

Ali continued. "After finding out who Abe was, I made a bad decision and decided not to tell him he had a daughter." She took a deep breath to hold back the tears. "I think it's safe to say that the hormones made me very insecure and I wasn't up for seeing the rising country star at that moment. Then time just slipped away and it felt like it became too late to get in touch with him." She wiped at her eyes. "My biggest fear was he'd resent me so much he'd take my baby from me." She whispered.

"No one is taking our Ana-girl from us!" Stated Sam the brother that was a year younger than her.

Everyone nodded in agreement. Ali noticed her mom looking very upset. Ali wasn't sure if it was because she never confided in her about Abe or if it was the thought of losing Ana that had her close to tears.

She explained how Jake found Abe and they met up. She went on to inform them that after talking to Abe her worry was for nothing. Abe had no intentions of taking Ana from them. She asked Jake to take the floor and explain why he was in town and how this was all connected. He would know how to tell them and put them at ease at the same time.

Jake took the next ten minutes and explained to them about everything that went down at the school. He read them the contents in the note and how the kidnapping flopped after Ali rescued her daughter. The boys were impressed with their sister. In closing Jake explained how he had agents watching Ali and Ana around the clock and how Will would be staying at the farm. He wasn't sure if Ana was their only target or if they would attempt to go after anyone related to Ali and Abe. He explained that everyone needed to be on guard and let him know if they see anything suspicious.

"Al, do you have anything to add?" Jake motioned for his sister to take the floor.

"I want to add that before this all happened, I already planned to ask Jake for help getting a hold of Abe after Christmas. Ana has been asking a lot about her father. So now that Abe knows he's a father he's planning on coming to Ramona tomorrow and spending some time with his daughter."

Everyone was quiet for several moments. Her brother Sam was the first to break the silence. "That's why you gave her a second middle name of Parker!" he exclaimed. "I always thought that was an odd middle name."

"Actually, her last name is hyphenated Parker-Mason but I mainly use Mason unless it's something important."

Once again everyone started talking at once. The boys huddled together to get all the facts from Jake about the kidnapping. Regan was laughing at Granny. Ali finally looked at her father. He was silent the entire time. She would be crushed if he was disappointed in her. She pleaded with her eyes that he not be upset with her. As if understanding her look he rose from his chair and walked over to her and pulled her into a bear hug. Loud enough for everyone to hear he stated, "I don't care about the past. The only thing we need to worry about is keeping you and my granddaughter safe. And you know, if you changed one thing about the past that little girl may not be as perfect as perfect gets!" he stated.

Ali wiped at the tears in her eyes and saw the hurt look on her momma's face. She walked over and sat next to her mother. "Mom," she covered her mother's hand with her own. "I'm sorry we didn't tell you we recognized Abe in the hospital. Regan and I were shocked at first. Then I didn't want anyone to know until I decided what to do. I wanted to tell you but I was afraid you would talk me into doing the right thing by letting him know. And I just wasn't ready to do the right thing."

Her mother tucked her daughter's hair around her ear. "You are probably right. I would have wanted you to do the right thing but that's water under the bridge. I'm just glad it all worked out."

Ali gave her mother a worried look. "What do you think the town is going to say?"

Lana smiled. "Well first they are going to be in awe that a famous country singer is in town. Next they are going to say how they all have been your best friend for years. Third you are going to be bombarded."

Ugh, Ali thought, the last thing she wanted to deal with is people in her face and business. She wasn't sure she wanted Ana involved in all the hoopla. Isn't that part of the reason she didn't tell Abe? What next? Was there going to be reporters on her doorstep? Was her life going to be in an uproar? How did Abe plan to get to know his daughter if they never had any peace? Ali decided stressing about it was a waste of time and she'd just deal with it as it comes along.

Jake gathered everyone's attention and stated how Abe's agent got a hold of him earlier that morning and explained to him how they were tweaking the story a bit. He filled them in on what to say. Ali agreed it was a good plan to say she never told Abe's name to everyone in order to protect Ana. Plus everyone would know he was on tour a lot and that was why they never met him. And what better place to keep a child safe then good ole quiet Ramona, Illinois. Obviously, Abe's agent was good at this stuff. It made her wonder how many other stories he covered for Abe!

***

Todd pulled in Ali's driveway the same time she did. Once inside he grabbed their coats and hung them in the hall closet. He declined her offer of wine but agreed to a cup of coffee. As she prepared the drinks, he watched her with adoration in his eyes. He was crazy about her. Had always been. She was his first love. He loved her before he got the nerve up to ask her out. He loved her with something close to obsession after the first time they made love when they were seventeen.

His heart had never really healed when she ended their relationship right before high school graduation. He wasn't surprised she broke it off. He knew they both needed to go out and experience the real world, yet that didn't make it any easier.

It helped that she never threw a bunch of men in his face. If anything, she always kept a low profile on the dating scene. That was until she came up pregnant. Todd had been shocked when his mother told him that Ali was pregnant and wasn't married. Even then he thought about packing up everything in Chicago and coming home to play the knight in shining armor. He didn't care if he wasn't the baby's father. He would love any child that came from Ali.

Timing was everything. He didn't have anything to offer Ali at that time. He was working at a firm and studying for his bar at that time. He wanted a few years under his belt before he moved home and set up a practice in Ramona.

Then he met Tracey, one of the partner's daughter. They hit it off, first as friends, then as lovers. He loved spending time with her. She was fun, witty and very charming. Yet the one thing she wasn't was Ali Mason.

He hated to think about how he never gave Tracey a chance. In a sense he used her. He knew she was having serious feelings for him. Yet he still strung her along. When he passed his bar and was ready to move home, he pushed her away without a backwards glance.

Finally home, he set up practice and gave Ali a little time to adjust to him being back in town. He knew precisely when it was time to make his move. Timing was everything and when his practice immediately started booming it was time to reintroduce himself to his high school sweetheart.

Watching her, he couldn't believe how well his plan worked and she was in his life again. Now he just had to figure out how to keep her. Deep inside he felt like she didn't quite feel for him the love he felt for her, but he was doing everything he could to show her. Hanging with her daughter was one easy way since the little girl could charm a snake. She was wonderful and Todd had to admit that he hoped there would come a day when she would call him daddy.

Ali brought him back to reality when she started asking about his week. They hadn't seen each other since Sunday, when he dropped her off the day after her work Christmas party, because Ali had a lot going on. He could see in her eyes she was tired. He was glad she was finally on winter break...she looked like she needed a break.

Walking over to her, he pulled her in his arms and gave her a long sweet kiss before putting her head to his chest to embrace her for several minutes. She seemed to relax in his arms. That made him smile. God, how he loved this woman!

He told her to get comfortable on the couch and he would pour the coffee. She smiled her thanks and walked into the other room.

Todd sat the cups on the table before sitting next to her and looking around for Ana. "Where's my buddy, Ana?" he asked.

"She's staying at Grandma and Grandpa's house. You know how she loves being spoiled by them," she sighed with a smile.

"I would have spoiled her."

"I know." She loved that he was crazy about her daughter. "I wanted some alone time with you."

"You did?" he grinned. "Well, why didn't you say so in the first place?" He moved toward her as if to pull her in his arms.

Ali chuckled and pushed her hands against his chest. "To talk Todd...to talk!" she laughed.

Taken back a bit, he looked in her eyes. He could see the seriousness there. Damn, he thought, was she ending it again? He didn't know if he could handle that. Everything was going great. He knew these past few weeks she was happy with him. Hadn't she kissed him back earlier? That had to mean something...right? He hated the feeling of dread coming over him!

"What's up?" he asked hesitantly.

Ali stood up and walked over to sit in the chair across from him. "I think it's time to tell you about Ali's father." She took a deep breath. "I want you to know I respect that you never questioned me about her father."

"Ali, I didn't ask because I didn't need to know. I don't care who her father is." He leaned forward and put his elbows on his knees and put his hands together. "I don't care because I want to be her father."

His declaration startled her. Before she could stop him he held his hand out and asked her to let him finish. "I know it's too soon to blurt that out but I want you to know that no matter what the story is I'm good with you being a single mom." Looking deep in her eyes, he smiled. "To tell you the truth I'm glad he's not in the picture. I've come to love that little girl as much as I love you."

Tears sprang into her eyes. That was the first time since high school Todd had ever used the word love. Anxiety was sitting in on her heavily. This was not going the way she expected.

"Todd, I think you need to hear me out before you say anything more."

Misunderstanding what she meant, he replied, "No matter your past I plan to love you forever!"

Ali stood up and started to pace. "Okay, let me restart this over." She almost rushed her words so he couldn't interrupt her again with declarations of love. "In a nutshell, almost five years ago I met a man while I was on a trip to Nashville. Well I'm going to put it out there...I fell pretty hard. It was quick and fast. We met, we hung out and had a wonderful time together. We talked, we laughed and things happened." She looked him in the eyes. "I promise you this was out of character for me. I don't pickup and hookup! I'm being honest here, there was something between us." She blinked back the tears. 'Damn,' she thought, 'this is hard.' "I'm not trying to hurt you or rub it in your face but I want you to understand how it all laid out." Taking a deep breath, she continued. "Anyhow, the next day he had to leave early and I was dead to the word and didn't realize he left. A few hours later I was awakened by the maid and rushed to checkout. Once I checked out, I wondered where he was. I knew nothing about his life, just stories of growing up, his likes and dislikes, stuff like that...but I was too stupid to get his last name and he didn't get mine."

Ali stopped pacing and sat back down across from him. "Needless to say, I came home and found out I was pregnant and no way of knowing how to get a hold of the father. So I lied and told people the father and I met online and I went to Nashville to be with him and you know the rest." She looked him in the eyes. "I'm not proud that I lied. I had to do what I did so people didn't judge my daughter…and me!" Ali rubbed her hands down her face. "The day I delivered Ana I found out who Ana's father was. I actually saw him being interviewed on the television." She sighed as she sat back in the chair. "I'm not sure if you are familiar with country music, but he's a singer named Abraham Parker."

Todd's eyes became large and round. He sat back and rubbed his hands down his face. Wow, he thought, he didn't see that coming! He didn't know what to say. How does anyone compare themselves to a famous, good-looking star?

Ali watched the emotions play across his face. She could see his pain. She walked over and sat next to him.

"Todd?" She put his hands in hers. "I've shocked you. I'm sorry."

"It's okay. I'm just a little overwhelmed." He smiled and squeezed her hands. "It's a bit surreal! So I'm taking there's more?"

She nodded. She told him about the kidnap attempt. She was patient and answered all his questions. He was a lawyer through and through. His anger was apparent. It took her a bit to reassure him that Jake was handling it.

She decided to toss the last bit of shock his way. This part was the worst. She knew he wasn't going to be happy with Abe staying at her house. "Earlier today Jake and I met up with Ana's father and explained everything."

Todd sighed. "And? Did he tell you why he left without any word from him?"

"He actually was wondering why I never got in contact with him. It seems he left his number on the night table. But I guess in my hurry to leave, because check out time had already passed, I overlooked the note." She looked him in the eyes. "Anyhow, he was shocked and a bit upset that he missed out on his daughter's first four years of her life."

"I'm confused as to why you didn't tell him when you found out who he was?"

She went on to explain all her fears and anxieties about seeing him again. How she worried about him taking her baby away. Todd could understand her worries. Being a lawyer, he knew there was never any guarantees in the system and money usually talked.

"I understand. So now what?"

Ali stood and walked over to the other chair and stood behind it and put her hands on the backrest and faced him. "So now he wants to get to know Ana." She felt terrible watching the hurt register on his face. She hated that she was going to have to hurt him even more. "He's actually coming tomorrow and is going to stay here for a few days…I'm guessing until after her Birthday."

Todd stood and walked over to stare out of the French door window. "As in staying here?" he asked without turning around to look at her.

"Yes, but I didn't invite him. My brother Jake did. He felt that Abe needed to get out of the public eye and not draw too much attention to himself and Ana. Even though I believe Abe being in town is going to draw all kinds of attention and gossip, possibly even reporters, I have to do what's best for my daughter." He heard the dread in her voice.

Turning around he looked at her. "Can I ask what your feelings are right this moment?"

She looked at him long and hard. She didn't know what she felt. From the moment she spoke with Abe earlier in the day she hadn't had a minute to think. From the guilt of having to explain everything to Abe, her family and now Todd, Ali realized she was absolutely exhausted.

She answered what was in her heart. "I don't know what I feel right now. I know I have a ton of guilt for keeping him from her for four years. The pain I saw in his eyes today was real. After seeing that, if I could go back and change it I would. But I can't! So the next best thing is to let Ana and Abe have a relationship. I don't know what I feel for him. Hell, I only knew him one day and then I don't believe I knew him at all." She walked to him and put her arms around him and hugged him hard. "I do know right at this moment I'm glad I'm with you!" She meant it.

Todd hugged her back. He was so happy to hear her say she was glad to be with him. He'd take any hope she gave him. Pulling back, he put her hands in his. "As I said earlier, I love you." He reached in his pants pocket and pulled out a beautiful princess cut diamond. "I've had this with me for the last week. I figured I'd wait until Christmas, but I'm thinking that it may be a bit crazy then." He paused and let his words sink in on her shocked face. "Ali Mason, will you do me the honors of becoming my wife?"

Ali didn't know what to say. She almost panicked. This was the last thing she needed. She didn't want to hurt Todd but she needed to sort through things with Abe first.

Todd could see the hesitancy on her face. It hurt...but he wasn't giving up. "Ali," he slipped the ring on her finger, "just think about it for a few days. Wear it and see if it fits into your heart." When she nodded, he kissed her. He explained that he needed to get going, yet stood there hugging her until they heard the front door open. Jake walked in and paused, thinking he was interrupting.

"Sorry!" he stated as he tried backing out of the room,

"It's okay, Jake," Ali said. "Todd was just heading out."

"Hey Jake," Todd said as he crossed the room to shake hands with Ali's brother. "Good to see you again."

Jake shook his hand and commented about the upcoming NFL game. Ali smiled. Todd knew all her brothers from dating Ali in high school. It was nice that they all recently got reacquainted when she and Todd started dating. It was funny though, she loved football as much as they did, but her brother's never talked football with her.

After seeing Todd out, she walked back into the living room and plopped down on the recliner across from the couch that was being occupied from one end to the next by her giant of a brother.

"Did you just get back from the ranch?" she asked.

"Yes. I actually just finished talking to Regan. She confirmed that she never spoke of Abe to anyone…not even her dog! So I'm clueless on who could know. I'm thinking it has to be the birth certificate. Only the birth certificate has Abraham Parker as the father, right?"

"Yes, but I used Parker in the hyphenated form on Ana's name. So unless someone really put thought into it they probably didn't think much of it. Plus because I was a little embarrassed about having a baby out of wedlock, I requested that no birth announcements be sent to the paper or the internet."

"You don't think anyone would notice Abraham Parker's name on the birth certificate?"

"I don't know! It wasn't like he was a household name back then. I've raked it over and over in my head…I cannot figure it out. Even when I enrolled her in Peak's Landing Pre-K, I didn't use Abe's name as her father and I didn't hyphenate her last name. I put her in as Ana Grace Mason."

"I had Will go to the Paducah hospital where you had Ana and see if he could get us a lead. He got back early this afternoon and said there wasn't much to go on. It seems that Medical Records are the personnel that comes to a new mother's room and obtains the personal information from the mother."

Ali remembered there was an older lady who sat with her after she had Ana and she verified the information Ali wrote down for Ana's parents and Ana's name. She remembered because she almost panicked because she wasn't sure if she should use her name or Abe's. That was when the lady suggested she hyphenate the name. "I remember the lady I just don't remember her name. But she knew I was using the baby's father's last name because she was the one who suggest I hyphenate it."

"Actually the lady, Anita Kreah, still works there. She's the one who handled Ana's birth certificate. Will waited for her shift to start and they must have chatted for a while. According to her she handles so many births there was no way she'd remember a baby four years ago. She assured him she filed

115

the papers through the state and no one else would have had access to her cases." Sighing, he ran his hand through his hair. "Will ran her through as she's as clean as a whistle."

Ali saw on Jake's face the frustration she felt. "I guess it's a disappointment when a lead doesn't pan out?" She smiled at him, "Thank you for being there and helping me out."

"Al, it's my job. You know the big brother thing. Anyway, we have other leads to look into. Problem is it takes time." Because he didn't want to stress her about the kidnapping, he changed the subject. "So what are you going to do about Todd?"

"What do you mean? Todd and I are fine. I told him everything and he is fine with Abe and Ana getting to know each other," she stated in a matter-of-fact tone.

"So that explains why he suddenly tossed a ring on your finger tonight instead of at Christmas…which happens to be the second biggest engagement day of the year."

Ali threw a pillow at him. Sometimes it was annoying to have a brother who knew who, what, where, when, why, and how before you did. That was why he was good at his job. "I think he is a bit worried. And I didn't say yes. He just asked me to wear it and let him know in a few days."

"You know I think Todd is a great guy, but because I'm your big brother you have to hear my opinion." He stood and walked over to her chair. "I think there is a reason you ended it with Todd years ago and I think there is a reason you couldn't finish speaking with Parker today," he stated as he bent down and kissed her forehead before saying goodnight and climbing the stairs to his bedroom.

Ali sat in the recliner a long while, trying to sort all the feelings and emotions spinning around in her head. By the time she made her way to her own bed she had a headache and what felt like a heartache.

Chapter Fourteen

Abe couldn't sleep. So around four in the morning he decided to take the scenic route to Ramona, Illinois. Even driving under the speed limit, he was pulling into the town before the chickens woke. He smiled as he drove around the sleepy little town. He forgot that places like this still existed. Being on the road put him in the big cities. Anymore he took a charter to his concerts. So small towns were something he rarely ever visited.

Driving around the town courthouse, he figured this must be the main focal point. It was stuck right in the middle of town. And by the look of the place, Abe was sure it had some historical value. The building was huge with extremely tall windows that curved at their tops. The clock tower erected from the middle of the building and had a clock facing all four directions. Abe was sure the building was somewhere in the eighteen-hundreds. The tall pillars gave the place its historical charm, which was something Abe loved. If things would have turned out differently and his music career hadn't fallen in his lap Abe liked to think, other than agriculture, he would have done something with architecture.

Across the road from every side of the courthouse lined shop after shop. The road was one way all around with angled parking spaces in front of the shops. Abe parked in front of a little cafe with an open sign placed on the corner of their curtained window.

Deciding he was hungry, he put his ball cap on, locked his car and went into the establishment. The quaint little cafe had a few patrons and one waitress who yelled out that he could take a seat anywhere. As was his habit, he sat at a table in the back. Only this time he didn't turn his back to everyone, but faced the entrance and pulled his cap down further.

He wanted to watch Ali's little town. He hoped this early in the morning he wouldn't be very recognizable to anyone. So far none of the patrons paid him any mind.

He smiled and thought about how his mother was going to love this little town. Knowing her she would probably set up shop here. Since turning the majority of her 'Booming Boutique' business over to someone else, Sandy was looking for her next chapter in life. He had an odd feeling that she may be finding it when she arrived in town a few days from today.

The waitress, Clara…according to her nametag, approached his table and gave him a once over. By her expression. Abe didn't think she recognized him. Of course, she had to be all of seventy years old and moved like she wasn't in any hurry as she handed him a menu. With an accent that sounded northern, yet with a hint of the south attached to it, she asked if he would like a drink.

Abe ordered coffee as she left the table and he looked over the menu. It didn't take him long to make a decision, but it took Clara a while to bring his coffee. After ordering he looked around the tiny little cafe and had to admit he felt right at home. The town was nothing like he expected. There was true charm and history here. When he got time, he planned to read up on this little town that sat out in the middle of nowhere!

After the waitress sat his plate down, he was deep in thought. The question that kept circling around in his head was what he was going to do about Ali? He still wanted her! He knew that just by the way he reacted to her yesterday. Not just in a physical sense but he wanted to get to know her with no secrets between them. Yet how could they make it work? He wasn't sure what he wanted anymore. Singing was all he knew. Was he willing to give it up for her? He didn't know. He did know she wasn't the type to follow him all around the country. He didn't want her to. He liked that she was home every night taking care of their daughter. He knew that made him sound like a chauvinist but the road was no place for a family. He's seen enough families split up because of the nightmares that went with a traveling band.

After paying his bill and leaving Clara a nice tip, Abe decided to walk around the little town. He made his way to the gazebo that sat smack dab in the middle of the courthouse's courtyard. The rather large white structure was decorated for the holiday season. Sitting down on the bench inside the gazebo, he looked around and noticed the entire town was decorated to the hilt. Every light post had garland wrapped around it with big red bows. The buildings also had garland and bows draped across them. He was sure there were lights under the garland that lit up at night.

Looking around he noticed that many of the shops were starting to open. That surprised him because he remembered his grandmother always saying that most shops didn't open on Sunday because that was 'The Lord's Day'! An hour passed and Abe still watched as the town woke up. He was glad he had the sense to wear a thick coat because the air was chilly. He didn't mind though. He was too fascinated with Ali and Ana's little town.

People would call out greetings to one another. A gentleman pulled into a handicap spot and two people paused in the chatter to help him out of his car into his wheelchair. Kids were running through the town square, past the shops and in the direction of the steeple that poked its head above the buildings lining the square. By the way they were dressed, and with hardly any parents following, Abe assumed they were going to their religion classes. He smiled and felt really good inside knowing his daughter was being raised here. On impulse he walked over to the florist across the street and decided to purchase some flowers for a special girl!

***

Sunday mornings in Ali and Ana's house usually were relaxing and fun. Church first, then breakfast after. Today that wasn't going to happen. With about two hours before Abe was expected to arrive, Ali decided to explain about Abe to her daughter. Sitting her daughter on the couch, Ali didn't know where to begin or how to explain to a four-year-old about the father she never met but was soon going to meet.

She was glad her brother was out trying to find a lead because she wanted to talk to her daughter alone. Not that they were really alone, Jake posted an agent outside her house twenty-four hours a day. The feds didn't take light to an attempted child abduction.

"Did I's do something bad momma?" Ana asked looking worried as to why her mother wanted to talk to her.

Ali kneeled in front of her and gave her a hug. "Not at all baby girl."

"Are you sure. You gots a worried look on your face."

Ali smiled, "Not at all. Actually I have some great news. Remember how we talked about your daddy a few weeks ago?" She continued when Ana nodded. "Well in a few hours you are going to get to meet him!"

Ana jumped up from the couch and threw herself into her mother's arms. "Yippee!" She pulled back and took both hands and squeezed her mother's cheeks. "For real, momma?" she asked.

Ali had tears in her eyes and said, "For real, Ana!"

It took Ali a minute to calm her daughter down. Sitting her back on the couch she said she needed to explain a few things. "Mommy liked your daddy a lot a long time ago. His name is Abe."

"Abe..." Ana said as if trying it out.

Ali shook her head. "Yes, you can call him Abe until you feel comfortable calling him Daddy...okay?"

At Ana's nod she continued, "Ana, do you remember the music mommy lets you listen to. You know the singer Abraham Parker?" she asked her daughter.

"Yep, he's gots a…I mean got a name like me," the little girl exclaimed.

"Yes, he does and do you want to know why?" she asked. Ana nodded her head. "It's because Abraham Parker is your daddy."

Ana did a funny thing with her face when she was amazed…she opened her mouth in a big 'O' and put her hands to her cheeks and asked, "Really?"

Ali smiled and said, "Really! He actually likes to be called Abe though. Do you think you can call him that?"

Ali was surprised when Ana just nodded and didn't ask a ton of questions. Instead she jumped up and started pulling her mother upstairs.

"Where are we going?" she asked her daughter.

"I have to find a pretty dress to wear!" she exclaimed.

Ali laughed. Typical female has to look her best when meeting a man…even if that man is her daddy.

***

A couple hours later the girls heard the doorbell ring. Ali let Ana get the door because she asked her mother earlier if she could. Ali stood back and observed the meeting from a distance. Ana opened the door wide and stared up at her father for the first time. Neither moved for what seemed like eternity but was actually only several long seconds.

Ali watched as Abe bent down to be eye level with Ana. "Hello," was all he said.

Ana smiled and said, "Hello!"

Abe smiled at her. "You must be Ana?" When she nodded, he brought his hand out from behind his back and handed her a bouquet of pink tea roses. "Then these are for you!" he stated with a smile.

Her smile was big. "I' never had so many flowers before," she whispered.

She turned to run to her mother. "Momma, Momma, Abe gives…I mean gave me flowers…Look, Momma!" she exclaimed.

Ali looked at her daughter's smiling face before she looked at Abe as he walked through the door. "Hi," was all she could think to say.

He smiled, showing his dimples. "Hi." He pulled his other hand out from behind his back and handed her a bouquet of beautiful wild flowers.

"Mommy, Abe gave you flowers too!" Ana exclaimed.

Ali, never taking her eyes off him said, "Thank you…you didn't have to do that."

"Yes, I did for acting like a complete jerk yesterday." He gave her a lopsided grin. "And for thanking you for the album. It meant a lot, Ali."

"Abe, Abe…" Ana tugged on his hand. "Can I show you your bed?" she asked.

Smiling down at the beautiful little girl, he was sure this was how Ali looked when she was Ana's age. He picked up his suitcase from the porch and gave her his hand and let her lead him to an upstairs bedroom he planned to call home for the next few days.

Ali walked into the kitchen to put the flowers in water and to regroup. After several minutes she went upstairs to join father and daughter. The layout of the upstairs was two rooms on the left and two on the right with a bathroom between each set of rooms. Ana pointed out that her room was the first one on the left. She hinted that he should know that in case he wanted to read her a bedtime story at night. She went on to explain that her mommy's room was next and across the hall was his room which was next to her uncle Jake's room'

After the tour of the upstairs, Abe followed his daughter downstairs and into the kitchen. She told him that was where her and her mommy does lots and lots of cooking. Ali waved at them from behind the island as she opened a can of corn.

Abe was charmed by his beautiful daughter. She showed him the rest of the house like a little tour guide. She led him back to the living room and asked if he wanted to watch TV. He said he would enjoy that. She turned on the television and sat right next to him on the couch, not leaving room for a piece of paper between them. Unobserved from the kitchen Ali had to smile. It was cute to see Abe watch 'Beauty and the Beast.'

Ali went on to prep food for supper. She didn't want to interrupt this important father daughter bond that was happening. He was here to spend time with his daughter and she wasn't going to stand in his way.

A half hour later Ali went to quietly check on them. She came up behind the sofa to see Ana fast asleep with her head tucked inside the crook of her father's arm. Abe was just staring at her and softly running his fingers down the side of her face and into her hair. Ali knew that look; it was a look of true love. It was the look she had on her face so many times when she looked at her beautiful baby daughter.

She came around the sofa and looked at Abe. For some reason she knew she needed to share this moment with him. He looked up and she saw what she suspected…Love!

"Ali, you did good. Our little girl is perfect." They stared at each other for a moment when he said, "Thank you!"

She knew he was forgiving her. She knew he realized she was giving him the greatest gift any woman could give a man and he was thanking her for it.

Not wanting to break the moment, but feeling she needed to ask, "Do you want me to take her to her room? She'll be out for a couple hours."

He smiled. "Can I? I want to tuck her in," he asked.

"Of course." She led the way to her daughter's room. She pulled down the blankets and watched as he put her in her bed and pulled the blankets up and around her. He reached down and kissed her forehead.

Standing upright he turned and almost bumped into Ali. On impulse he reached his arms to steady them. There was that same jolt that passed through her that she felt years ago when they first met and again in his agent's office the day before. They paused and stared at each other for several moments.

Ali was the first to break the spell by pulling away and walking out the door while Abe followed her. She led him to the kitchen where she was preparing the ingredients for dinner. She offered him a drink, which he declined, as he took a seat on the barstool across the island from her. She decided if they were going to be spending time together over the next few days, she had better set some ground rules.

"Abe, I think we need to make this situation the least amount of awkward for Ana's sake," she said.

He looked at her and nodded. "I agree."

"Good. So coming from my end I want to start by saying I want you to feel at home here the next few days. So if you are hungry or thirsty please feel free to grab whatever you want. Nothing is off limits so make use of any of the rooms," she stated.

Abe lifted his eyebrows and grinned. "Any room?" he questioned,

Ali's heart gave a jilt. He had a very sexy smile and was he flirting with her? Then it dawned on her what he was implying and she blushed. "I'm sure you know what I mean. I wasn't suggesting…" she stammered, "whatever, you know what I mean."

He chuckled. "Yes, I know what you mean." He nodded to the vegetables she was chopping. "Can I help with that?"

She was happy to change the subject, so she nodded and slid the cutting board across the island to him. Grabbing a bowl and ingredients for a marinade, she continued her ground rules when he finished washing his hands.

"I want you to know that I plan to give you as much time as I can with Ana. I will try to stay out of the way. I've even decided I have some last-minute shopping to do so maybe you two can hang out then?" she questioned. "Also, before I forget, there is FBI all around the place. I'm sure you noticed that when you came in."

Two things came to Abe's mind…first, he didn't see FBI outside but figured they must be in hiding. Of course, Jake would have told them Abe was expected to arrive today. Second, he realized he didn't really want Ali to desert him and his daughter. It wasn't that he was afraid of spending time alone with Ana, he just found that he wanted to spend time with Ali also. It made him wonder about his feelings for her. With someone like Ali, it was long term. Was that what he was wanting…long term with her? If so, then what? Was he willing to trade one life for a different life? He didn't think he'd mind that. He really was starting to believe he might be done with the fame. He liked the idea of being a normal person. Yet there were so many factors involved he just wasn't sure what he was going to do.

Abe had no idea why these thoughts kept popping up. It was the same thing that happened to him when he met her years ago. Was it a sick infatuation he had with her? And why her? He knew the obvious…he was attracted to her and she was beautiful. Yet what was it about her that made him want to toss his entire life away just to be with her? He knew he had to take control of his thoughts before he did something he would regret. He had to think things through!

"Ali, I don't mind you being around. I'm not sure Ana is going to be comfortable being alone with me."

She smiled. "She can hardly contain her excitement with you being here. So we can leave it up to her to decide."

He looked at her long and serious as she prepared the steaks. Feeling his eyes on her, she looked up. She was curious to know what he was thinking. "Ali you did good! I mean with the way you raised her. I've only been with her a few hours but I'm crazy about her. She's adorable, charming and funny…I see a lot of you in her!"

There was joy in her eyes when she looked back at him. His words meant a lot. "Thank you!" She chuckled. "She, of course has some of you in her as well. You need to ask her to sing a few of your songs. I know I'm biased, but she's good."

"She knows my music?" He seemed shocked at that.

"Well of course." She smiled at him. "I know she's only four but it's amazing how quick she catches on to music. I figured it was because she was your daughter."

It dawned on her that he must have figured she had no intentions of ever letting her daughter know who her father was. It disturbed her that he thought her so cruel. "Abe, I knew one day, maybe not this early in the game, but while she was young that the two of you would be together. I never wanted to hurt either of you. I just didn't know what to do. And I'm not going to lie when I tell you I was scared."

"You know, I kind of get it. Maybe not happy with your choice, but I do try to understand it. I'm sorry you were scared. I want you to know that if I would have known, I would have been here," he stated.

Ali's reply was interrupted by the arrival of her brother Jake. He walked into the kitchen and gave her sister a kiss on the cheek before shaking hands with Abe, and snatching a baby carrot off the tray. He leaned against the cabinet and asked where his niece was before popping the carrot in his mouth. Ali explained she was napping and asked him to fire up the grill in the garage.

"I take it I'm grilling those steaks? Isn't the whole cooking thing a woman's job." Jake grinned as her eyes narrowed.

"If you don't want any laxatives in your chocolate cake, you'd better take back those words!"

"I got it," he stated before turning to Abe. "Come on buddy, us men-folk are needed elsewhere and if I have to freeze my ass off in the garage because the door needs to be open then I'm going to need some company!" He walked out of the kitchen with a reluctant Abe on his heels.

***

Todd arrived a few minutes later. Ali let him in and he followed her into the kitchen to finish up the meal. He was looking at her intently to see how she was faring with Ana's father coming and staying at the house. She looked and acted fine but a bit tense. "So I take it he's here?" he questioned.

"Yes, he's in the garage grilling with Jake," she stated as she finished stirring the iced tea.

He walked over and put his arms around her waist. She turned and let him pull her in for a comfortable hug. He could feel how tense her hug was and that worried him. Were her feelings already changing or was he just paranoid?

Both turned to the sound of Abe's voice. "Excuse me, I didn't mean to interrupt," Abe stated. "Jake forgot a flipper for the steaks."

The men sized each other up. Abe was no fool. By the way this guy was holding Ali, they were obviously involved. Why didn't he think that was even possible? He never once wondered if she was involved with anyone. Hell, maybe she was even married. Looking briefly at her hand he saw a ring. What did Jake say in Max's office yesterday about her being in a relationship? He couldn't remember because he was too shocked and pissed to focus on everything Jake said.

Nothing like the feeling of a cannon ball landing in the stomach. Wow, he wondered, where did that come from? She wasn't his. Why was he reacting so strongly to her seeing someone or even being married? He had his confirmation when he looked at her hand and spotted the diamond on it.

Ali pulled away from Todd. She looked back and forth between the two men. "Abe this is Todd…Todd…Abe." Turning to a kitchen drawer she pulled out a flipper and handed it to Abe while avoiding his eyes.

"Abe…Mommy, is Abe still here?" He heard before he saw his little girl rushing down the steps. She smiled when she spotted him. "You're here. I thought it was a dream."

Abe smiled and leaned down while she rushed into his arms for a hug. "I'm here. Your momma is putting me to work by helping with supper!" He tossed her in the air and caught her. "I bet you have to work for your supper as well?" She smiled and nodded her little head while her floppy curls bounced every which way before she used her arm to push it out of her face.

"She does," her mother stated. "Ana sets the table."

Abe let her go before heading out the door to give Jake the flipper. He had questions and Jake was just the person to ask. Funny, but he liked and trusted the FBI agent. Even though he didn't know him long, he felt like Jake had his back.

He wasted no time once he entered the garage. "So I just met Todd."

Jake looked at him. "And?"

Abe lifted his eyebrows. "So what's the deal?"

Jake wasn't going to make it easy on him. He wanted to feel Abe out on what his feelings truly were for his sister. "What do you mean?"

"Well obviously they are together. How long have they been married? And why didn't you let me know that before I arrived?"

"Would it have mattered?" he questioned. "If you knew ahead of time would you not have come here?"

"Of course I would have come, I just would have found a different place to stay."

"Why would it matter if you are only here for Ana?"

Abe sighed, feeling frustrated. "I wouldn't intrude on a married couple. Especially considering I was once involved with the female."

On one hand Jake liked his answer because it showed morals and values, but on the other hand did it imply that Abe wasn't interested in Ali and him picking up where they left off? It wasn't that Jake had any ill will for Todd. It was just that after seeing the reaction Ali and Abe had when they set eyes on each other the day before told him they needed to finish their ending…or beginning!

He decided to relieve Abe of the stress he was feeling. He looked closely at him to see his reaction to the news. "They aren't married!" Bingo, the look on Abe's face said volumes. Relief and what Jake thought might be hope. "They are recently engaged." He went on as he flipped the steaks on the grill. "So if you feel there is something long term in your future with her you better act quick."

Abe leaned against Ali's car and took it all in. So recently engaged? Did she love this guy? Why did he feel relief when he realized she wasn't married? Was it hope? Did he want to give up his crazy, exciting life to settle down and be a normal human being? How could he tell Jake it was long term when he didn't know what he was going to do about his career? So many unanswered questions. One thing was for sure, he thought with a grin, Jake apparently wanted him and Ali together.

Chapter Fifteen

Inside the kitchen, Todd was asking himself a lot of questions also. The first was why in the hell was this happening? All these years he waited patiently for the perfect time to sweep back into her life and 'Boom' her baby-daddy appears. Of course, he has to be a freaking famous country star…really? To top it all off he's good-looking and put together great. Millions of women flock to the star. Yet Todd knew by the way he looked at Ali, when he interrupted them in the kitchen, the man still wanted her. Plus, little Ana didn't even acknowledge him when she came downstairs. That bugged him. He liked the little girl and thought she liked him as well. Now he wasn't sure of his relationship with either one. Of course, Todd wasn't giving up the fight. He was determined to get her to the altar quickly.

Jake and Abe came in carrying the steaks just as the two girls finished setting the table. The tension in the air was so thick it could be sliced. Thank goodness there was a four-year-old in the house. Ana was the first to break the tension. "Abe, I can sing all your songs," she stated proudly as she made sure she sat next to him at the table.

He smiled at her. "You can? After supper will you sing for me?"

She blushed and shook her head. "I'd be too embarrassing for me," she stated while tripping over the word.

"Maybe it would help if we sung it together."

Her face looked as if she thought he hung the moon. She nodded and exclaimed they should start tomorrow. Ali looked like she was on the verge of tears by the beautiful bond her baby and baby's father were sharing. Jake was observing it all and also taking in Todd's angry face.

Todd was trying to keep it together but wasn't doing so well. Not to feel left out and wanting the little girl's attention to be directed at him, he asked Ana if she wanted to go see the new animated moving coming to the big screen the following evening.

"What's animated?" she asked.

Todd smiled. "A cartoon."

She smiled and looked at her father. "Can you come?"

Todd hadn't expected this. He wanted it to be just the three of them. He knew he was acting like a spoiled brat but he didn't care.

Ali looked between the two men and didn't know what to say or do. Abe was here to spend a few days with his daughter. Todd knew that but acted like he was in competition with the man over Ana's attention. Todd deserved Ana asking if Abe could go just because she knew he was acting immature.

Thankfully Abe took control of the awkward situation. "Actually Ana, late tomorrow night my mother and sister are coming up from Nashville to meet you. They won't arrive until later and I want to get them checked in and settled in their hotel. So why don't you go to the movie with Todd and then he can bring you to the hotel where you can meet them?" He looked at Todd and Ali. "Is that alright with you both?"

Todd didn't know what to say. He didn't expect the man to be so accommodating. Now Todd was ticked off. The star made him look like a complete ass. Of course Todd was going to have to put a good spin on it to save face. "That would be great." He looked at Ali and said, "I'll text you the time for the movie tomorrow. If I get out of court early, maybe the three of us can do dinner first." He looked at Abe. "You can just let Ali know when and where they arrive and the three of us will meet you after."

Abe was trying to keep his temper in check. How many bloody times did the man have to use the term 'the three of us' to get his point across? And why was he going to court? Did he do something wrong? He decided there was only one way to find out. "Court?"

Todd smiled. So the star knew nothing about him. Good! Every lawyer knows that gives him the advantage. He didn't want to touch base with the nagging question in the back of his head…how much information did Ali tell the other man about their relationship? "I'm a trial lawyer."

Abe wondered if he was supposed to be impressed. Well he wasn't. So the guy was decent looking and probably had a lot of money. Well Abe was doing fine in both those areas. He wondered if Ali was in love with the lawyer?

Ali could feel the tension between the two guys and felt it was best if she changed the subject. She told everyone to finish their meals so she could get the cake served. Walking over to her island she silently said a prayer asking Him to get her through this evening without the two men coming to blows.

The tension was so thick it made breathing hard. She was frustrated with Todd for acting like a brat and baiting Abe. She was just as upset with Abe for acting like he didn't care one way or another if he was being baited or not. She wouldn't admit it to herself but she wanted Abe to act a little bit jealous to see her with someone. She knew it was childish but she couldn't help it. To top it all off she was ready to beat her brother for smiling at all the drama.

After dessert was finished, Ana jumped off of her booster and grabbed Abe's hand and asked him to come with her. It was cute that she thought of him as hers. Ali was amazed at how well the two of them took to each other.

"Come on Abe let's color pictures," Ana said as she tugged him out of his seat.

"Hold on Ana," he stated. "Don't we need to clean up after supper?"

Ana nodded and started grabbing the dishes off the table and was about to toss them in the sink…food and all. Ali laughed and told everyone to clear out of the kitchen. She would take care of the task all by herself.

Ana asked Jake and Todd if they wanted to color. Jake declined, he needed to call Will and see if anything more was found out about the investigation. Todd wasn't going to be left out when it came to the competition of winning Ana…or Ali, so he joined in the coloring.

Ali smiled when she walked into the living room and watched the threesome coloring. It was comical to see two grown men sitting on the floor, coloring in a princess book on the top of a coffee table. It was also ridiculously sexy in her eyes. Finding her eyes drawn to Abe, she smiled and wondered what the world would think if they were looking at what she was looking at. Hell, they would think what an incredibly sweet and sexy picture Abe made. She had to admit she still found him incredibly sexy.

Ali thought Abe aged nicely in the last five years. His messy, spiky brown hair only added to his appeal. The lean, firm, tanned body made her catch her breath. She remembered the first time she saw him. Remembered thinking how handsome he was. Back then she didn't know he was a big superstar. She wondered how different things would have played out if she would have recognized him as a country singer that day?

With her eyes turning to Todd, she thought he was very handsome also. He may lack that natural sex appeal Abe had but he was the safe bet. He was that guy that wasn't going to ride off into the night and not be seen for months. He definitely didn't have half of the world's female population knocking on his door. Ali didn't think she could handle the competition that came with Abe.

"Mommy, Mommy look what I color," Ana announced. She ran up and showed her mother the picture she colored. It was Rapunzel in a tower with her prince climbing up her hair.

"That's beautiful!" she declared.

Ana whispered as she pointed to the prince. "That's Abe." Ali smiled and looked to see if the men heard Ana's declaration. She could tell by the look on Abe's face that he heard it. Todd seemed oblivious because he was too into his coloring to pay any intention. Ana whispered once more, but loud enough for Abe to once again hear it. "And that's you." Ana was pointing to Rapunzel.

When Ali looked up, she caught Abe's eyes. They stared at each other for several moments before he asked Ana if he could see the picture.

He stared at the picture and started to grin when he looked up at Ali's red cheeks. "You did good Ana. I think you should have your momma hang it on her fridge."

"Okay." She turned and asked her mother to hang the pic. Ali agreed, anything to get away from Abe's laughing face.

The next hour consisted of Ana and Abe playing with Ana's toys in her playroom and she and Todd watching television on the couch. Ali would have rather been in the other room with her daughter but she felt Todd and Abe needed some space.

Ali, not being a television watcher, wish she had something to occupy her time with. The show on the tube was some crime scene/courtroom drama series that reminded her that the outside world wasn't always a safe place to be.

She was relieved when the show was over. She explained to Todd that it was bedtime for her and Ana. He was reluctant to leave. He didn't like leaving her alone with Parker. As she walked him to the door, he pulled her into his arms and just as he was about to kiss her, Ana and Abe appeared in the living room. All it would take was for either one to look over and see what was about to happen. So Ali pulled back and Todd leaned in and gave her a kiss on the cheek.

Since getting back together, they only shared that one night together. It was a sweet night of holding, touching…making love. He hoped she thought about that night and not about the superstar in the living room. "I can't wait until I can hold and touch you again," he whispered. "Please tell me it won't be long until we can have a night together."

Ali looked at him and smiled, even though deep down she wanted to cry. Why couldn't she desire him? It wasn't because Abe was here that she felt this way. Abe just made her remember passion. The night she was with Todd she felt attraction, but not passion. Would it be enough to be with him and not desire him? Not sure what to say she just smiled and reminded him to text her about the movies the following day.

"Okay, I love you," he stated. He was heartbroken when she said 'thank you' and kissed his cheek and sent him out the door.

Abe kept busy picking up in the living room but his hearing was alert. He knew he shouldn't eavesdrop but the time he realized Todd wasn't quite out the door and they were actually saying their goodbyes, it was too late. He did get two things out of the thirty seconds he stood in the room. Ali has been intimate with the man and she hasn't told him she loved him yet.

This made him bummed and happy all at the same time. He didn't want her to think he was listening when she turned back toward the living room and asked, "Was that Todd leaving?"

"Yes," she replied.

Walking into the living room she reached for her daughter's hand. "Time for bed." Ana ran ahead of them to brush her teeth so she'd be ready by the time they climbed the stairs to her room.

As Ali headed for the stairs, he stopped her by putting his hand on her arm. She looked up at him. "I find it weird that Todd didn't want to tell Ana goodbye when he left." At her frown, he continued. "I'm not trying to stir the pot, but if he wants her to be his step-daughter, don't you think he would make a conscience effort that was genuine."

She looked angry. "What do you mean? He just didn't want to interrupt your time with her."

"Really, then why in the hell did he suggest you all go to the movies tomorrow night...on a whim...and I stay away? Sounds like he's trying to win an Ana popularity contest." He knew he was baiting her, but seeing her with that guy's arms around her set him off.

"Well he knows you are out of his league as far as a popularity contest is concerned. The entire female population is in love with your image. That is all but one and that's me. So I don't know what your beef is with Todd, but he loves Ana like his own and you are going to have to accept that." She had to defend Todd. He was her safe haven that prevented her from falling all over Abe...a much more famous Abe than the one she fell all over five years ago.

"Really!" He lifted his eyebrows. "You sound jealous." He gave her a slight knowing grin.

Ali had to mentally shake her thoughts. Ugh...this man could make her crack with just a look. She shook her arm from his hand and stated. "Never, because I could not handle the hoopla that comes with you!" Glaring at him with her piercing green eyes she continued. "It seems to me you're the one with jealousy issues!" she quietly yelled.

They both were interrupted by Ana calling out for both of them. Abe followed her up the stairs to Ana's room. Ana was jumping on her bed in her night shirt and leggings. Ali knew she probably shouldn't let her jump on her bed but she always felt a kid should be able to act like a kid. So they played a bedtime game where Ana leaped off her bed into her mother's arms and then Ali would act like she was throwing her on the bed a few times before tossing her on it and then tickling her until Ana said uncle.

"Abe catch me," Ana said and leaped into Abe's arms only seconds after he realized what she was doing. She giggled and Ali had to scold her that Abe wasn't ready and he probably didn't want her jumping all over him.

Abe declared he wasn't mad, he just wanted to get even. He tossed her in the air a few times acting like he almost dropped her each time before tossing her on the bed. Ana shouted, "Tickle me…tickle me." Abe and Ali both tickled her until she was laughing hard and saying "uncle!"

When she calmed down, she said to her mother, "Can Abe read me a bedtime story?"

Ali was completely happy with the idea of the two bonding further over a story. She smiled and nodded her head. As she started to back out the door, Ana stated, "No Mommy, you stay too. Abe reads us both a story." She jumped off the bed and grabbed her favorite book and then climbed under the covers. She patted each side of the bed. "Mommy lays here." She patted her left side and then patted the right side. "Dadd…I mean Abe lays here."

It didn't go past her parents that Ana almost slipped up and called Abe her daddy. Ali wanted to bring it up but figured that was between the two of them. She was sure in time Ana would be calling Abe daddy.

After ten minutes of listening to Abe's soothing voice read the bedtime story, Ana was fast asleep. Ali covered her up and turned her light off before following Abe out the door and down the steps.

Neither said much as they cleaned up the coloring mess and straightened the living room. Abe's phone went off and he excused himself to answer it. He walked into the rear of the house toward the toy room to take the call. Ali couldn't help but overhear bits and pieces. It was obviously a girl he was talking to. Apparently, they left things on a bad note because he was telling her that because she couldn't accept things for what they were they were done. Then she heard him say something about a ring.

Ali went into the kitchen so she wouldn't be tempted to listen to any more of the conversation. She remembered Jake saying that rumor had it Abe was engaged. She hated to admit it but it disturbed her to think of him with someone else. She also wasn't sure she liked the idea of her daughter having a stepmother.

Looking down she stared at the ring Todd slid on her finger the night before. What was she going to do about the proposal? She wondered how Abe would feel about his daughter having a stepfather? By the way the two men avoided each other earlier she doubted he would like it very much.

It was weird how she never thought about all the little things. Like step-parents and separate households. Or even Ana staying with Abe on weekends. That truly made her want to panic. She didn't mind her daughter spending the night at her parents once in a while, but tears sprang in her eyes when she thought about her little girl leaving for long weekends or even week-long road trips when he was playing. She was suddenly afraid Ana would eventually want to go on the road with her father.

Abe found Ali wiping at her tears when he walked into the kitchen. Too late to pretend she wasn't crying, Ali lifted her chin and met his eyes when he asked, "What's wrong, Ali Cat?"

She looked into his eyes and thought about how incredibly handsome he was. Of course, he knew it. He had women throwing themselves at him every day.

His thumb moved softly back and forth over her chin. She felt that lightning jolt again. How was he capable of driving her senses wild? No man has ever affected her like this man. Looking at his lips, she wondered if he tasted like he did all those years before.

Abe looked at her glassy eyes staring at his mouth. It was all the invitation he needed. Bending forward he leaned into her mouth with his lips touching her. The contact stirred a strong tingling sensation through both of them. The softness of her lips made him want to taste more of her. His tongue pressed against her lips wanting her to open her for him.

Ali gave into his demands and slid her hands up his chest and wrapped her arms around his neck before pressing her body into his. She wondered if he would taste the same as he did in the past, but no memory came close to the feelings going through her mind and body at this moment.

Abe's hands rubbed up and down her sides as he pressed her closer. What was it about her that made him feel things he never felt before? Like never letting her go. He just wanted more and more of her. It was part of the reason he went crazy when he couldn't find her.

Ali didn't want the kiss to end but knew she had to. Pulling away she backed up a few steps. She couldn't let this happen. She didn't need a repeat of what happened five years ago. She had to keep her distance so she could sort through all these changes occurring. Her daughter leaving for weekends, step parents, someone else making decisions for her daughter. And let's not forget women flocking to the superstar. It was almost too much to be deal with.

Abe leaned back against the island facing her. His look was intent when he asked her with his southern drawl, "Why did I just see tears in your eyes, Ali?" She looked at him and started to deny anything was wrong but he shook his head. "I know what I saw pretty lady!" he stated.

She figured she might as well clear the air about what was worrying her. "What now Abe?" At his confused look she continued. "With Ana, what now? I guess I didn't give it much thought before. Probably because everything in the last week happened so quickly. But what are you hoping for? Every other weekend? I'll be honest…I don't know if I can handle you taking her for days at a time."

They stared at each other as if in a standoff. Finally Abe asked, "Do you not trust me to take care of her?"

"It's not that at all. It's just that the last four years it's been the two of us…"

"No fault of mine!" he stated a bit heated.

"I know that. I'm just trying to get you to understand. I rarely let her stay the night at my parents. It's just that my heart breaks when I think of her leaving me for the weekend…or longer if that's what you are hoping for. The typical two weeks in the summer kind of thing makes me sick." She was wringing her hands. "I know in time I may need a break and will look forward to some 'me' time. But as of yet I haven't felt that."

"What about when you and your boyfriend get married? I'm sure he's going to want you to himself from time to time." He nodded to her ring.

"Well that brings me to the next thing bothering me. Stepparents! I never thought about sharing the mommy role with someone else. I will admit that the thought of that kills me!" Her eyes were filled with unshed tears.

He wanted to comfort her and wipe away her tears, but because he was talking about that little girl upstairs, he knew he wasn't going to make Ali promises that would interfere with his relationship with Ana. He had his rights and after meeting her he knew he was going to be a part of her life for the rest of his. Ali was the one engaged. As far as his relationship went with Shea, it was over. He just wished she'd quit calling and texting. He took the call from her earlier because Max informed him he needed to let her down easy. He didn't want her passing around a lot of BS about their relationship.

He spoke from his heart. "Ali, I'm not the one with a ring on my finger. If you are asking me to back out of Ana's life minutes after I got in it just to make you happy…I can't and won't." When she started to interrupted, he stopped her by putting up his hands. "Wait, please let me finish." When she backed down and nodded, he continued, "But I will do everything in my power to make this comfortable for you." He ran his hand through his hair. "I'll be honest with you, I don't know from one day to the next what is happening with my career."

She gave him a doubtful look. "Why? I figured you would be in it for the long haul!"

He had been thinking about quitting here and there. He's even voiced to Max a few times that he had burnout. Yet never said he wanted to quit all together. He wondered if he said that because it's what he felt or was it because she implied earlier that she didn't want to be involved with a famous musician?

Not wanting to imply false hope he twisted his meaning, "I'm not saying it's a done deal. I'm just saying that musicians come and go. One minute you are on top and the next you are a has been." He walked over to stare out the kitchen door window. "I'll be honest though…the last few months I've wondered what life would be like not dodging the paparazzi and traveling nine months out of the year." He smiled and finished, "At this point, I'm either in for the rest of my life or I'm stepping out for good. I'm not going to lie though…stepping out has been winning on the scale."

Ali didn't know what to say. Was he blowing smoke or was he serious? She felt like she was even more confused now than before. She wondered what the woman on the phone thought about him quitting. She wished she would have asked Jake more about this fiancé he brought up to her a couple days ago. Was she real or was it tabloid talk?

"So while we are on the subject of steps…when are you and Todd making it official?" He looked directly at her mouth, wanting to remind her that even though she was engaged, she had kissed him long, hard, and passionately a few minutes ago.

Ali decided that since he came clean, she could do the same. She looked into his face. "We technically are not officially engaged."

"Really!" he stated, nodding to her ring.

"Well, he did propose," she paused, "I just didn't give him an answer."

"Why not?" Her cheeks turned red at his question. "I'm sorry, I shouldn't pry, but I'm a bit confused here. You kiss me like there's something between us, yet you're wearing another man's ring. I'm just trying to figure us out. And that kiss wasn't a woman in love with another man kiss!" He didn't like the feeling of anger he felt every time he thought about her being engaged to the lawyer.

Ali started to resent his accusing attitude. She owed him nothing when it came to her personal life. How dare he try to make her feel like a cheat? "I guess I can say the same for you. Did I or did I not hear you have your ring on someone else's finger?" her tone was slightly bitter.

"No." Then he realized that Shea was probably still wearing his ring. "Well I mean she probably still is wearing my ring." Realizing that didn't sound good. He tried rewording it. "I mean it's off but she won't believe it's over." Running his fingers through his hair. "What the hell!"

"Exactly. There is a ring…and on her finger. Yet you kissed me like someone not very engaged." She walked across the kitchen and turned around. "You know, Abe, our circumstances are a bit odd. I don't want to spend your time here fighting with you. What happened between us earlier shouldn't have happened. We both need to figure out how to go from here as parents…not anything else." Taking a deep breath, she finished by adding, "I think I'll go to bed. Good night."

She left before he could reply. He didn't know what he would have said anyhow. He could kick himself for being an ass about her kissing him when she was wearing someone else's ring. Especially when someone else still had his ring on her finger.

Chapter Sixteen

The next day brought cold weather low into the teens. Illinois was known to go from sixty degrees one week to ten degrees the next. The joke in Ramona was flip flops one day, boots the next. Yet the weather was the last thing Abe had on his mind when he walked into Ali's kitchen at sunrise. Apparently, the girls were sleeping in. Well it was only seven and they were on winter break.

Abe wanted to give Ali a peace offering and the best way to do that was breakfast. Cooking wasn't his specialty, yet he knew his way around the kitchen. He assumed they enjoyed breakfast because there was plenty of bacon and eggs in the fridge.

He dove into some serious cooking and a half hour passed before Jake appeared in the kitchen doorway. Lifting his eyebrow, he asked if there was coffee. Abe nodded to the filled pot. Jake poured a cup and sat at the island.

"So cook by day, country star by night...who would have thought," Jake stated.

"Whatever, it's the least I can do with Ali letting me stay here."

"Yep..." He popped a chunk of bacon in his mouth. "The best thing about it is I get to benefit from it!" Jake grinned.

Abe looked at him. "Maybe...but only if you answer me a question."

Jake gave him a suspicious look. "What?"

Abe decided, after a sleepless night of flipping and flopping, he wanted another chance with Ali. If he wanted to be honest with himself, he'd admit he wanted her the second she walked into Max's office two days ago. What was it about her that the more he was with her the stronger this attraction was? He wondered if it was because whenever they were together, he always felt the 'normal life' he missed since he found fame. She seemed to bring him back to the basics.

No matter what the reason, he knew there was something between them and he needed to figure out what it was. He also knew he needed Jake in his corner. "Between you and me..." He looked Jake in the eyes before he continued. "Do I have a shot with your sister?" he asked in a hushed tone in case Ali walked in.

"Well that depends if your intentions are honorable or if you are looking for a fling?" Jake wasn't afraid to put it out there. "If it's a fling…you won't like the consequences when dealing with me. Yet if you are sincere in your pursuit, hoping for long haul, then I'd say you have a hell of a shot."

Abe smiled at him. "Not looking for a fling. Trust me, spend a few years on the road and you will find all the 'flinging' going around can put a real bad taste in your mouth." Looking around Jake to make sure his sister didn't come into the room. "I'm not sure about a long haul. I mean if that happens then I'm good going with the flow, but if we try and we just can't get it together then at least we tried. I'd say for Ana's sake…but it's more than that. From the moment we met there has just been something between us. I can't explain it!"

Jake was pleased with the other man's confession. He would like for Ana to see her parents together. Yet before he could comment any further the girls walked, or in Ana's case…ran into the kitchen.

Ali smiled. "Are you guys making breakfast?" She watched as Ana ran to Abe, who picked her up and gave her a hug before putting her back down.

"Not me. Abe here is doing all the work, while I…" Jake bit into another piece of bacon, "reap the rewards!"

Ali and Abe's eyes met for a few seconds before she asked if he wanted help.

"Not with breakfast. But I would like to have you and Ana help me after breakfast."

"With what…with what?" Ana exclaimed with her hand stretched out wide.

Abe walked over to the island where she was kneeling on the barstool next to Jake. "Well, I need help doing some Christmas shopping."

"I can do that. Momma says I'm a good shopper." She looked at her mother. "Right, Mommy?"

Ali smiled at her daughter. "Yes, ma'am. You are a great shopper."

"So…?" Abe asked, drawing her attention back to him. "Are you free today?"

"No plans for us. We just have the movies tonight."

Abe didn't want to be reminded that Todd was taking them for the evening. Yet to avoid an argument he decided to be quiet. He didn't want a repeat of the two of them arguing like last night.

"Great, then let's leave after breakfast." He ruffled his daughter's dark curls sticking out all over her head. "Thanks girls."

Ali asked Jake if it was okay to go on the excursion? He agreed but assured her he would be close by at all times. He grabbed her phone and explained that he was going to put a tracker on it in case something went awry.

Several hours later, while sitting in an ice cream parlor, Abe was happy at how well his day went. Their shopping adventure landed them at a mall in Paducah. He never would have believed shopping with his daughter could be so much fun. Abe was able to get his mother a beautiful pendant of diamonds circling a sapphire. Ali assured him any mother would love it. She also agreed that the princess cut diamond earrings would guarantee a 'brother of the year' award with his sister.

Sitting on the parlor's heart-shaped stool, he smiled with excitement because he really pulled a fast one on his daughter and her mother. He excused Ana and himself away from Ali as she stood in line waiting to purchase Ana a Christmas dress. The plan was he and Ana would meet Ali at the mall ice cream parlor at a designated time. Ali agreed because it would be a perfect time for her to shop for Ana.

Ali waved goodbye to the duo as they walked away hand in hand toward the mall's big toy store. Keeping an eye on his daughter as she looked at a shelf of dolls, Abe asked for the manager. The manager appeared a few minutes later and Abe explained, out of Ana's earshot, what he was hoping to accomplish.

The plan was he would nod at all the toys he wanted purchased and wrapped. He asked the gentleman to be inconspicuous. His other request was for half the gifts to be wrapped in Christmas paper and the other half in Birthday. On the Christmas gifts, he asked that they label half from Santa Clause and the other half from Daddy and Mommy. The birthday gifts needed to say from just Mommy and Daddy.

While watching his daughter across the room he asked that the purchases be delivered to his mother's hotel room in Ramona. The manager didn't mind because Abe assured him it was going to be a large sales purchase. Plus he promised to compensate them for any expenses, plus a bonus to the manager and clerks as a way of saying thanks. Abe was unaware that staff didn't mind helping because they knew he was good for it because they knew exactly who he was. The manager promised to personally deliver the gifts himself!

The toy store shopping was premeditated. The idea came to him early this morning while he laid in bed. Before they left for the mall, he stopped off at the hotel his mother and sister were occupying and checked them in. He explained to the hotel manager that several packages would be arriving and delivered to their room. He even called his mother to let her in on the surprise.

The hard part was trying to get Ana to be honest about which toys she liked and which she didn't. In order for him to get her to tell him what she liked without telling her they were for her, Abe came up with a plan. He explained that he needed to buy for a little girl in his family and needed her help in choosing the right gift.

He smiled at how well the plan went. They went through every aisle of the huge toy store. Whatever Ana admired Abe indicated to the clerk. Six times the clerk had to get another cart. Three times the items were too big to fit in the cart.

Abe had a great time shopping with her. What fun it was watching her show delight over a doll or a stuffed animal. She fell in love with one particular doll with green eyes and dark hair. She said it looked like her momma. It reminded him of her. He smiled and told her he was sure the beautiful doll wanted Ana to take her home today. She was so excited she hugged the doll close and thanked him with a hug also.

She showed an interest in a small bike and the manager pulled him aside to explain the model was a demo and a new one would be in pieces if he purchased it. Abe told the man to not wrap the new one but go ahead and deliver it.

On their way to meeting Ali at the ice cream shop, Abe stopped back by the jewelry store and made a purchase of a pendant and chain that outlined a mother and child's image that was encrusted in diamonds. He spotted it earlier and thought of Ali. He also spotted a pretty little locket he wanted to purchase for his little girl. The engraving on the outside said 'Daddy's Girl!'

After putting bags inside of bags, they made their way to the ice cream parlor. Ali was sitting at the table on the phone. Noting she hadn't ordered yet, Abe and Ana walked over to the counter to order three cones before joining Ali.

When they made it to the table, Ali was hanging up the phone. "Well, did you two get all your shopping done?"

"Yep," Ana stated as she started spooning ice cream in her mouth. "Abe has a cousin girl he buys for. She's like me so I helped him find toys for her. He didn't like the toys 'cuz he didn't buy them. But look..." she pulled her doll out of the bag. "He buys me this. Isn't she beautiful? I think she looks like you, Momma!"

Ali smiled when she looked at the doll. "I think she looks like you...imp," her mother said as she swiped a finger down her daughter's nose.

Abe smiled at the exchange. "I agree!"

Ali looked at him and smiled back. "Thank you for getting her the doll." Her smile made his stomach flip a little. "But don't you think you should have waited until her birthday Sunday?"

Abe almost laughed. She obviously thought his only purchase was the doll. Well he might just have to let her think that. He was sure she was going to be upset when she sees all the gifts he did purchase.

140

Ali looked at her daughter and gave her a frown. "I'm sorry to disappoint you Ana, but Todd is going to be held up at court today. So I think going to the movies is out of the question."

Ana looked at Abe. "But can't Abe take us?"

Ali looked at Abe with a 'sorry she's putting you on the spot look.' "Honey, Abe has to meet his mommy and sister, you know your grandmother and Aunt Amanda. Remember Abe told you all about them yesterday?"

Abe interrupted. "They won't get her until after eight. What time is the movie?"

"Six."

"Then I think we will have plenty of time." He looked at Ali. "Are you okay if they come to your house after to meet up with us? I have a feeling this one is not going to go much longer after meeting them."

Ali nodded in agreement. It was in that moment Abe realized the day had gone perfect. Now he could have the girls all to himself. Todd cancelling made the day complete. Nothing could dampen his mood...or so he thought.

As he was joking with the girls, he noticed Ali looking behind him as his back was to the entrance. Slowly turning around, he spotted four teenagers approach their table. Ali was taken back when they asked him if he was Abraham Parker? He tried not to look aggravated because he knew they were fans and because of them he was where he was today. Yet he just didn't get why they couldn't leave a man in peace to eat some darn ice cream with his little girl!

Ali watched him in action. She knew he wasn't happy he'd been spotted, but he was polite as he gave them his autograph. He asked the kids how they knew he was at the mall and they informed him that pics of the trio were already posted all over twitter and Instagram. They went on to say Facebook was tagging everyone they knew in the area to get to the mall. They also explained that there was a line outside of the ice cream parlor of fans waiting to meet him. The only reason they didn't rush into the parlor was because a couple of mall security were aware he was there and keeping crowd control.

There was nowhere Ana and Ali could escape to without being noticed. Frustrated, Abe had to think of something really quick to get his girls out of the mall without being followed.

As the teenagers thanked him and left, he started texting Jake. When he finished he turned to her and said under his breath, "I'm going to act like we are saying our goodbyes. Like we're old friends. You take Ana and grab the car and pull around to the loading zone outside of Dick's. I'll be out there ASAP. Don't be paranoid, remember Jake and his guys are out there watching. When you leave here walk around for a few minutes and act like you are shopping. Then go and get the car. I'm going to have one of the security guards follow you."

Looking down he read the incoming text from Jake. "Jake will meet you at the entrance we came in. He said he has all entrances covered. Even though I don't think anyone will follow you…text me when you get to the car. I noticed the loading dock when we came in and I'm sure I can figure out how to find it. Sadly in this line of work you get use to fast escape routes."

He motioned to one of the security guards right outside the door of the parlor. He thanked him for the crowd control and asked if he could help out the situation further. At his nod he handed the man Max's card. He asked if he would follow the mother and daughter to the entrance of the mall. He explained they would be meeting a tall, dark headed man who would accompany them to their car. The officer was happy to oblige. Abe told the man to send an email to the address on the card and he would receive a nice gift for helping.

Abe turned to Ali and gave her a brotherly hug and kissed Ana on the cheek. He whispered to his daughter that they were playing a fun 'hide and go seek' game. Ali noticed he quietly dropped his keys into the side of her handbag before she walked out the parlor doors.

Looking around Ali came up short. She almost panicked because there in front of them was a line of at least one hundred people just waiting to meet him. Photos were snapping over and over. Ali pulled Ana close. It was overwhelming to see all these people wanting to meet one man.

Ali looked at her daughter and could see she was confused and scared. Ali knew she had no time to calm her daughter's fears as she quickly pulled her along. What was done was done. Abe was Ana's father and with that came the hoopla.

Looking back to the crowd she was making sure no one followed her. What she saw hurt deep inside. Abe was looking at his fans with ease and charm. He smiled like he was excited to see them. She didn't realize he was just as upset as her. That he put on the charm so no one would think to follow them. Ali wouldn't understand that because no one paid her or Ana any mind. She figured it was probably because no one could believe he'd be with some small-town little mouse like herself.

Abe on the other hand couldn't get away from the crowd fast enough. He was glad to see that as far as he could tell there wasn't anyone following them. For the next twenty minutes he signed autographs and answered questions about his upcoming album. He even turned down three marriage proposals. Two from a couple twenty-year-olds and one from a white-haired seventy-year-old lady.

Abe was relieved to receive the text from Ali stating they made it to the car, she was parked by Dick's service exit, with Jake in his car behind her. He motioned the security guard over. He explained to the crowd that he needed to use the restroom. He hated lying, but he had to do what he had to do. He asked the security guard to make sure there was no line cutting. He knew most wouldn't follow him because they didn't want to lose their place in line. As he dashed into the nearest department store, he made a mental note to text Max so he would set the security guard up.

Several minutes later, Abe all but ran through Dick's and out the back exit. He waved at Jake in the car behind her before jumping in with Ali. He had to hold on as she took off like there was paparazzi on her tail. Abe chuckled as he looked back and mentioned that no one was behind them.

She looked at him with smiling eyes. "What?" She shrugged. "I always wanted to drive the getaway car!"

He laughed. "That's fine, but don't forget we have precious cargo in the back."

She slowed down. "I know. I wasn't driving that crazy!"

They didn't relax until they were out of the parking lot and on the freeway. Ana was fast asleep within minutes. Ali was the first to break the silence. "Is it always like that?"

"Well, as a rule, I don't hang out in malls. Usually everywhere I am is in a controlled situation."

"That seems almost sad…I'm sorry to put it that way but your life seems a bit restricted!" She really didn't think she could handle the lifestyle he led. She was really worried about her daughter. There has already been an attempted kidnapping. What next?

As if reading her thoughts he tried to reassure her. "Ali, I can't promise Ana and you will always be safe. But I can promise I will try to create the safest environment possible for you both." He grabbed her free hand. "I don't like all that back there. I want you and Ana's environment to be safe. I hate this waiting around to see what the kidnappers will do next and I don't like feeling useless." Taking a deep breath, he continued, "How was Ana?"

Ali gave him a quick look and grinned. "At first I thought she was startled by all the people. Then she stated that it wasn't fair that all those people got to play 'hide and go seek' with us. She was hoping it was just the three of us that were playing!"

Abe looked at her incredulous. "You've got to be kidding?"

As Ali shook her head and grinned Abe became serious. "Would you let me boost the alarm system on your house?" He could tell she was going to protest. He stopped her by saying, "Please let me do this. I'm the reason for such actions…please Ali Cat?"

She glanced at him before looking back at the road. He was relieved when she nodded. He was already making plans in his head about what kind of security system would work for her place. He just needed to go over it with Jake!

"Abe," Ali squeezed his hand before letting it go, "We really are going to have to discuss the safest way for her to grow up. She's fine going to the Pre-K program at my school…which is extra safe now because Jake is making it so. But in a couple years she will be in kindergarten and will have to attend school within the district she lives in. I won't be there to keep her safe. I just think we need to make a plan."

"I know." He ran his hand through his hair and looked out the window. "It's crazy. We really didn't have time to think about how this could all affect her. The paparazzi is going to get wind of it soon and when they do there is no stopping them." He looked back to make sure Ana was still asleep. "Ali, I don't want to not publicly claim her as my own…but I will if you think I should. I'll do anything to keep her safe. But before you reply, I said publicly, not privately. She's mine always, we just don't have to let the world know if you think it's for the best."

This was her out…if she wanted to take it. She could have Ana mostly to herself. Abe would be the quiet father from a distance. Ali knew in her heart she couldn't do that to Abe or to Ana. "I don't think it will matter. We both know it's going to get out. There are kidnappers out there who found out about her. People took pictures of all of us today. Plus her birth certificate has you as her father. Yet the biggest reason is I want her to have her daddy at her recitals and school programs."

"Thank you for that!" He let out the breath he was holding and smiled at her before turning to the window. After a few moments, he looked back to check on his sleeping baby in her car seat. "Sadly, it's probably good that she calls me Abe. That will throw people off for a bit." He paused a few seconds. "I just wish I could hear her call me daddy!"

Ali reached for his hand again and held it for several miles of complete silence. She broke the silence as they entered the city limits of Ramona. "Actually I think we probably shouldn't hide the fact that you are Ana's daddy. If we hide it people are going to want to know why. So I think we should just go about our lives like we aren't hiding anything." She squeezed his hand before stating, "Abe, I bet she will be calling you daddy soon. She will when she's completely comfortable."

After they pulled into her driveway, they unloaded the bags from their day of shopping and regrouped for the evening. After refreshing, they headed to a small diner in town. Keeping a low profile was the plan but they agreed they shouldn't look like they are in hiding or hiding something.

Ali knew the way to the town's heart was to make the townsfolk feel Abe was one of them. With him being Ana's father that pretty much made him a part of the town. A town the size of Ramona didn't have much excitement, so Ali was banking that once they got to know Abe, they would protect him like their own. In turn they would keep their eyes and ears peeled.

The diner was usually busy and tonight was no exception. Ali felt nervous but wasn't letting on that she was afraid there was going to be a repeat of what happened at the mall earlier. She smiled at several people as they entered the eating establishment. Trying to be nonchalant was hard when paranoia was setting in. Did everyone in town know Abe was her guest? It sure felt that way because the diner was packed. She had to admit it was probably busy because it was Christmas Eve, Eve! Most people had the following day off and was stopping in for a bite to eat after finishing up their last-minute shopping.

After several minutes she realized she was being paranoid when most people she acquainted herself with gave her a wave and went back to their dinners. Lily, the waitress, did eyeball Abe up as she asked the trio to follow her to an empty table. Ali wasn't sure if it was because the teenager knew who Abe was or because she thought he was hot!

Several tables called out a greeting to her and Ana on their way to the table. Merry Christmas was greeted from across the room by old friends. After sitting down she looked around to see if those greeters were looking at their table. As it was, they were not. There were several tables calling out greetings to the Filmores as they followed Lily to their table.

Ali smiled at how proud she was to belong to such a wonderful community. She loved the small-town charm Ramona represented and was proud to have so many people to call friends. Yes it was a bit of a gossipy town and there was that group that thought they were the town elite, but in the end, Ramona was the typical small-town America that she was happy to call home.

Ali waved at a few people who acknowledged her from across the room. It didn't take long for many people to become aware of the man sitting across from her. By the time they ordered Ali knew most people were wondering about Abe's presence. Or maybe they were wondering where Todd was? Ali pushed the thought to the back of her head. She didn't want to think about Todd at the moment.

Had Ali looked closely she would have noticed not everyone was happy to see her. It would have amazed and upset her because she really did try to get along with everyone. She knew not everyone liked her, but she also felt if they had a beef with her then they just had issues in general. She could think that because in the end she always tried to be kind and good hearted to everyone.

It was amazing she didn't feel the heat from Jena's glare at the back of her head. If Ali would have looked behind her booth, she would have spotted her nemesis having dinner with a big, shady looking guy with dark glasses on. It was to Ali's benefit she couldn't view the pair from her angle.

Jena was seething. She knew exactly who the guy with Ali was. She recognized Abraham Parker the second he walked in the diner. Her heart leaped until she spotted who he was with. That almost set her over the edge. How did that bitch get the men? First Todd and now a country music star.

She wondered if he knew what a slut she was? How she didn't even know who the father of her kid was? He probably didn't know she was seeing someone else. Or did she dump Todd for him? The gutsy bitch just showed up in the middle of town prancing her new man. Wanting to show everyone she snagged a star. Well she was tired of Ali Mason and maybe her new beau needed to know a few things about the woman he was hanging with. He might even decide to thank her for letting him know what a tramp Ali was.

Jena made her move a few minutes later when Abe walked down the bathroom hallway. Jena waited a few minutes and made it look like she was exiting from the women's restroom at the same time he exited the men's. She made a point to bump into him as he stepped into the hallway. "I'm sorry." She backed up like she was going to fall.

"Sorry!" he said as he grabbed her arm to keep her from falling.

She smiled at him and grabbed his arms to prevent from falling. "Hi." She gave him a surprised look. "Oh, aren't you Abraham Parker?" At his panicked look she asked, "I thought that was you with Ali Mason."

Abe was trying to figure out what to say. He hadn't been prepared to be put on the spot with questions about Ali. When she suggested they eat at the diner to 'get it over with,' did she mean the town finding out he was in town or that he was Ana's father? "Yes," not liking to lie, so sticking with the truth without giving anything extra. "Well she's an acquaintance of mine. Are you a friend of Ali's?" he asked.

"Well, not exactly." She batted her overly painted eyes at him and gave him a sad, pouty look that made her pathetic. Jake had an instant dislike for the woman. "Ali and I don't see eye to eye."

"Well, that's sad. If you'll excuse me, I need to get back," was all he said. He didn't like the woman. She gave him a bad feeling.

She acted like she didn't hear him. She put her hands on his chest to stop him from retreating. "It is, but between you and me, I don't like how she keeps stringing her lover along. She needs to just marry him and give that little girl a daddy. It's sad how she knows he's the daddy but is holding out on..." she looked him up and down, "bigger and better!"

Abe felt his heart drop. Who was the woman referring to as Ana's 'daddy'? It killed him to give her the satisfaction of asking who she was referring to. Yet he had to know. So nonchalant he asked who she was talking about. "Why her boyfriend Todd Evans, of course." She rolled her eyes. "It's sad that she keeps stringing him along. I think she's holding out on a bigger score than him. For that kid's sake, I think she should do what's right and let her kid know Todd is her daddy." Smiling, she put her card in his hand. "If you are in need of someone...single, to show you around, here's my number." Giving him a head to toe look over, she smiled and turned around to return to the dining room.

Abe just stood there for several moments looking at the card but not really seeing it. He never once doubted Ali about his role as Ana's father. Should he have? Was that hard woman correct? 'What the hell' was all he could think. What an idiot. He should have requested a paternity test. Who in the hell would try and pass off their child as someone else's? Someone wanting money or in his case money and fame?

He needed to think about what to do about the situation. He didn't know how to approach Ali about having a DNA test done. He wasn't sure he wanted to. He was already in love with the little girl. To find out it was all a lie was almost too much. Plus, to think about Ali being a liar and schemer was something he just couldn't believe about her.

What was he to do? His mother would be meeting her granddaughter in a few hours and what if it was all a hoax? Abe put the card in his pocket and went over to the table where the girls were sitting. He smiled and pretended everything was okay. He found himself watching Ana closely to see if there was any resemblance between himself and her. Unfortunately, in this case, all he saw was Ali.

Chapter Seventeen

The next few hours went on forever. He was stressed to the gill by the time the movie was over and they were pulling into Ali's driveway. Ana was wide awake and ready to meet her grandmother and Aunt. Ali seemed more nervous than excited to meet them. Abe wondered why. Was it because she was being deceitful?

As the doorbell chimed, Ana pulled on her momma and wanted to be held. With Ana in her arms, Ali watched as Abe opened the door to his mother and sister. She wondered what was bothering him? Was it his worry for Ana's safety? She wasn't sure, but something had him quiet all evening. The stress was giving her a headache. Plus now she had to face the woman who probably has no respect for the girl who slept with her son the same night she met him and then didn't tell him he had a daughter until four years later.

As the two women entered Ali groaned inwardly. Of course they would be beautiful, he was...so why not his family? His mother was tall, thin and looked way too young to have a child in his early thirties. Her smile was warm and gentle when she hugged her son.

His sister was 'holy cow' beautiful. Stunning, actually. She was tall, long blonde hair and shared the same light green eye color as her brother and mother. Abe mentioned his sister was a professional model a few years back and Ali understood how she did so well at the career. She was perfectly posed and charming. She almost smiled at the thought of what her brothers were going to say Sunday when they got a look at her. She couldn't wait to see Jake's reaction when he showed up in a little while.

Ana slid out of her arms as Abe introduced Ali to his mother. "Mom, I would like to introduce you to Ali Mason." He led them over to where she and Ana were standing. His mother came over and grabbed Ali into a hug. She backed away a bit to look into her face. "I'm so glad my son finally found you. And I want to thank you for giving us the greatest gift ever. I will be eternally indebted to you." She hugged her again with tears in her eyes.

"Mom, let her breathe a minute before you crown her." Abe chuckled. His mother pulled back and he introduced his sister to her. Amanda shook her hand and smiled.

Next came Ana's time to be introduced. Abe grabbed her hand and brought her forward to meet her grandmother and aunt. Ana smiled at her grandmother. Sandy bent down to Ana's level and smiled at her with tears in her eyes. "Hello." Sandy said.

Ana looked at Abe. He nodded to her. She smiled. "Hello…grandmother." Everyone, included Abe, was shocked that she instantly called her grandmother. Abe didn't want to admit he was a bit hurt that she called her grandmother, but hadn't called him daddy yet.

Ali saw the hurt flash in his eyes. She was guessing that Ana called Sandy grandmother because no one told her the lady's name. Ali would have to fill Abe in on that later.

Sandy smiled at her beautiful granddaughter. "I'm so happy to meet you." She pointed up at her daughter. "This is your Aunt Amanda." Amanda bent to meet her niece. Ana said the first thing she thought of when she looked at her aunt. "Are you a princess?" her little voice was filled with awe.

Amanda laughed and said, "You and I are going to get along very well missy! And I'm thinking it's you who is a princess."

"I am. Momma says I must be Snow White because she has my hair! Even though I have the little sister's name from Frozen. I know…confusion." Ana rolled her eyes and shrugging her shoulders.

Amanda laughed and offered her hand. "Come sit with me and tell me about Snow White." Ana was happy to follow her beautiful aunt anywhere.

Ali smiled at Sandy. "Welcome to our little town. I'm sure you didn't get to see much considering it was dark out. Maybe tomorrow we can show you around. Christmas Eve is a festive time to visit."

"I'd like that very much, but please don't feel like you have to entertain us. We plan to be here through the New Year…no pressure. Just hoping to spend time with you all whenever you have some free time. Amanda and I can explore when you are busy or just need some quiet time."

Ali smiled. "My house is open to you whenever you'd like. I promise you will not be a bother to us. Ana, and myself, are going to love having you both here. As a matter of fact, please don't make plans for the next two nights. We have a town celebration tomorrow evening and Christmas Sunday morning then Ana's fourth birthday Sunday evening."

Sandy was excited. "Only if I can help." Ali smiled and stated that would be wonderful. She offered coffee and Sandy followed her into the kitchen.

Abe stood back and watched how all the women in his life just took everything over. It was funny how Ana took to Amanda and Ali took to his mother. He knew they would like each other. He was now just hoping it wasn't all for nothing.

Leaning against the mantle, Abe turned as the front door opened and Jake walked in. It was really funny to Abe to watch as men stop dead in their tracks when they see his sister for the first time. Jake was no exception. His face registered surprise and pleasure.

"Uncle Jake, Uncle Jake." Ana yelled as she hopped off the couch and ran to her uncle, who caught her in his arms. After peeling his eyes off of Amanda to give his niece a hug, he sat her back down. Ana took his hand and pulled him to the couch. "This is my Aunt Amanda," she stated proudly. "Isn't she look like a princess?"

Abe laughed at the awkward moment. He decided to save his sister and Jake by making the proper introductions. They were both polite but quickly avoided each other. That seemed to be a bit odd. Amanda was a notorious flirt. Why start acting shy now? It just confirmed to Abe that a woman's mind was the most complicated thing ever!

Next Jake was introduced to Sandy and of course they hit it off. Jake charmed the older woman with his beautiful smile and flirting skills. Abe was glad his sister was in the toy room playing dress up with Ana, and Ali was acting the perfect hostess by acquainting herself with his mother. It gave him time to ponder what the lady in the restaurant said earlier.

Still brooding an hour later, Abe joined the group as everyone came into the living room. Amanda and Ana made a grand entrance from the playroom. Ana asked everyone to have a seat so she and her aunt could put on a modeling show. They were wearing boas and hats. Ana changed into a spaghetti strap princess dress and plastic high heels. Amanda was showing her the proper way to walk on the fake catwalk. Ana mimicked everything her Aunt did making everyone laugh.

In the next instance everything about Abe's demeanor changed before Ali's eyes. The two models were still parading across the living room when Amanda flipped off her boa and turned her back to the crowd and looked back to blow a kiss to her audience. It was when Ana turned that Ali heard his intake of breath.

Abe softly grabbed Ana's arm as she walked by. He didn't think anyone paid him any attention as he turned her around and looked at the birthmark that was identical to his. Ali acted as if she was listening to what Sandy was saying, but was really watching the exchange between her daughter and Abe. She was confused as she watched him rub his thumb over her birthmark then give her a big hug.

Ali was more confused when Ana ran to follow her aunt to the playroom and Abe looked at her with wonder in his eyes and stated, "She's really mine!"

Sandy, not seeing the exchange but hearing his remark stated, "I know, I just can't believe she's ours. We are so blessed that you gave us such a delightful little girl. You have taught her well. For that I thank you again."

A little while later, Amanda reentered the room holding a sleepy Ana in her arms. "I think it's getting late. Mom, we need to be getting back to the hotel." Nodding to the tired little girl. Ana started to whine about her grandmother and aunt leaving. She laughed as she hugged her. "Don't worry Snow White, we will be back tomorrow."

After seeing them out, Ali went upstairs to give her daughter a bath. Abe joined them when it was time to put her to bed. Ali grabbed a shower while Abe read Ana her bedtime story. It was a half hour later when she found Abe in the kitchen picking up.

Ali was steaming. She kept it all in, but now that they were alone she wanted the truth from Abe. "What was that 'she's really mine' statement earlier?" Before he could answer she continued. "If you weren't sure from the get go why do all these fatherly things in the last two days?" She started pacing. "If you questioned it...why not get a DNA test to begin with?" She stopped and looked at him. "What made you change your mind in the living room?"

"Ali, please let me explain." He sat at the island and asked her to sit. She almost told him no but decided it might help her calm down. "I, up until a few hours ago, never doubted she was mine. And now when I think about it, I realize I was stupid to doubt it at all."

"When and why did you doubt it?"

"While we were at the diner."

"The diner?" She gave him a confused look. "I'm lost."

He pulled out the card Jena gave him earlier. She looked at it and then back at him with a confused look on her face.

"She cornered me at the bathroom. She recognized me. She asked what I was doing with you. I didn't know what to say because I didn't know how we were going to connect me to you two. She preceded to tell me Todd was Ana's father. That you were holding out for a bigger prize. She said Todd didn't even know Ana was his."

Ali got up to start pacing again. She was livid. She has finally had enough of Jena's meddling. How dare she approach Abe and spread such lies? "I can't believe she wasn't afraid you would tell me what she said." She continued to pace. "Hell, she probably didn't care. She wanted you to tell me." She stopped and looked at him. "What else did she say?"

Abe gave her a sheepish grin and had the grace to blush. "She would show me around town if I was interested."

"I just bet she would." She sat back down and spent the next fifteen minutes telling him about all the horrible things Jena had done to her over the years. Abe felt like a real ass for believing such a malicious woman.

"Ali, please forgive me for doubting." He reached across the island and put her hands in his. His eyes pleaded with her.

"Only if you tell me what made you realize she was lying."

She watched as Abe stood up and took his shirt off, slowly, as he stared into her eyes. Ali didn't know where to look…his eyes or his body! Damn, he had a beautiful body. It was flawless. His body looked even more contoured than the first night she met him. Mentally clearing her thoughts she stated. "If you're hot," 'of course you are,' she thought, "I'll turn down the heat."

Abe knew he was making her hot. She had the same look in her eyes that he remembered so well from their night together at the Gaylord. He chuckled and turned around. He heard Ali gasp as she saw the birthmark on his shoulder blade.

He turned back around and put his shirt on. "The best thing about this is…I know it sounds a little vain, but she's everything you and now I feel like she did get something from me. So you can imagine how happy I was to see we share the same stamp."

"Abe," Ali smiled at him, "she has so many traits from you. She holds her head like you do when you are trying to make someone smile. She runs her fingers through her hair when she frustrated. My favorite, plus the one thing that worries me the most, is she's a natural born entertainer." She smirked, "But, then again, that may have come to her through your sister. After tonight's fashion show, I can say that your daughter has a new career choice to add to her 'when I grow up' list."

"Lord help us all!" he stated.

Ali laughed and wished him good night before heading up the stairs. Her last thought was after seeing him without his shirt on she wished she would've waited to take her shower. She would have made it a cold one.

***

Christmas Eve morning arrived with the promise of a wonderful day for a sweet little girl. Abe smiled as he heard her little voice in the kitchen while he descended the stairs. He stopped to eavesdrop on their cute conversation. He

152

knew his heart could never feel a stronger love than what it felt at his daughter's words.

"Mommy, can we make heart-shaped pancakes for Abe?" Ana apparently was helping her mother make breakfast.

"Sure baby. You can help me," Ali said.

"Mommy…" There was a pause. "Do you think Abe will be okay if I call him daddy?"

There was another pause before his daughter spoke again. "Mommy, why are you crying?"

"Come here baby girl…I'm crying because I need a hug." He heard a sniffle. "I can promise you that the best present you can give Abe is calling him daddy!"

Another pause then the little voice melted his heart completely. "Mommy…I think I love him lots," she said in a quieter one.

Abe stood on the stairs and rubbed at his eyes, trying to prevent them from filling with tears. He didn't know what was coming over him lately. Tears were definitely a new thing for him.

That was how Jake found him, standing on the stairwell, rubbing at his eyes. Jake paused behind Abe as he descended the stairs. Jake smirked as he looked at the Country Star and lifted his eyebrows. "What in the hell has gotten into you?" grumbled Jake. He didn't think the other guy was overly soft, but was beginning to wonder.

Abe looked at him for a moment. He wasn't too manly to admit to Jake what had him all unmanly. He nodded into the kitchen and whispered, "Ana just told her mom she thinks she loves me and wants to call me daddy!"

Jake smiled. "I get it." He slapped Abe on the back. "She does get right to the heart, that niece of mine, doesn't she?" He put his arm around the other man's shoulder and led him down the steps.

***

For December, the temperature was mild and the day was beautiful. Jake didn't pay any attention to the beautiful day. He was pumped up and ready to roll. Day five of investigating any and everything to do with the kidnapping, he felt he might have his first break. The lab found a partial fingerprint on the typed letter left for Ali. They believe the typist may have accidentally put the print on the paper while possibly loading the printer…maybe before they knew their next print would be a ransom note.

Now he had to run it and see what matched. He hoped it led to the kidnappers. As of right now they had no other leads, and with the print being a partial there would be no absolute proof of the owner being the kidnapper except for Ali and Ana identifying him or her.

He tried to run it in Ramona, but their system was outdated and wasn't digging in deep enough to run a partial. So now he was heading back to Memphis Headquarters to run it through there. He wanted to get there so he could get back in time to relieve the evening agents from stakeout duty. He'd hate for someone, who was expected home, to be stuck on the job on Christmas Eve.

When he was in the house for the night, they only placed one agent outside. The same went for his parents' house as long as Will was in for the evening. As for the hotel where Abe's mother and sister were staying, they had an agent inside the lobby and one outside at all times. The good thing is the Bureau had men in the Paducah area so the boys didn't have far to drive to get home.

His rushing back home definitely had nothing to do with getting back in time to go gaga over Abe's sister. No way he was getting involved in that! How screwed up and uncomfortable would it be for everyone if they hooked up and it went south. And he was sure it would go south because long-term, even marriage was out of the question for him. Being a detective was hard on his own family, he didn't want to bring a wife and kids into it knowing there was always danger around every corner.

***

The holidays had a way of putting smiles on everyone in the Mason and Parker families. There was a lot of sneaking around. Ana was excited to wrap her daddy's watch. Just knowing she was going to be able to actually give it to him made her extremely happy. Ali was trying to separate Christmas from Birthday for Ana. Jake loaded his trunk and backseat with wrapped Christmas presents from himself and Santa. Amanda had a pile of Birthday gifts, from the stash Abe had sent to the hotel, packed in her car. Everyone had special gifts for each other to open the next morning.

The evening was spent having dinner and going to the town square for the lighting of the town square Christmas tree with his mom and sister, Ali's parents, and Todd. Abe found he really enjoyed talking to Ali's father. They had much in common with Abe being raised on a ranch. He was actually excited when Frank invited him to the ranch during the following week to show him around. It was a bittersweet moment that reminded him of a time when he hung out at his own ranch with his father.

Later, as everyone gathered around the town square, Abe, while holding his daughter, was focused on Ali and Todd who were standing in front of him.

He hated the feeling Todd put inside him. It wasn't that he disliked the guy. It was just that the guy had his girl. Yes, he admitted to himself, he thought of Ali as his. She and Ana were his girls. He wanted a chance to be a complete family. Yet the only thing stopping them was Todd. He knew Ali was going to have to figure out what she truly wanted.

He finally understood the saying 'all's fair in love and war.' The two of them were not married. That pretty much said he had a chance and he planned to take his chance and help her realize what she really wanted. He knew she had feelings for him. He felt it when they kissed. Also their relationship from the beginning never had closure. They were never given the chance to see where they were heading and if they were right for each other. He knew she would have to make some sacrifices. He also realized he was willing to give it all up...his career and the hoopla, for these two beautiful females that became his entire life in a few days.

In the center of town was a gazebo with a band set up inside it. People were dressed for the cold weather. Hot chocolate was being offered under a tent and children were running around as children like to do when outside. The small park was lit by thousands of Christmas lights. It was bright enough for Abe to see that many of the locals were looking at him and whispering among each other. Damn, he thought, he was busted. How long before the paparazzi would find out he was here? It was Christmas Eve, hopefully they would be at home with their families.

When the band went into an instrumental and the caroling came to a halt, many of the locals approached the Masons. Ali came up from behind him with a stunning little blonde next to her. Ana leaped out of his arms into the blonde's arms.

"Abe," Ali stated with a smile, "I'd like to introduce you to my very best friend Regan...Regan...Abe."

"Hello Abe," Regan shook his hand after shifting Ali on her hip. "It is very nice to finally meet you."

Abe returned her smile as he shook her hand. He knew he had an instant friend in her. Earlier in the day, when Ali was explaining who they were meeting with tonight, she told him all about her best friend. The girl who was there every step of way during and after her pregnancy.

Looking around, Regan whispered, "I wondered how long it would take before the natives became restless and make their way over to meet the famous Abraham Parker!" She nodded as the crowd slowly approached. Jake came out of nowhere and grabbed Ana, not wanting her mixed up in a crowd. He had the area on full alert. Even though he knew most everyone in the large crowd, he didn't know if any of them were capable of kidnapping. Will was covering the crowd. Two other agents were in the crowd. So Jake felt it was safe but didn't want his niece overwhelmed.

Ali looked surprised. "Wow, it's not that bright out here, how did they figure out who you were?"

Regan answered. "Well from what Mrs. Russ told me when I walked up earlier, Jena has been telling everyone within hearing that Abe is in town hiding out. She's even been saying you are trying to put your claws into him just to give your kid a daddy." Seeing the anger in their eyes, she continued quickly as the crowd approached. "Sorry, you can ask Ali, I don't sugar-coat anything and by saying that I'll tell you Jena is a cold Bitch!"

The threesome turned as a crowd approaching them. In the lead was the town mayor, Mr. Thompson, a robust man with thinning hair and a rounded belly. There were approximately thirty locals lined up behind the smiling Mayor.

"Ali Mason," Mayor Thompson shook her hand. "Please introduce us to your friend."

Todd approached Ali and could tell she was upset. He decided to take control of the situation and made the introductions. "Mayor…Abe, Abe…Mayor Thompson."

The Mayor was excited. Reaching out, he shook the country star's hand. "Nice to meet you Mr. Parker." Swiping his arms toward his surroundings, he stated, "Welcome to Ramona!" Ali almost laughed. The mayor knew exactly who Abe was. He didn't even need clarification of a last name.

Ali watched as Abe put on his country star charm. Todd put his hands on her shoulders from behind her and she looked up smiling a thanks for being kind in the introductions. The next few minutes they listened as Abe answered question after question about any albums or concerts in the future. She was surprised to hear him evade the questions by saying he was taking a break.

Ali was distracted by a few locals who chatted with her about Christmas. She was relieved when the orchestra started back up. Everyone turned toward the gazebo to wait for the Mayor to announce the lighting of the tree. Instead he declared he had an announcement to make. "Ladies and Gentlemen, I dare say what a wonderful Christmas Season we are having this year." Everyone clapped. When they quieted, he continued, "So as a few of you may know, we have a real-life celebrity in our midst!"

Ali panicked at the mayor's words. She looked at Abe but he just smiled at her. She wondered why he wasn't bothered at the Mayor's words. It didn't take her long to figure it out as the Mayor continued with his speech.

"The gentleman I am talking about is the country singer Abraham Parker." He nodded in Abe's direction as he led the crowd in applause for Abe. Abe smiled and waved. The young girls all around started whistling and doing that annoying scream thing that girls did. Ali noticed many eyeing him up…including Jena, who was making her way to him like a woman on a mission. As she approached him, Abe gave her a look of disgust that had her instantly backing off.

The Mayor continued, "I took it upon myself to ask Mr. Parker if he would bless us with one of his songs." The Mayor chuckled. "He has agreed. So ladies and gentlemen…Abraham Parker!" The crowd applauded.

Abe took the stage and was handed an acoustic guitar. While he tuned it, Ali noticed Jena glaring at her as she moved to the back of the crowd. Ali wished she would just leave.

As Abe started singing, Ali's breath caught in her chest. He was singing the unplugged version of the song they danced to at the Gaylord. His voice was so beautiful. He was mesmerizing to every female at the park and made every man want to be him. Her chest tightened and her heart was beating rapidly. She was glad Todd was behind her and didn't see the tears in her eyes. Blinking, she was relieved to see Jake and Ana approach her. She reached out and pulled her daughter in her arms hugging her tight as she listened to Ana sing along with her father.

When she finally looked at the gazebo, she stared right into Abe's eyes. He was looking her way but she was sure he was just looking at his daughter. She hoped Todd took it that way as well. The last thing she wanted to do was hurt Todd.

When the song ended the crowd applauded and whistled. Jake and a few other guys, she assumed undercover agents, protected the gazebo to keep fans at bay. Ali watched as Abe whispered to Jake and he nodded his head.

Ali looked up when Abe grabbed a microphone and spoke to the crowd. "Thank You all for letting me perform for you tonight." The crowd started cheering again. It took several minutes for the cheering to quiet down. "I want to add that I love Ramona. It's a great little town. Most especially because it's home to my little girl." The crowd started murmuring and Todd tightened his grip on Ali's shoulders. "I want to thank you all for keeping her safe for the last few years. Unfortunately being in the position I am, it was only logical to keep her tucked away in a community that I know would always keep her safe and happy."

Ali knew what he was doing. He was convincing them they were his special friends and he was sure they would always look out for his child. 'He's amazing,' was all she could think. He was making them believe he always knew she was there and he had always been in his daughter's life. He was going to have her town wrapped around his finger. Everyone but Todd. She knew by his grip, not hurtful but firm, he wasn't happy about the declaration and devotion.

Abe looked at her and Ana, who was grinning at her father. "So on that note, I'd like to ask my little girl if she would like to come up and sing a Christmas song with me."

Ana's eyes were wide. Ali didn't need to look around to see that half the crowd was curious and the other aware of who his daughter was. She whispered Abe's request to Ana. She looked at the crowd shyly. She wiggled out of her mother's arms and ran to the gazebo and up on the stage into her father's arms.

Ali kept her eyes on her daughter as most of the crowd turned in her direction after seeing who Abe's daughter was. Regan, her parents, and Abe's mother and sister all came to be around her.

As the father and daughter started in on 'Rudolph the Red-nosed Reindeer' many people smiled, several had tears in their eyes. Ana had been shy, but within moments she was charming the audience along with her father. Abe sang it with the silly twist he taught Ana over the last few days. Ali wiped her eyes and smiled. She always suspected her daughter was a natural…but now there was proof. With a heavy heart she was almost sad at the thought of her daughter being in a world she herself would never feel comfortable in.

At the end of the song everyone cheered for several minutes as Abe and Ana approached her. She, along with nearly everyone at the park, praised the father and daughter. Jake walked over and announced it was time to get to mass then home. Ali knew he didn't like all the attention directed at them. She assumed that Abe okayed it with Jake before bringing Ana to the stage, and he just wanted them out of the public eye ASAP.

***

It was pushing midnight by the time they arrived at Ali's with Abe carrying a sleeping Ana inside and up to her bedroom. She was asleep before Christmas Mass even started and slept on Abe's shoulder all throughout the ceremony. Abe waved goodbye to his mother and sister as they followed their agent out of the church. They promised to be at Ali's late morning for Christmas brunch.

Abe got to tuck his daughter in bed after Ali put her PJ's on, never waking her. As Ali headed to the shower, Abe headed down the steps to meet Jake in the garage to help him unload the Christmas gifts from his SUV. He was humming a Christmas tune with a smile on his face as he thought about what Ana's expression was going to be like when she saw all her gifts under the tree the following day.

He paused briefly when he spotted his nemesis at the bottom of the steps. He didn't realize Todd came back to Ali's after church. Abe could tell by the look on his face Todd was in a confrontational mood. Damn, he didn't want to have a one on one with the other guy. He had things to get done before morning. The last thing he needed was the other guy dampening his good mood.

"Where's Ali?" Todd snapped at Abe as he descended the stairs.

Abe was a bit taken back by his tone. "Jumping in the shower...what's the problem?"

Todd was tired and he was jealous. Everything was working his way until this guy came along. Mr. Perfect was ruining his well laid plans. Why did he have to show up now? Why couldn't he just stay the hell away? Ana and Ali were Todd's future not this big music singer. What was the big deal singing some damn songs anyhow? Being a lawyer was hard work and something to be proud of.

Todd knew the entire town would be rooting for Ali and Abe to be together. Hell Todd was nobody's fool, he knew Abe still wanted Ali and he was pretty sure Ali still wanted Abe. He was also sure that when Abe left to go back to his glam life, he could make Ali remember she had feeling for him before this jerk showed up.

Looking at Abe, Todd couldn't hide his anger! "My problem is you putting Ali and Ana in danger tonight by letting the entire town know about her parentage."

Abe was a bit surprised at Todd's outburst. Did he think Abe was never going to declare Ana as his? "Todd, first of all Jake was okay with it." He could tell that admission only upset him more. "Plus there were several agents everywhere. Did you not know that?" He could tell by the other man's surprised look he had no clue about half of what was going on as far as the FBI's involvement in the kidnapping. Everyday Abe and Jake went over and over what was being done, who was where they were supposed to be, and any new evidence that popped up. "I'm not sure whatever gave you the impression I wasn't going to let it be known I was her father. It's already been leaked, hence the kidnappers know about her. Hell, they knew about her before I did."

"Which is the reason she was taken in the first place. Now the world will know she's your child and there will be many kidnappers coming for her. Did you even think about that before you selfishly had to declare her as your daughter?" Todd stated angrily.

Abe was trying to keep his cool. "So what do you think I should have done Todd? She is my daughter...nothing can change that!"

"She's only your daughter in the eyes of the world if you declare her as so. If you didn't exist for her, she would never be in any danger!" Todd knew his words were harsh but they would solve his problem so he didn't really care.

"Are you seriously implying that I should walk away from my daughter?" Abe looked at him incredulous.

"No," he stated quietly, "I think you should walk away from both of them."

Before Abe could reply, Ali retreated down the steps. One look at her and the anger on her face indicated she heard everything the other man said. She looked at Abe a second and asked if he would excuse them before turning back to Todd. Abe almost felt sorry for the guy as he retreated to the garage door to make his exit.

Chapter Eighteen

Ali was fuming! Who did Todd think he was to tell Abe he needed to step back from being in his daughter's life? She made that mistake four years ago and she would be damned if she allowed someone else to make decisions for Abe again. She held up her hand as he started to explain himself. "I don't want to hear it. You had no right!" She started pacing. "I don't want to hear it was out of concern for us that you asked him to walk out on his daughter. It was out of concern for you and only you."

She stopped and looked at him. She was trying not to shout. "Do you have any idea what that would have done to that little girl?" She gestured toward Ana's room. "Her heart has cried for her daddy so much in the last year. Then she meets him and you think he should up and leave her?" She started pacing again. "I get it, he comes in and he disrupts your life. For that I'm sorry, but I took four years from him and I'll be damned if I let someone else guilt him into leaving her." She wiped at the tears filling her eyes. "This isn't about hurting your feelings, it's about the feelings of a four-year-old."

"Ali, I'm sorry. You are right. You're right about everything." He sat down on the couch and put his elbows on his knees and hands on his forehead. "I'm not going to lie. I feel like I'm losing you." He looked up at her. "I can't compete with that." He motioned toward the garage door. "But I don't want to lose you. Not when I just got you back."

The sadness in his eyes almost crushed her. She knew she couldn't lead him on any longer. She walked over and sat on the chair across from the couch. "Todd, I don't know what you want me to say." She had tears in her eyes. "I love you, I truly do. It's just not the kind of love you deserve." He started to shake his head as he watched her remove the ring from her finger. "I have no idea what tomorrow will bring. Yet right now I have my past to deal with."

"We have a past." He was crushed. "What about our past?"

"Todd," she hated hurting him. "I shouldn't have let us start up again. I mean I'm glad we got to know each other as adults." She gave him a sad smile. "We have shared some beautiful memories, but I am being honest when I say the reason I never dated anyone since him was because I never got over him."

Todd looked at her with doubt. "Come on Al, you knew him one night. All you two had was infatuation. No one falls in love after just meeting someone."

"Maybe not for most, but I came darn close." She walked over and took his hand and placed his ring in it. "I have to find out if what I feel is real or if it's what you called it…infatuation."

He stood and looked deep into her eyes and knew he lost her. Giving her a hug he whispered in her ear. "Take care Ali. I love you." He turned and walked out the front door.

Ali wiped at her tears. Her heart was breaking for hurting him. After several minutes she took a deep breath and walked to the garage door and decided to see where Abe was at. Pulling the door opened, she jumped a few feet and yelped when she spotted Santa Claus standing near the entrance. "Oh my, you scared the tar out of me." She had her hands pressed to her chest. She started laughing when she noticed it was Abe in the costume. "What are you doing?"

Jake answered from behind him. "The easy part if you ask me."

Ali wondered what he meant until she spotted her brother by the work bench. Beside him was a mess of bolts, screws, bars, and wheels. "Are you putting together a bike?" she asked incredulous.

"Trying. Country King over there buys the kid a bike and it comes in pieces. I'm not sure why I was designated to put it together while he gets to play good guy and get all the credit," he grumbled.

"We flipped a coin…remember? I won, I picked Santa," Abe stated as he looked closely, through the Santa hair, into Ali's face to see if she was okay after what he was sure was a confrontation between her and the boyfriend. Abe almost stayed so the three of them could just hash it out. Yet it was Christmas Eve and he truly didn't feel like getting into a shouting match. Plus, he knew he had nothing to be ashamed of. He didn't do anything wrong even if the boyfriend wanted to make him feel guilty.

Her face didn't tell him much. She looked composed but her eyes were damp. Maybe a bit of anger there as well. She wasn't giving him a thing, but he did notice the vacant ring on her finger. He knew he should feel badly for her…but he didn't. In fact it made him as happy as a boy at Christmas. Which was what he pretty much was at the moment.

"Okay," she was afraid to ask. "So why are you dressed up?" she asked him.

"I'm trying to see if it fits," he answered as she looked him up and down and chuckled.

"I think it's all good. So what are you going to do while you are wearing it?"

"Actually it's a test run. Tonight I'm going to put most of the presents under the tree. The rest I'm going to put in my Santa sack and about a half of an hour before Ana usually wakes I'm going to put the suit back on and you are going to wake her and let her see the back of me putting her gifts under the tree and drinking the milk and eating the cookies."

Ali had to laugh. "I am...am I? You have this all planned out. So what happens if she wakes before you do?"

He grinned. "I already explained to her the rule in my family is that on Christmas morning we always woke our mom up first. That way Santa wouldn't think we were peeking and be put on the naughty list for next year. I'm sure if this happens you will shoot me a text and give me about fifteen minutes." He flashed her that sexy grin that always made her heart flutter.

Ali chuckled. "Sounds good. Well she usually wakes up about six-thirty so wake me before you put on the suit and we will let your plan roll." Ali yawned and excused herself and went to bed.

At her retreat Jake spoke, "Come on, you lovesick fool...let's get this bike together so I can get some sleep!" Abe didn't comment, he just smiled as he discarded the suit.

***

Christmas and Ana's Birthday felt like the celebration of all celebrations. Everyone had a festive day. When one of her uncles asked her what her favorite gift was she stated it was her new daddy, grandma, and aunt. This brought smiles to everyone, including her manly uncles. Of course they were sheepish acting whenever Amanda was in the room. And overly doting to their niece in her presence as well.

Abe's Santa Claus plan worked out perfectly. Ali 'shushed' her little girl as they peeked down the stairs. Ana almost couldn't contain her excitement while she watched him put the many presents under the tree. Ali rushed her back up the stairs while Santa was enjoying the milk and cookies and told her they needed to wait until he left. They didn't want Santa to catch them.

The most priceless moment was when the girls 'woke' Abe up several minutes after they returned to Ali's room. Ana was tugging on her over-dramatically-tired father to hurry up and go downstairs with her and her momma. The little girl was jumping up and down with excitement at all the presents under the tree.

Looking at Abe, Ana shouted, "Daddy, look at all the presents Santa left us!"

Abe stopped in his tracks and was startled. He smiled at his daughter and opened his arms and she ran into them. Ali's eyes swam with tears when she noticed the raw emotions on Abe's face. She was sure he had a few tears in his eyes.

It was amazing to see all the gifts Abe bought their daughter. When she pulled him aside to scold him about spoiling her, he made her feel guilty by saying he was making up for the last four Christmases. He then handed her the box with the necklace he purchased for her at the jewelry store the day they went shopping at the mall. Ali was so touched by his lovely gift she was shaking when trying to put in on. Abe took over and put the necklace on her neck.

Ali, remembering how much he liked the album she gave him when he found out about Ana, she made him a larger, more detail album loaded with many pictures of Ana's four years. Plus she copied all the videos from Ana's birth to present time so he could watch his baby grow up. He loved the gift not only because it helped him feel like he was with his daughter the last four years, but also because Ali took the time to make such a great gift for him.

Abe was a complete goner when his daughter shyly gave him the watch she picked out for him. He almost cracked when she stated she bought it for him even before she met him. That she was going to keep it for years and years and years…but didn't have to now.

No one mentioned Todd the entire day and Ali was grateful for that. She prewarned her mother and Regan, who sent a heads-up to the rest of the family. He didn't try to contact her in either. Not that she expected him to. It wasn't that she was angry any longer. If anything she felt guilty. Guilty because she didn't feel for Todd what he felt for her. She realized she should have never led him to believe she had more feelings for him than she did. It scared her to think how close she came to settling.

Abe liked Ali's brothers. Ali's brothers liked Amanda. Ali and Lana laughed at how gaga each one acted over the beautiful model. Of course she was charmed and made each and everyone feel like he was a king. Well, except for Jake. Ali observed the two of them completely ignoring each other. She thought that was odd but didn't have time to think about it. She was too busy playing hostess.

Ana's uncles loved the long red underwear their niece picked out for them. Ali laughed at how easy Ana could get them to do her bidding. She had all five uncles and her grandfather put the underwear on and come out to model them. Ali noted their cheeks were as red as the fabric. She was sure that was because Amanda was there to see their embarrassment.

164

As the night came to an end and she and Abe tucked Ali into bed he suggested they watch the videos she put together for him. They laughed and joked while watching his comical daughter learning to crawl, walk and climb. She was wondering how Abe felt about not being in any of the videos. He never said anything but she was sure it was there in the back of his head.

Later that night as Ali laid in bed, she vowed to herself to video Abe and Ana together as much as possible to make up for time lost. She was touching the necklace Abe gave her and smiled a bittersweet smile. She wished there was a chance for her and Abe. Yet she was a realist. There was no way she could ever fit into his world. She didn't want paparazzi following her and her daughter around hounding them. She knew she could only protect Ana for so long. Her daughter may eventually want to be a part of the glamorous life that Abe led, but until then, she would try to keep her as perfect as she was at this moment. Ali just prayed that her daughter always made good choices.

***

Choices were also on someone else's mind. The choice between killing the momma and the kid or just the momma. Either way the Mason whore must die! When it came to revenge one really had no choice but to do what must be done.

Her strung out eyes watched as her lover played with his new little handgun. He was excited to see it had a silencer on it that kept the pops to a bare minimum. It made her smirk to see how excited he was with his new toy. He had better be happy. It was hard obtaining it on the black market, but she had connections and the gun was needed if he was going to wipe out the girl.

It irritated her that she was even remotely dependent on the man. He turned out to be just a big lazy demanding thug who felt she was put on this earth to cater to him. If she had her way, she'd kick the bastard to the curve and handle the Mason bitch all by herself. Miss High and Mighty was only a means to an end. It was revenge she was seeking and killing one to hurt another was the plan. So in order to bring everything to a head she needed the help. Then she'd kick his ass to the curve…or to a grave. He wouldn't be much use to her once her revenge was over.

There wouldn't be any guilt over killing his lazy ass right along the side of the Mason lady. It would be a pleasure considering she did the whore a favor and caused her to be reunited with the famous baby daddy. It pissed her off to think that the little innocent school teacher is all over town parading her one-night stand.

She was taken back to see them together at the diner a few days ago. She figured the Mason chic met up with baby-daddy because of the kidnap attempt. It was funny that because of her the bitch decided to come clean to the kid's father.

She was glad her man hadn't gone with her that day. What are the odds that the first time in public since the kidnapping attempt, besides work, she runs into the source she was hiding from? It was a good thing she never let him out of the house which was fine with him because he enjoyed sitting on his ass watching Netflix all-day…every-day! She felt she needed to find out if there was any gossip spreading about the kidnapping attempt and knew the diner was the place to go and catch up. It was notorious for the close tables to have neighbors chit-chatting about this and that.

She was relieved the Mason whore didn't identify her. They made brief eye contact but there was no shock of recognition on the other woman's face. She had been pretty sure the whore didn't get a good look at her in the van the day Mac screwed up the kidnapping. …but couldn't be positive. It was a relief not to be on guard and hiding out. The bad thing was Mac couldn't unless he wore a disguise. At least not until the whore was six feet under. And that was going to be soon!

***

By late morning, post-Christmas, Ali was picking up the toys that overtook her living room. She was trying to figure out where to go with everything when the doorbell rang. Ali opened the door without thinking. She paused when she looked at the FBI agent standing next to a petite little brunette who Ali recognized as the one the tabloids labeled as Abe's fiancé. After Ali nodded to the agent that it was okay to let the woman in, the girl rudely pushed her way past Ali and walked into the living room.

"Where's Abe?" she asked as she whipped around and looked at Ali.

"And you are?" Ali wasn't going to be intimidated by this girl. She was guessing the boys, which is now how she thought of the agents, let her pass without too much hassle because they also recognized her.

"I'm his fiancé…now where is he?"

"He's in the back yard with his daughter."

She glared at Ali when Abe's daughter was mentioned. "I just bet." She took a step toward Ali. "That's good, because that gives me a minute alone with you." Her eyes flared as she looked at Ali. "I want you to know that I don't believe this bogus BS about Abe and you conceiving a baby and him being in her life the entire time. But whatever. I just want to let you know that

166

I will not have you stand in the way of the two of us getting married and living our dream." She looked Ali up and down making Ali wish she would have given a little bit more care to her appearance this morning. "Trust me babe…you will not fit into our world." She turned her back on Ali and asked in a snotty voice. "Now where is the backyard?"

Ali was ticked. How dare this she-devil come in her house and talk to her like that. It took all of Ali's control not to kick the woman out. Instead she told her to wait there while she went to get Abe. The last thing she wanted to do was put her daughter in the line of fire from this woman.

Walking out through the back porch, Ali spotted Abe trying to teach Ana how to ride the bike. If she wasn't so upset, she would have enjoyed the sweet view of father and daughter in front of her.

When she approached Abe she stated, "You have a very rude visitor. I really hope you can take her somewhere else for your visit."

"Who?" he asked and looked confused.

"Not sure, but she's in my living room as we speak." She smiled at her daughter. "Mommy will finish practicing with you." She took the reins and made herself busy helping her daughter.

Abe was disappointed when he stepped into the living room to see Shea near the front door. How in the hell did she find him? He couldn't remember if he gave her Ali's name when he explained Ana to her a week ago.

Shea turned when she heard him approach. "Sweetheart!" She rushed into his unopened arms. "How I have missed you." She smiled sweetly at him.

Abe wasn't amused. "How did you find out where I was?"

"Abe," she pouted, "are you not happy to see me?"

Abe looked at her and wondered how he ever thought she would make a good wife. She was so perfected and unreal. She was nothing like Ali…genuine and just all around good.

He pulled her away and walked over to the recliner, giving her no choice but to sit on the couch across from him. "I want to know how you found me?"

She was startled at the anger in his voice. He was never short with her. The last thing she wanted was to come here and fight with him. She was here to win him back. Not throw him over to Mary Poppins. "Honey…" she couldn't think of a lie quick enough so she had to tell him the truth. "Remember when I programmed the phone locator on your phone because you always left it here or there? I had it set to alert me to wherever you were…or I mean wherever you left it so we would always be able to find it." Her face looked innocent but her eyes were lying.

Abe wasn't buying her bull. He would never have allowed her to have that kind of control over him! "Are you kidding me? You were keeping track of me like a parent to a teen. Give me a break." He stood and started pacing while running his hands through his hair. He was sure Jake would know how to unload the track app from his phone. He now had to figure out a way to get rid of Shea before she started all kinds of trouble.

Turning to her he asked, "What do you want?"

She stood and walked over to him and tried to put her arms around him. He backed away and she started pouting again. "Abe, why are you doing this to us? I'm sorry I came off strong about your little girl, but I was in shock. You have to understand, I love you." Her eyes filled with tears.

Abe could see through the fake tears. He could see through everything about her, but he felt he had to test it. "Great, if you love me then you will be fine with my decision to get out of the music business."

Her expression was priceless. "Are you freaking kidding me…are we back to that again?" Clenching her hand at her sides, she shouted, "You would throw it all away for some kid?" She watched as his eyes went into a glare. She glared even deeper. "It's not about the kid, it's about her homey momma. One look at her and I knew you were struttin' after her."

She grabbed her handbag off the end table and walked over to the door. She could tell he was done with her. She was okay with that. Plan B was play the victim if he didn't come begging back. Putting her hand on the doorknob she had to give him her final say. "You're an idiot. Together we could have had life by the balls and you ruined it. Well I will make sure the entire world knows what an ass you are. So have a happy fucking life…you bastard." She turned and opened the door to flashing lights from several photographers standing on Ali's lawn. Before she closed it, she turned and looked back at him and smiled before putting on a hurt, humble look as she turned back to the paparazzi and dabbed at her eyes. She slammed the door and let the world see what terrible Abe just put her through. Abe was sure she was going to fill the newspapers and magazines with a bunch of BS.

He started to turn toward the back door that led out into the fenced yard when he heard the front door reopen. Thinking it was Shea, he was relieved to see it was Jake with his partner Will.

Jake asked where his sister was. Abe explained in the backyard. Even though Jake was relieved the fence was high enough to keep out the cameras he wanted the girls to stay inside for the time being. After retrieving the girls he planned to fill everyone in on the security breach they were facing with twenty paparazzi on the lawn.

Abe was pacing again. Will had to smile at the poor fellow. He really looked like he hated all the hoopla that came with being a celebrity. There was no way Will would trade spots with the poor sucker.

Ali and Ana arrived in the living room with Jake on their heels. After Ali turned on cartoons to distract Ana, Will described how he threatened a reporter to explain how he knew Abe was at this address. The man admitted that they were tipped off that Shea was planning to meet him in Ramona, so they followed her here.

Jake peaked out the window while talking on his phone. He was calling in the locals to get the mess of people off of Ali's lawn. "Abe..." Jake nodded toward the door, "what's the deal with your little friend? It looks like she's out there holding court. What's up with that?"

Abe looked into Ali's eyes and answered her brother. "She's no longer my anything."

Jake, understanding what Abe was implying, let out a soft whistle. "Well I guess she's filling them in on every nasty detail with the way she's dabbing at the waterless tears filling her eyes."

"Trust me, they are waterless. She's just trying to further her career," Abe said with bitterness.

Ali was relieved to hear the crazy woman wasn't going to play stepmom to her little girl, but she was also a bit panicked to see all the reporters on her lawn. Several minutes later the Ramona Police Department had the reporters moved back to the other side of the street. She watched, from behind the living room curtains, Shea and her fake tears finally get into her limo and pull away.

Jake decided that everyone, including Abe's family, Regan, and her father, needed to meet out at the family farm for dinner to discuss the steps needed to be taken in order to control the chaos and keep everyone safe.

Abe was given the okay to call a company about fencing for her front lawn, driveway, and making the entrance gated. Since the house sat on a two-acre lot, with neighbors at a distance, the gate wouldn't look out of place. He also called a local landscape business that Jake recommended to put in some large trees to make the house and yard more private. With the promise of an extra bonus if the job was done quickly, he was reassured it would be done in a few days.

Jake beefed up the security cameras and placed another unmarked agent on the street at all times. Ali didn't think she ever felt any safer. She hated that a chunk of their freedom was taken away, but she understood that there was no going back and the safety of her child was top priority.

Chapter Nineteen

That evening as everyone gathered at the Masons family farm for dinner, Granny Ellie was having the time of her life. She flirted shamelessly with Abe and Will. Ali laughed and shook her head when her granny proclaimed to Will that if she were younger, by a few years, she would teach him what it was like to be with a real woman. A red-faced Will laughed and said he didn't doubt it.

After she finished with Will she decided to turn her attention to Abe and Ali. She asked them if they started working on giving her a great-grandson. They sputtered and stuttered and Ali explained that their relationship was strictly platonic. Ellie lifted her old bushy eyebrows and asked Abe if he had a problem 'getting it up.' Ali's brothers' laughter erupted the kitchen. Abe was shaking his head while his face turned as red as Will's had been a few minutes earlier. Ali was sure her granny knew what she was doing and was definitely playing the 'I'm old and I can get by with anything' card. Ali tried giving the older lady a pleading look but Granny was too busy staring at Abe...waiting for his answer.

The evening wasn't just about taking Granny Ellie's abuse. Many decisions were made including Abe setting up a press conference in Max's office. It seemed as if it was the only choice to keep the paparazzi at bay. To everyone's dismay, it was decided that Ana would go along. It came down to giving the press what they wanted only it would be under Abe and Ali's terms. So putting her in front of the world and declaring they had nothing to hide seemed like the best choice. Of course then they planned to keep her out of the public's eye as much as possible!

The next hour it was decided what would be said at the conference. Abe was hoping to set it up in two days. He knew the people of Ramona would have questions for the Masons and Regan. Everyone was on board with how they should handle the town...including commenting to the people how they hoped Ana would always be safe while she lived here. The goal was to get the small town to be their eyes and ears and to want to always protect the little girl from the outside vultures!

Ali told the family that she and Todd were no longer an item…which Granny Ellie was very vocal about being relieved because she didn't think Ali should be messing around with two men at the same time. Ali didn't even try to defend herself. Ellie would probably ask her if she had something wrong with her if she couldn't get either man to take her to bed. She learned long ago it was sometimes better to just change the subject.

The topper to the get together was the chemistry in the air between Abe's mother and Regan's father. No one mentioned it but everyone could see the way they took to each other minutes after meeting. It was as if they were old friends running into each other the way they chatted most of the evening. Out of earshot from the couple, Abe and Regan both commented how their parent never showed an interest in dating anyone, but it was as if the second they met sparks started to light.

The final topic of the evening was the plans for New Year's Eve the following Saturday. It was decided that the Mason brothers, Ali, Abe, Regan, Amanda, and Will would go to Lisa's Bar to celebrate and introduce the locals to Abe. This would give the locals a chance to feel like Abe was a part of them and they would keep an eye on any outsiders coming into the area. That was one of the many things Ali loved about her town. People from Ramona took care of everyone they considered 'insiders' and that included Ana Masons daddy. Famous or not he was now one of them because of his little girl! Plus they would get to declare Abe as their own town celebrity.

When all of the important issues were finally decided, Abe excused himself so he could call Max to discuss the press conference scheduled for the following day. At the beginning of their conversation Max started off by telling Abe that Shea was trying to cause trouble. He went on to explain that she was running Abe, Ali and Ana through the mud. He chuckled and said that sadly it was backfiring because she was trying to make herself look like the victim, but it seemed no one really knew what to believe because she was talking out both sides of her mouth.

She changed her story so much the media was exhausted even listening to her. 'Did Abraham have a child or was he just dating someone with a child?' Which was what she implied in one interview. Or that he wanted to throw everything away with Shea because he had a child. Yet in the next instance she implied the child wasn't his! And what upset the fans the most was she couldn't understand him giving her up for a child? According to twitter these comments disturbed thousands of fans.

Max went on to say that as of this evening Abe's record sales were flying through the roof. It seemed as if the fans were rooting for Abe and his daughter. It apparently made everyone want to meet the little girl after watching Abe and

Ana singing at the town gazebo. Apparently, someone posted it and it went viral!

Sadly, according to Max, his fans weren't getting a good impression of Ali. Apparently a 'long-time friend' of Ali's was saying some not so nice crap about her. Whoever this 'friend' was, was telling the paparazzi that Ali wasn't a fit mom and was looking for a sugar daddy. She went on to being quoted as saying that Ali was never sure who the daddy was.

Abe filled Jake in on the mysterious friend and now he was on the lookout for this so called 'friend' of Ali's that was spreading the lies. He wondered if she didn't have something to do with the attempted kidnapping? Ali believed it could only be one person…Jena! Jake planned to find out if her belief was true.

The next day Abe, Ali, and Ana left for Nashville. With all the construction going on Jake felt it would be safer if the trio stayed away. It was a hassle to monitor everyone coming and going. Every man or woman working to install the fence, trees, or cameras had to have a special pass and have gone through the FBI's security system. This was to avoid anyone trying to get to them that wasn't a part of a work crew.

Ali was relieved her brother was FBI just for the simple fact that he was able to monitor the work being done at her place. She couldn't believe the work was going to be complete after a few days. She was happy when she got to return home, but frustrated because she realized it was going to take some time to get used to the security system just installed.

Sadly, having a brother in the FBI didn't protect them from all the speculation coming from the media. Many rumors were going around. Shea was doing everything she could to portray Abe as a liar and a cheat. Ali watched a video on social media that had Shea dabbing at her eyes and stating that when they got engaged, he never told her about any long-lost daughter. She went on with her fake crying act and blamed Abe for ruining her life. She actually implied that she couldn't believe he deserted her for a four-year old? She wanted everyone to think she was the victim. She believed the fans loved her above all else. Little did she know her words only made her look like the self-absorbed diva she was.

***

It was decided that the trio would stay at Jake's ranch for two nights. It worked out perfectly because most of the work at Ali's place would be finished by then and the press conference was scheduled for the following day so there wouldn't be much rushing. Abe's mom and sister decided to head back also just to regroup and catch up on things they've put off the past few weeks.

Ali had to admit she was curious to see Abe's place. She didn't know what to expect but it definitely wasn't this adorable, charming cabin in the middle of the woods.

From the outside the place looked like a picture you'd find on a puzzle. Almost surreal. Ali kept pushing back ideas of how well she would fit into this part of Abe's life. Yet this was her dream place. Out of town, a big yard and a handsome man to sit with on the porch swing.

Ali made her thoughts go away. Ugh, she thought, why did she keep having fantasies about him? The last thing she needed was something else to add to her overactive imagination of her and Abe.

Abe watched Ali's reaction to his home. He didn't realize he was holding his breath until she turned, smiled and raised an eyebrow and stated, "I'm impressed!"

With pride, Abe gave the girls a tour inside and out. Ana declared that the only thing missing was a puppy and kittens. Abe picked her up and tossed her in the air and stated that puppies and kittens were a must.

Considering Abe and Ana was so very much in the public's eyes at the moment, it was decided they stay in and Abe would grill up some steaks. Ana was happy that he was going to make hot dogs just for her. She stated at least a dozen times that she loved her daddy's home!

After supper was finished, to Ali's dismay, she found herself swinging on the front porch with Abe. Ana was playing in the yard in front of them. Ali hated feeling so at home and content.

"Look at her." Abe broke into her thoughts as he nodded at their daughter. "She does need a puppy!" he stated with a grin.

Ali smiled. The picture in front of her was great, but she'd had to admit a puppy would have made it perfect. His little girl was picking up sticks and digging in a mudhole and explaining how she was making them supper.

"I agree," she replied. "But as much as I dread it, I have a feeling, with the exception of school, wherever she goes the puppy will go."

Abe chuckled. "I bet you are correct!"

Ali hated thinking about weekend visitations and the separation that she was sure was going to be coming soon. About how sad her little girl was going to be when she had to leave one parent or the other. Just the overall change they were going to have to go through.

Announcing to her daughter that it was bath time and then bedtime because they had a long day tomorrow, Ali told the little girl it was time to go inside.

Ana groaned but climbed the steps to her momma. Looking at Abe she asked if he was going to read her a bedtime story?

"Of course Imp!" He patted her butt and stated he'd be up in a few minutes when her bath was done.

A sadness washed over him as he watched the girls retreat into the house. Tonight, on this porch, he finally experienced everything he needed to be complete. Sitting next to Ali and watching their daughter play in the yard was everything he craved in life. It was more important to him than a music career of any sorts. This was what he wanted now he just had to figure out how to convince her she wanted it also.

Leaving the music industry was going to be a bit tricky also. He had Max to think about, even though Max was more friend than agent. He was sure Max would understand especially because he was married with three children. All of which he adored and always put first.

His fans were very important to him also. He needed to let them down easy. Plus he had concerts scheduled throughout the spring and summer and he wanted to finish them out. His label contract was up in the fall so he had to ride it out until then.

Overall that was the easy part…the hard part was getting a stubborn school teacher to admit she had feelings for him as well. He knew she felt something for him. It was just getting her to admit it and act on them!

***

The afternoon of the press release brought on a bundle of nerves for Ali as she walked into the same room she entered several days ago to explain to Abe he had a daughter. She wasn't nervous for herself, but mostly for Ana. She wasn't happy with the idea of her child going in front of a room full of people, but she knew she had to trust Jake. She tried to relax a bit after Max smiled and told her she was going to be great. Obviously, she looked nervous if Max had to point that out.

Stepping in front of the microphone was terrifying for Ali but Ana was all bows, lace, and an unbelievable bundle of charm. The little girl's parents couldn't be any more proud of her. The press fell in love.

"So Ana, what is it like to be the daughter of a big country star?" asked a gentleman with a Nashville News label on his microphone.

Ana smiled sweetly before replying. "I don't know but I love having Abe as my daddy!"

The crowd was putty in her hands after that.

When the questioning turned to Ali, she almost panicked. Taking a deep breath, she stuck with the story they decided on. Abe had been in Ali's life all along. They just didn't advertise it because they didn't want to put his daughter in danger.

The interrogation, at least that's what Ali thought it felt like, went on for several minutes before they jumped to Shea. Abe didn't run the woman down. He just played it as if Shea was upset and that overtime, she will see that it was better for everyone if they went their separate ways.

"So Abe..." The next question was shot at him. "What are your plans for your music career? I mean can we expect to see these two beautiful ladies at your concerts?"

"Absolutely!"

Ali wouldn't admit to the disappointment she felt with his answer. So the few hints that he dropped about maybe retiring from his singing career was just a bunch of smoke. What did she expect? He didn't really owe her anything. Did she think he was going to declare a deep love for her after all these years? She needed to be a realist! She also knew she needed to come to the fact that the two of them needed to stick with the role of Ana's parents and nothing more. So no more front porch swings and definitely no flirting. She planned to stay away from anything romantic when it comes to him.

After the conference Jake drove the trio to the Nashville FBI Branch to have Ali look through photos and try to identify the man who tried to abduct her daughter. Abe had the Memphis office run the fingerprint and there was now a list of people the print could belong to. The list consisted of four criminals, each with a fingerprint that closely matched the very partial print.

As Ali looked at the four pics, Jake realized it was a longshot that the partial was connected to an actual piece of crap who tried to abduct his niece. He was surprised when Ali stated one of the pics seemed familiar. Jake asked her if it was okay if Ana looked at the pics and she agreed. She'd do whatever it took to catch the man who tried to take her daughter.

Abe brought his daughter in from the other room and Jake asked her if any of the people in the pics looked like the man who tried to grab her. Ana pointed to the same pic as her mother did. Jake and Ali looked at each other. Was it him or was it a coincidence? Jake knew the guy was an ex-con by his record. He should be reporting to a probation officer in Tennessee where he served time. Jake promised as soon as he knew something, he'd run a report of the guy and he would let Ali know what he found out.

That evening, back at Abe's ranch, she retired to her room early and informed Ana and Abe that the evening was for the two of them. She explained that she was curling up with a good book and would only bug them when it was Ana's bedtime. The two girls were sharing one of Abe's guestrooms. Abe just wished Ali was sharing his room.

Good to her promise, Ali retrieved Ana a few hours later. Abe couldn't shake the feeling something was wrong. At first, he thought it had to do with the investigation. Yet something told him it had something to do with them.

He felt her withdraw from him. Her smile was polite as she stated she'd let him know when Ana was done with her bath so he could read her a story. He smiled back but wondered what was going through her mind as he watched the girls climb the steps to their room.

The feeling only grew stronger the following morning on the car ride back to Ramona. Ali was exceptionally quiet. He just wished for the life of him he knew what was wrong with her. In the back of his head he was sure it had to do with the two of them. He was almost in a panic because he was afraid he was losing her before he really ever had her.

Arriving at Ali's house they found Jake in the kitchen. He was fixing a sandwich and offered them some. As they declined, he motioned for Ali to occupy Ali so they could talk. After turning on the television for her daughter, Ali returned to the kitchen.

Jake opened a folder and showed Ali more mugshots of a man Ali thought, the day before, was very similar looking to the man who tried to abduct her daughter. He explained the man's name was Ronnie MacDonald and he was an excon. He was sentenced to sixteen years behind bars for murdering his drug dealer. He was released out of a Tennessee federal prison about six years earlier on good behavior. As of a year ago he no longer needed to check in with a probation officer. His last known address was Paducah Kentucky. Yet as of this morning they were sure he didn't live at that address any longer.

Ali couldn't be one hundred percent if the man in the pics was the man who tried to abducted Ali. She didn't want to wrongfully accuse someone. She explained to her brother that she just couldn't be sure. Jake decided to show the rest of the clan the pic and see if anyone remembered ever seeing this joker.

Minutes later Jake was out the door with two things on his agenda. First, to pay a 'visit' to a local and put the fear of God in her! Second...to find the SOB in the pics. He needed to talk to his family, Regan & her father...maybe Dan had spotted this man at the casino at some point. And third was to Abe's mother & sister, who he was just informed by his boys, had just returned to town. Grinning, he decided to start backwards and go with the tall blonde first. He knew she was off limits, but a little flirting wouldn't hurt. Besides, maybe seeing her would get her out of his head.

***

Ali spent the day cleaning her closet and several other useless chores. She was relieved when Abe suggested he and Ana should go to a matinee and get out of her hair. Of course minutes after they left, she wondered if he was trying to put distance between the two of them. This led to a feeling she refused to touch on. She knew it was all for the better. Taking a deep breath she decided her laundry room needed cleaning…for the second time today.

As her quiet day continued, she became more down in the dumps. Who was she kidding? She wanted Abe. She wanted to touch him. She wanted to joke and flirt with him. She wanted him in her everyday life. She wished he'd let her know what he wanted. She would never dare ask him. But she knew he was attracted to her. She could feel it as strong today as it had been the first day they met. She just wished she knew where they went from here.

***

Jake arrived at the house later that evening and informed Ali he tracked down the rag magazine that posted the lies about her. Come to find out it was just as she guessed. Jena was the one who filled their ears with a bunch of lies. Jake said in a few days he was going to have a little talk with Jena. First, he was going to see that she publicly declared herself a liar. Then he was going to do some digging into her lifestyle.

He wasn't ruling her out as a part of the kidnapping scheme. He knew the girl for most of her life and he was very aware of her devious nature…especially when it came to his sister. He was betting she was into something illegal. Word on the street says she likes her cocaine. Of course no one in her surroundings knew she was addicted to the nose candy except for the friends she did it with. Seemed to him she probably had a great motive for sending a ransom note. Money was usually the reason, but if she was involved how did she know Abe was Ana's father? That was something he intended to find out.

Chapter Twenty

New Year's Eve in Ramona was always a festive time. Ali was especially happy because she was going to hang out with her five brothers, her best friend and her newest friend, Amanda. It was bittersweet becoming close to Amanda, because she was Abe's sister and would always be a reminder of Abe when he left. So Ali decided to just think of her as Ana's aunt and Ali's new friend.

She was excited because Abe was going along also. The last few days she avoided him, but deep down had to admit she missed him. Missed hanging out and laughing with him. They went from flirting buddies to just roommates. It was her fault but she didn't think she had a choice in the matter. It came down to knowing her heart couldn't live in his world. She knew she was selfish, but she wanted the two of them in her world. More of an equal foundation. Yet that was impossible when you were someone like Abraham Parker. And Ali didn't want to be his reason for leaving his world and resenting her for it down the road.

The plan was for Ana to stay the night at the ranch with Ali's parents, Sandy and Dan. Jake even made sure he had extra agents posted at his parents. Ali and Abe were going to go to the hotel and pick up Amanda and meet Regan, the Mason men, and Will at a nice steakhouse in town. After the dinner, the plan was to head over to Lisa's and do a little drinking and dancing.

Ali was nervous when she looked in the mirror. She hoped she wasn't overdoing it with the new dress she bought for especially tonight. Then again didn't most people go overboard when going out for New Year's Eve?

She put on a sleek little black halter dress, that was only attached by one button at the nape of her neck. The dress hugged her body and accentuated her slim waist and curvy hips. She was afraid she looked too leggy considering the dress was several inches above her knees. The three-inch heels only made them look longer. What made her a bit insecure was how low cut the front was. There was just a hint of curve of her breast to make her wonder if the dress was too much. She decided not to think about it and just go with it!

She softened her curly hair into pretty waves that flowed freely past her shoulders. She even spent extra time on her makeup and took a shot at contouring her features and had to admit she didn't do a half bad job of it. She wondered what Abe would think?

She had her answer a few minutes later when Abe watched her walk down the steps into the living room. She smiled as his mouth opened. Ali wasn't sure she ever felt sexier than she did at that moment.

Jake thought she was stunning. He couldn't take his eyes off her. She was just down right gorgeous. 'God,' he thought, 'you made her perfect and she's the mother of my baby. How did I ever get so blessed?' Clearing his throat, he stated, "Ali…you are breathtaking!"

He didn't want to share her tonight, but he was excited about the upcoming evening because he felt like it was their first date. Even though it wasn't technically a date, because the evening was planned by the family a few days earlier, he still felt like she was his date for the evening.

Ali devoured Abe with her eyes as much as he did hers. He was wearing black pants with a long sleeved, baby blue shirt that brought out his beautiful eye color and showed off his nicely cut upper body. It was opened at his neck only a few inches and complimented the stylish black sports coat that was definitely tailored to fit him perfectly. His hair had that sexy messy thing going on. Yep she didn't know if she could keep her hands off him tonight! She was getting hot…fast.

Abe couldn't stop staring at her. He had to shake his head as if to clear it. He grabbed her wrap from her and turned her around to drape it around her shoulders. Ali closed her eyes when she felt his gentle kiss on the side of her neck below her ear before he whispered, "We need to leave at this very moment or we will never make it out of this house tonight."

Ali slowly opened her eyes and turned to stare into his. She glanced at his mouth then backed up a step to look into his eyes. Meeting his look and taking a deep breath she nodded her agreement. In a daze she walked around him and headed to the garage door.

Abe realized he quit breathing for a second and started panting a bit. 'Damn, she's going to make this one hard night!' he thought as he followed her out the door.

***

Dinner was nice at 'The Flame Grille.' Their party was seated immediately due to the reservation Regan prearranged. Everyone was in a festive mood, especially Ali's brothers. Well three of the five anyway. Ali grinned as she watched Adam, Sam, and Jon make fools of themselves over Amanda. Will seemed to be interested in her also, but then again Will was a bit flirty with Regan and even Ali herself.

She thought it was sweet that Amanda made her three younger brothers feel like they were family. She made a point to let them down easy but making sure they weren't offended. The boys took it all in stride and continued to flirt with her like they had no clue to take the hint.

Ali was surprised to see that Regan showed an interest in Will. She never would have thought the dangerous sexy detective would be Regan's type. Her friend usually went for the quiet broody type.

It reminded her that she hadn't really had time to hang with her friend in the last week. So she wouldn't know if there was something between them. She decided to feel out the situation later in the evening.

Looking at her two older brothers she wondered what was up with them. Frank had been especially quiet all evening. As a rule he was a quiet guy, but around family and friends he usually liked to relax and cut up. Tonight he seemed preoccupied. Almost angry. Funny, but it looked like Will was the target for his anger. She couldn't understand what would make Frank angry at Will. According to Jake, the detective was a fun, easy going guy, when he wasn't catching bad guys. Odd, but it seemed to her like Will was enjoying the pissed off looks Frank was passing at him.

Jake was also brooding and Ali was once again clueless to what was going on. Even though the evening dinner was fun and no angry words were being passed around, Ali felt like she was in the twilight zone. Taking a drink of her beer she decided tonight was her night to have fun and she wasn't going to worry about anything.

A few hours later Ali came to the conclusion that the evening was supposed to be bizarre all around. Dinner was nice but there was tension in the air. After dinner they arrived at Lisa's Pub. Abe was impressed that the small town had such a large bar. He loved the huge dance floor and the bar's long 'L' shape. The place could hold a large number of people.

Ali knew most of the people living in Ramona. She wasn't surprised when many stopped by their table to say 'hi' and hoped to be introduced to Abe. She was glad they weren't acting like starstruck groupies. After the introductions they would tell Abe they love his music and give him a 'welcome to Ramona' or a 'nice to meet you' and go on their way.

Lisa, the owner of the pub and a longtime friend of the Masons, stopped over to say hello. Ali introduced the pretty blonde to Abe, Amanda, and Will. After some small talk and thanking Lisa for the round of drinks she ordered for the table, Ali started to relax.

That was short-lived because a few minutes later Ali looks up to see her old buddy Jena come strolling in. She watched as her nemesis strutted to the bar and took a seat on an empty barstool. Ali hated how Jena was making her dread the evening.

Ali decided as a New year's resolution she was going to give Jena no more of her thought time. From now on she didn't care what the woman said or did. And heck with starting her New Year at midnight. She was starting her resolution now.

Turning, Ali looked back in the direction of the band. She glanced over at Abe checking out the band as well. She wondered if he was thinking about his own band. She was sure this four-piece country band wasn't anything like what he was used to. The lead singer on the stage was a large man, well over six feet tall, with an impressive belt buckle that had a large part of the man's stomach hiding it. His face was bearded and he wore a cowboy hat that looked too large for his head. The rest of the band was very similar to this man only minus the beard.

Ali couldn't remember what Abe's band members looked like whenever she creeped up on him over the last four years. She was sure it was because she only had eyes for him. Shaking her head she needed to move her thoughts away from Abe. She decided thinking about how her family was acting looney was a great distraction.

Looking around she spotted Jake flirting with half the women in the bar, asking several to dance when a slow song came on. Amanda was getting quite the attention from many admirers. Her other brothers were all over the place flirting and dancing. Regan and Will were talking at the bar and looked to be doing some shots.

When the next slow song came on, Abe asked Ali to dance with him. She was happy to oblige. Making small talk she confided in Abe about how weirdly Jake and Frank were acting. "I just feel like things with my family are happening around me and I am clueless to what is going on." At his grin she continued. "Do you know something I don't?" She glared at his grin.

"Ali love, are you really that unaware of what is happening?"

She almost smiled when he called her 'love.' "What is happening?"

Turning her to look at Jake, he answered her. "Watch Jake." He nodded in her brother's direction. Jake was leaning against a pillar talking to a short, petite girl who was hanging on his every word. Ali watched as Jake kept looking at something across the room. Ali turned to see where he was looking and was surprised to see he was looking in Amanda's direction. She watched Amanda talking to a tall good-looking cowboy. Ali was astounded to see

Amanda's eyes stray to Jake. If they made contact, they would quickly look away from each other.

Ali looked at Abe with a startling expression. "Oh." Was all she could say.

Abe smiled and said, "I spotted the chemistry between those two the minute they were introduced." Grinning he continued, "I wonder what it is about the Masons and the Parkers? There's some underlying attraction that jumps out and slaps them when they first meet."

Ali didn't know what to say to his comment. She just stared at him for what seemed like forever. Abe decided to break the ice by filling her in on the rest of the twilight zone happenings tonight. "So let's see if you are observant about another chemical reaction." At her confused look he nodded to the bar where Regan and Will were doing a shot. "So what do you think is happening there?" Nodding to the couple.

"This one is obvious...Regan and Will are hitting it off," Ali gloated.

As Abe shook his head, she stated, "What do you mean? They obviously like each other!"

"Sure...but not how you think. Look over by the bathroom."

Ali looked to see her brother Frank glaring at Regan and Will as they laughed together at the bar. She could see her brother's anger even at a distance. After a few moments, she watched her brother walk over to the couple and slam his beer bottle on the bar between the two and glare at Regan before turning and storming out of the place. It took Regan about thirty seconds to follow him out the door.

Ali made a move to go after the two, but Abe stopped her. "Al, let them figure it out."

Looking at Abe she replied, "But what if they need me?"

"I think right now they need each other." He put his finger and thumb to her chin and coaxed her to look at him. "Let them work it out."

Ali took a deep breath and smiled at Abe as the song came to an end. "Okay, so who wants someone else here that I'm clueless about...Mr. Observant?"

Abe looked into her eyes several seconds while standing in the middle of the dance floor. "I think the last one is obvious," he stated in a matter-of-a-fact tone.

Ali knew he was referring to the two of them. She looked from his eyes to his mouth, silently asking him to kiss her. Abe moved forward...

"Excuse me, Mr. Parker." They were interrupted by the lead singer of the band. Abe and Ali stepped back and turned to the man.

"Yes, can I help you?" Abe was polite but his tone had a sharp edge to it that Ali knew was from being interrupted.

"Hi," He gave Abe his hand. "My name is Dean." He smiled as Abe shook his hand. "Well I know we decided…well that is the town decided to not bombard you with hoopla while you are here." Ali and Abe had no idea what the man was talking about. At their confused look he explained, "Well there was a special meeting after your press conference and it was decided, by most everyone in attendance, that we need to treat you like a normal person and not make you uncomfortable with always wanting your autographs and asking a million questions."

Ali thought it was sweet that her town was going out of the way to make Abe feel at home. Looking at Abe she could see this pleased him also.

Dean continued. "So I hope I'm not imposing to ask if you want to sit in for a few songs tonight?" Before Abe could reply he went on to say, "No pressure."

Abe looked at Ali to see what she thought. She shrugged and said it was all up to him. Abe agreed to sit in for a few songs. It was decided when and what he was going to sing before Dean left to rejoin his band.

Ali and Abe walked over to the bar to grab a couple of beers before going back to their table. Of course who would they run into but Todd. He was as startled to see them as they were him.

Ali noticed two things in that moment. First Todd was sitting next to Jena. She wondered if that was a coincidence or were they in cahoots together. Lord she hoped not for his sake. The second thing she noticed was Todd was very drunk.

"Ali Mason," Todd Slurred. "Fancy meeting you here."

"Hello Todd." Ali didn't know what else to say to the guy.

Abe walked them down the bar a few spaces to where it was open enough to order their beers. Todd looked over and said to Abe, "Really Pal, you can't even offer to buy me a beer after the hell you made my life?" '

Abe paid the bartender and turned to hand Ali her drink. He looked at Todd and said, "I think you've had enough. Let's just say I owe you one." He took Ali's arm to direct her away.

Todd stopped them by jumping up and pushing Abe on the shoulder. "Don't tell me when I've had enough. What I've had enough of is you Parker," Todd slurred.

Abe looked ready to deck Todd. Ali panicked and almost got in between the two guys. She was relieved that Jake and Will walked up at that moment. Jake led Todd outside by grabbing his arm and shoving him toward the door to have a talk with him. Will walked with the couple back to their table and calmed Abe down by making light of the situation. Ali was relieved it ended before it began.

A little while later Abe was called to the stage to sing a couple of his songs. Minutes into the first song Ali watched as people took pictures of Abe as he completely captivated his audience. The upbeat song was one of his most popular and she was enjoying herself when Amanda grabbed her to join in the dancing on the packed dance floor. Half the floor line-danced the other just did their thing so she didn't mind shaking her booty!

Abe played three songs before making his way back to Ali a few minutes before midnight. Walking to the bar area they found most of their family and friends hanging out. Three of her brother's picked up a kissing partner for the midnight hour. Regan and Frank were back and at Ali's raised eyebrow her best friend had the grace to blush and silently mouth the words 'I'll explain later.' Amanda was still talking to the cowboy she met earlier while Jake was still doing his best to ignore them.

Midnight struck with the band's countdown. Hugs and kisses were given out to each other. Ali hugged her brothers and gave Will a kiss on the cheek. While Regan hugged her, she whispered that she expected a phone call the next day. She watched as Regan and Frank going in for a midnight kiss before she finally turned to Abe.

Abe was waiting for his turn to bring in the New Year with Ali. He'd been waiting all night. As she approached him, he said nothing. He reached out and put his hands on the sides of her face and pulled her to him for a long and passionate kiss. As the kiss ended and Abe felt like it was the perfect moment to tell her he loved her, he heard the words "you son-of-a-bitch!" Abe looked up as Todd came out of nowhere and started swinging in the direction of Abe's face.

All Ali saw was Todd aiming for Abe's face, Abe ducking and Todd's fist landing on Jena's face as she was coming up behind Abe. Jena fell back, Todd looked startled before Abe's fist landed across Todd's nose making him fall back into the crowd.

Everything went crazy after that. Camera flashes were everywhere. The man Todd fell on shoved him, causing Todd to retaliate and turn to throw a fist in the man's stomach. This made the man's friends angry and he took a swing at Todd causing a bloody brawl to break out.

Jake, taking it all in, yelled across the tables to Abe. "Get my sister out of here, I'll see to Amanda and the others."

Abe agreed he needed to get Ali out of there. This would be a perfect time for someone to snag her. He grabbed her hand and quickly pulled her through the exit to his car. Looking back he was relieved to see no one following them. He wasn't sure how due to there being paparazzi everywhere coming out of the woodwork as soon as Todd threw the punch that landed on Jena's face! He grinned as he heard glass crashing and wood splitting. Shit, he thought, Max was going to have a field day tomorrow when he opened the rag magazines. Abe would have to fill him in on the damages he was going to have to pay.

Once inside the car they waited for a few moments to see if the rest of their clan exited out the bar doors. Ali spotted Frank and Regan rushing out, hand and hand, making their way to Regan's car. Next came her three younger brothers laughing and running like little kids. Ali chuckled. After a few minutes they spotted Jake and Amanda rushing to Jake's truck and peeling away.

As Abe started his engine to leave, they noticed Will walking out like he didn't have a care in the world. He stopped and leaned against a street pole and watched as people started scattering about. Abe just grinned and shook his head. Hearing sirens, he decided it was time to hit the road.

On the way home Ali vented about the BS Todd pulled. Even though she felt terribly, he was apparently hurting, nothing justified him trying to sucker-punch Abe. Abe wasn't so sympathetic. He thought Todd was an ass and didn't mind saying so. Yet deep down he knew he'd feel as shitty as Todd if he didn't have Ali in his life anymore.

They both agreed on one thing…Jena getting sucker punched was the highlight of their evening. According to Ali that would be the highlight of her New Year. Abe hoped he would be her highlight.

Ali spotted the two familiar cars on her street. It was ironic how they became such a comfortable sight to her. The agents were always there. She wondered if they were on duty through the Bureau or if they did it as a favor to her brother. She wasn't sure how long the Bureau kept around the clock agents on a case but figured it had to be very costly to do it for a long period of time.

Parking the car in the garage, Ali followed Abe into the living room. Taking a deep breath, she wondered where this night was going to end. It was a startling revelation that she hoped it would end with her and Abe in the same bedroom. She wanted and needed the magic they somehow created. In the morning she would deal with the future. But tonight was for her and Abe.

Walking past him, she grabbed his hand and led the way up the steps to her room. Abe followed her like a puppy. Ali didn't mess with turning on the lights because there was enough moonlight coming in through her bedroom patio doors. Closing the door, she turned back to Abe and kissed him with all the passion she had built up inside her.

"Are you sure, Ali Cat?" Abe whispered as he held her in his arms.

Ali smiled and reached up and unbuttoned her one button and let the dress fall to the floor. Abe's mouth went dry as he watched her undo her skimpy little halter bra and let that fall to the floor as well. Staring at the beautiful woman in front of him, he had to tell himself to breathe. He reached out and cupped her full breast in his hand and stroked her nipple with his hand.

"I swear having our baby has made your body so much more beautiful than before and I don't know how that was even possible." He whispered as he caressed her breast. "I think your breasts are even more beautiful than I remember."

"Well," she ran her hands up the front of his shirt and started unbuttoning it. "I want to see what five years have done to the sexy man I remember." After taking his shirt off she ran her hands all over his slick chest. "Hmmm…" She looked at him as if in deep thought. "I think age is making you a little less firm in the chest area."

She shrieked as he grabbed her and tossed her over his shoulder. "I'll show you old age!" he stated as he tossed her on the bed and sat on top of her and held her hands over her head. Looking into her eyes he smiled. "I bet you I can get you to take that back and admit I too am as sexy as you remember!"

She laughed and shook her head back and forth. "No way!"

Abe preceded to show her he was everything he promised. He kissed her long before running his tongue all over her ears and neck. Next his mouth made its way to taste her breast while his hand massaged and rubbed her other one.

Ali declared uncle and admitted he was as sexy as ever before she did some exploring of her own. Her hands and mouth were over every inch of him. She wanted to taste every part of him. Abe let her explore until he almost lost control.

Against her will, he pulled her up to him and flipped her over so he could do some exploring himself. He grinned at her and said something about two can play at that game as he moved lower and took to her secret spot, the place that drove her crazy five years ago. Abe was relentless as he ran his tongue over it back and forth. He was glad she still went crazy when he touched her there. He loved the taste of her as he brought her to explosion several times before he stopped to protect himself.

Turning onto his back he grabbed her hips and slip her down the length of him. He needed to see if what he remembered of her riding him was as beautiful as was embedded in his brain from the last time they were together.

Ali didn't know how much more she could take when he laid back and put her on top of him. She moaned her pleasure as he filled her inch by inch. Nature took over as she moved around in a small circular rhythm. It didn't take long for the tempo to get faster and harder. She felt the pressure building and pushed down harder and harder, back and forth, to take it all in.

186

Abe truly believed he died and went to heaven. Watching her ride him with her breast out, her head back, and eyes half closed was an image that would never leave him. He loved this woman. He believed he loved her minutes after meeting her. She brought him to a place that only she could take him.

He didn't know how much longer he could hold one. He used every ounce of control to make sure she found pleasure when he did. Relief came second later when her body tightened around him and she shook long and hard from her head to her feet. His release was as strong as hers. He let the waves of passion shudder through him over and over.

Several minutes later Ali collapsed on his chest. Their bodies were hot, sticky, and wet. Her breathing was hard and quick. Abe looked at her and thought she had to be the most beautiful woman alive.

Ali grinned at him. "Next time you're on top!"

Abe pulled her to his side and asked, "Now who's acting old?"

Several minutes passed as Abe rubbed his hand up and down Ali's back. "Al, will you do me a favor?"

Ali, almost asleep, looked up at him and smiled. "Sure, what would you like me to do?" she asked in a seductive voice.

Abe smiled and stated. "Can you reassure your grandmother I can get it up?"

Ali laughed as she took a pillow and threw it at him.

***

Jake found the two of them in the kitchen making breakfast the next morning. It didn't take a rocket scientist to notice their relationship took a big turn since he saw them at the bar last night. Of course, considering Ali was his sister, he didn't want to think about what probably happened.

"Well look what the cat's drug in!" Ali said to her brother. "Just where did you stay last night big brother?"

Jake walked over to the pile of bacon on the plate, grabbed a piece and ate it before replying. "Wouldn't you like to know!"

Ali glared at him with a glint in her eye. "Maybe I do."

Jake smiled and leaned against the counter before looking her in the eye. "I'll let you...my sister..." he raised an eyebrow at Abe to let it sink in that Ali was his sister as much as Amanda was Abe's...so an eye for an eye, "whose bed I slept in if you tell me whose bed you both slept in."

Ali knew she was busted but would never admit it. She threw a hot roll at his head and called him a jackass. Jake chuckled at their red faces.

Grabbing a cup of coffee, Jake filled them in on Will's report of what went down when they all left. "Apparently the cops got called and a few people were arrested...including Todd."

Ali looked at her brother. "I don't know why he acted like such an ass. We only dated a few months. I never would have taken Todd as someone to act like he did last night. Why can't he let it go?"

Neither man replied. There were probably many reasons guys act like jackasses but there's no way to explain why they do what they do. Abe thought the man was head over heels for Ali because she was incredible. Jake thought it was because someone else snagged something he thought belonged to him. In this case it was Ali.

"It's okay Al, Will talked, or should I say charmed, Lisa out of pressing charges," Jake stated. "Even though the PD made him sleep it off at the jail. He is going to be released as soon as he wakes up and agrees to pay for the damages to Lisa's." Jake chuckled. "Last night was the most action Ramona has seen in a while."

"How did Jena fair? She was pretty pissed off when she was punched last night," Abe asked.

"Well now that's the funny part. She was arrested and booked for assaulting a police officer. She wanted the Ramona PD to find you both and arrest the two of you. So when the police talked to several witnesses, who confirmed the two of you were actually avoiding the fight, Jena went bat-shit crazy and punched an officer in the mouth."

At Ali and Abe's shocked expression he continued. "Here's the best part...after arresting her they found a buttload of cocaine in her purse." Jake loved shocking people and these two were no exception.

"Oh my Gosh!" was all Ali could say.

"Yep," Jake continued. "Of course she said she was set up. It didn't take her daddy's lawyer long to show up at the station." Jake grinned. "The kicker is she had to stay the night in jail because it's a federal offense to have that large of an amount of drugs in possession and you cannot be released until you stand in front of the judge." He grinned as he snagged another slice of bacon. "She has to go in front of the judge tomorrow morning, because today is a federal holiday, to see what bale is set at. Which also means she has to spend another night in jail."

Abe finally spoke. "If daddy is rich, won't this all just go away."

"Well, I plan to be there for her ten o'clock hearing tomorrow morning and have a little talk with her after. I need to explain that trash-talking to rag magazines was slander. And I want to see if she knows anything about the kidnapping!" At their confused look he continued, "I'm not sure she has anything to do with it…I'm just not ruling her out."

Ali was processing his words as he refilled his coffee and grabbed another slice of bacon before heading to the kitchen door. "Speaking of trash magazines…" He grinned at his sister. "Al you look good on the cover!" They heard his laugh as he retreated up the stairs.

Abe groaned as it dawned on him what Jake was implying. Last night's brawl made the cover of a rag and Ali was on the front. So much for getting the world to like her. If they follow their usual pattern, Ali was going to be made to look even worse.

He watched as Ali's facial expression registered what her brother meant. She groaned and looked at Abe. "Great! I can only imagine how I am portrayed." Tossing her hands in the air, she stated, "I don't care. I don't want to read about it or know of its existence." Stomping out the door defeated she shouted, in what Abe thought was good humor, "I'm going back to bed and fantasizing about Jena in jail!"

He grinned at her retreat and thought, 'Boy, do I have it bad for her.' He didn't care. He smiled as he turned back into the kitchen to clean up from breakfast.

Chapter Twenty-One

The next day Ali decided to visit Regan at *Mystique*. Since her friend hadn't returned her calls from yesterday, Ali decided to take the matter into her own hands. She knew her friend well enough to know something was up and that she was purposely avoiding her lately. It just bummed her out that she had so much going on lately that she didn't notice her friend needed her.

Her excuse for the visit was to fill Regan in on the Jena drama. Jake stopped by her house, after court this morning, and gave her the details of his visit with Jena. He had to use his badge to make her agree to talk to him before her lawyer ushered her out of the courthouse. After given a private room to chat, he got her to admit to spreading lies to the trash magazine. At first, she sneered and tried denying it but when he presented her with evidence and threatened to add to her current charges, she caved. Jake explained to her she had two days to retract her words and give a nice statement about Ali's character or she was going to be slapped with a slander suit.

When her lawyer started to intervene it was Jena who held a hand up to hold off the lawyer. She stated she was going to do what needed to be done. She stood up and thanked Jake before walking out the door with a defeated look on her face.

Jake explained to Ali that he wasn't buying her crap. It almost scared him that she was so agreeable. He went on to say she was going to have her day in court in a month but was released on a high bail. After dropping the name MacDonald to Jena, he was sure she wasn't involved with the con. He decided to go with his gut on this one and rule her out as a connection between the two. Yet, since he didn't know if MacDonald was even involved, he planned to keep a tale on Jena.

Ali text Regan earlier and gave her friend a heads up that she was stopping by. Regan's reply was that she was going to be too busy for a visit. Ali was mindful to the hurt feelings surging through her. Two days after the end of the holiday season was usually very quiet at the salon. This was the week most stylists took a few days off. The season was so crammed right up to the afternoon of New Year's Eve that by the time it was over most people had their look and they were good for a few weeks.

She decided busy or not...they were going to get to the bottom of this. She didn't like her friend avoiding her and lying to her. She knew it would distance their relationship if she didn't iron out all the creases. So Ali's reply to the text was, "Everyone has to eat so I'll grab lunch!"

Ali was relieved Regan was telling the truth about being busy. She had a client in her chair getting a foil. Ali recognized the lady instantly as the one who helped deliver Ana when she was born. She smiled after saying hello to the ladies and was trying hard to think of the woman's name.

Regan and Sue looked up as Ali approached and replied to her hello. Ali could tell Regan had a panicked look in her eye. It looked a lot like guilt to her.

Regan, out of common courtesy, reintroduced them. For the next ten minutes, after the formalities were done, Sue and Ali talked about Ana, Ali's class at school, and how Sue has been working at Ramona's small hospital for the last year. The entire time Ali kept sneaking peeks at her friend and could read the stress in her face as she continued working on Sue's hair. Yep, her friend had guilt written all over her face.

"Regan, I am going to grab lunch next door...would you ladies like something?"

"I don't think I'll have time Al. Sue will only be under the dryer for twenty minutes."

Before Ali could reply Sue spoke up. "Regan, I've got the night shift tonight so it's here, nap and then work with some downtime in between. Have your friend grab the food and if you run out of time just rinse me then go back to finish your lunch." Ali smiled a thanks and looked at Regan for confirmation.

Regan agreed and gave Ali her order of a salad and a mocha. Ali asked Sue if she wanted something and she asked if Ali minded picking her up a veggie sandwich and a mocha as well. Ali would have asked if anyone else wanted anything but *Mystique* was only occupied by the two ladies. Just as she thought, most everyone was taking a few vacation days.

After grabbing the lunches and drinks, Ali handed Sue her drink while she was under the dryer. Sue explained that Regan was in the bathroom. Ali went to the back room and started taking the food out of the bags. Minutes later, as Ali was nibbling on her salad, Regan finally made an appearance. One look at her friend and Regan burst into tears.

Ali walked over and hugged her. Regan sobbed for several minutes before she tried to compose herself. For several minutes neither said a word. Ali knew her friend would talk as soon as she had it completely together.

Regan looked at her best friend and felt like the biggest piece of dirt. "Ali, I'm so sorry. I didn't mean to keep things from you." She took the tissue Ali offered her. "You had a lot going on and I just didn't want to add to it."

Ali hugged her friend. "Regan, I love you. I'm not mad at you...even though I'm not sure what is going on."

"Don't you?" Regan looked up at her and asked.

"No, I don't know what's going on. I think I saw something happening the other night between you and Frank, but I'm not sure what that something is."

Regan pulled away from her and walked to the counter and leaned on it as she turned to her friend. "Well I guess to put it in a nutshell...I'm in love with your brother."

Ali lifted her eyebrows. "Wow, so when did all this happen?"

Regan shook her head. "I don't know...a few months ago. Maybe years ago." She ran her hands through her spiky hair.

Ali looked at her in confusion. Why hadn't she ever noticed her friend had a thing for her brother? Was she so self-absorbed she overlooked something as important as that?

Regan, as if reading her thought, rushed on. "Ali, I kept it very hidden from you. I didn't think anything would ever come from these feelings that started happening months ago."

"Why don't you start at the beginning?"

Regan started pacing. "It all started in the fall. Frank came in to see if your mom could give him a quick haircut. She was very busy so she asked me to do it. I was between clients so I didn't mind." She stopped and looked at her friend. "That's the first time I really ever talked to him. I mean we always were polite to each other but never had a real conversation." She gave her friend a watery smile. "He isn't the most social person out there you know?" Ali nodded in agreement. After a brief pause she continued. "The day I cut his hair it was a fun, flirty conversation." She looked away. "Then well, I don't know, I started thinking about him...a lot!"

She walked over to the table and plopped down on one of the chairs. Ali joined her. "I ran into him a few times and then one night we both happened to be at 'Lisa's' and something exploded between us. We had one incredible night," she smiled at her friend. "I'll spare you the details since he's your brother."

Ali smiled and rolled her eyes. "Thank you."

Regan chuckled, then the tears started falling again. Ali reached across the table and grabbed her hand. "What happened?"

Regan shook her head for a minute, wiped her tears and took a deep breath. "He just doesn't want me!" she whispered.

Ali turned mad…quick. "Are you saying he used you? If he did, I will personally kick…"

"Ali," Regan panicked. "Please don't say anything to him. It will only make it worse. This is why I didn't tell you. I didn't want you getting between your best friend and brother."

Ali got out of her chair and started pacing. "Regan, have you tried talking to him? Are you sure he doesn't want to go forward?"

Regan got her attention when she chuckled. "Well the morning after…that night, he was definitely feeling guilty and basically said it shouldn't have happened. How he hoped I would keep it between us." Regan sighed. "I felt like I was a dirty embarrassment to him. Like he was ashamed to be connected to me. I was confused." She wiped at her eyes again. "You know I have never had a one-night stand. I've only been with the three boyfriends of my past." She was starting to get mad. "I was pissed off and thought 'screw you' and I planned to move forward."

"Then what?" Ali asked.

"Well we started running into each other because of the few meetings at the farm. We have done everything we could to avoid each other. That is until New Year's Eve." Regan grinned. "I have to admit, Will acting like he was interested in me drove Frank over the edge. I never thought Frank capable of jealousy…but man he was that night."

Regan smiled at the memory. Ali asked what happened next?

"Well he walked over to us and stated, rather loudly, that Will was welcome to me. So I chased after him to give him a piece of my mind. We argued outside for a bit. He told me he was confused and blah, blah, blah. Like a fool I followed him back inside and stuck to him like a lovesick fool." She was angry at how weak she had been. "After all the chaos of the evening happened, he held my hand and rushed me to the passenger side of truck. We argued a bit in the truck on the way to my place and…" she chuckled as new tears fell, "we argued all the way to my bedroom where we had another incredible night."

"I take it you haven't heard from him since New Year's?"

She shook her head as her timer went off. In a sad, small, hurt voice she stated, "He left before I woke up."

Ali watched as her friend wiped her eyes and walked out of the room to rinse her client's hair. Ali was heartbroken to see her friend hurt. She was ticked also to know her brother was behind it. She wished she had answers for Regan, but the truth was she didn't know much about Frank's life. He was a great brother, son and uncle, but she had never known him to be in any relationships. Of course he worked and lived across the state line so she didn't see him much, except for Sunday suppers and Holidays.

Regan walked back into the room and explained that she only had a minute because Sue had to use the bathroom and was going to poke her head in the backroom when she was done. Taking a sip of her hot drink she looked over the lid to trying to guess what was going through Ali's mind. She didn't want her friend jumping down Frank's throat. She hoped Ali wouldn't let Frank know she knew about them, even though she realized Ali was his sister and Regan knew she couldn't control what siblings did.

Ali was cleaning up the table and put Regan's uneaten salad in the fridge. "What time are you done today?" she asked her friend?

"After Sue."

Just then Sue entered the room carrying her half-eaten sandwich and drink. "I'm sorry to interrupt girls but can I put my sandwich in the fridge? I want to keep it cold so I can have it for my shift at the hospital later." As the girls replied "of course" in unison. Regan explained she'd be out in a moment to finish Sue's hair. The lady replied that she wasn't in any hurry as she wrapped her sandwich in the paper before Ali set it inside the refrigerator door. Grabbing her drink, she thanked the girls and headed out the door to dry her hair. Both girls appreciated Sue understanding they needed a few more minutes.

At Sue's retreat, Ali knew she had to do something to help her friend. "Okay, I'm coming to your house at five and you and I are going to go have dinner and a bottle of wine. This will be good for us both. I start school back up in two days so there isn't a better time than tonight to hang out."

Regan was so relieved her friend wasn't upset with her. "Sounds good." Regan gave her a hug. "I'm sorry I didn't tell you."

"I get it. No worries. I'll pick you up at five." Ali hugged her and made her way to the front door, after waving to Sue who was bent upside down blow drying her hair. Ali chuckled and thought, 'Only in a small town could you get by with having your client dry their own hair.' Outside she spotted the agent parked next to her car. She wondered what the agent would do if they saw her strangle her brother? She may just have her answer when she gets her hands on him!

***

Abe was bummed that Ali was going to dinner with her friend. He decided it would be a great time to have some one on one with his daughter. That was until he spotted Ali coming down the steps with very tight jeans on and a shirt showing a hint of cleavage.

His palms started to sweat and his throat went dry. Flashbacks of New Year's morning started flashing through his head. 'Shit,' he thought. 'I have to calm down.' Slightly shaking his head, he smiled as she approached him. He pulled her to him and kissed her fast and hard. Ali looked startled and Ana giggled.

Abe looked down at his daughter who grabbed each of her parents' leg and looked up at them. "Daddy, you kissed Mommy!" she stated.

Looking down, he ruffled her hair. "So?" he questioned.

"So!" she stated. "Daddy?" she questioned.

"What Imp?" he asked.

"What's that taste like?" she asked with the curiosity of a four-year-old.

Ali and Abe didn't know what to say. Ali made a hasty retreat to get away from the conversation, but not before she heard Abe reply, "Lips! Slimy lips like on a frog! I'm going to find you a frog so you can kiss it!" Ali smiled at the exchange.

***

Regan lived a few minutes from Ali so the trip didn't take long. As it's always been, the two friends would knock and then let themselves into each other's unlocked house. Well that was before Ali had to be under lock and key.

"Regan, I'm here!" Ali walked into the kitchen and looked out the patio doors into the backyard. It made her sad to see everything brown and dead as winter tends to do to the outside world in this area. She wished it would snow.

A few minutes later she went to find her friend because she never heard Regan's response to her entrance. Looking throughout the house and calling Regan's name she wondered why still didn't receive a response. Ali knew she was home because her car was parked in the garage.

Opening closed doors on her way to Regan's master bathroom. Ali was shocked to see her friend passed out on her bathroom floor. Ali quickly shook her friend calling her name. There was no response. She checked her pulse and felt a slight beat.

Ali quickly ran outside the house and looked around for the agent who was her tail. It didn't take long for her to wave him to her and she reached in her car for her phone. The agent parked quickly and was running to her with his gun ready as she dialed 911. He heard her talking as he followed her in the house to the bathroom. He jumped into action as he searched her for wounds. Ali almost dropped her phone as she dialed Jake's number. The agent, after checking quickly through the house, went down the stairs to guard the door to make sure it wasn't a trap. Within minutes the ambulance was there and rushing Regan to the local hospital.

Ali rode with the agent right behind the ambulance. Jake was at the hospital before they were. He informed the agent to meet the rest of the men who were heading to Regan's house to search it. He called Abe and told him what was happening and for him and Ana to follow the outside agent to the farm. He was making sure it wasn't a trap to get to him and Ana alone at the house.

Ali freaked out as she watched her incoherent friend releasing bile from her throat as she was being transported inside of the ER. Jake quickly grabbed her and headed to the front desk to give them any information needed. Next they headed to the waiting room and…waited!

Ali paced for what seemed like forever. She was babbling on and on. Jake didn't know how to ease her pain. He was glad the room was unoccupied except for the two of them. Ramona Memorial had been a great hospital in its day, but over time hospitals became bigger and in larger cities. The smaller hospitals, like this one, was more for wiping scrapes or putting band aids on. In most cases people would head to Paducah before coming here. Unless it was an emergency like it was right now.

Ali finally lost it when Frank came running through the door like the devil himself was on his heel. "Ali, I just heard…" Panting, he continued. "How is she?" he shouted as he tugged on her sleeve. "Oh God if she doesn't make it…I didn't know…" Turning to Jake. "What are they saying?"

So that's how it was, Jake thought. Damn, how did he miss that one? "Calm down Frank. We don't know anything as of yet."

He had that lost boy look going on in his eyes. "What are her symptoms? I mean what happened? Abe called Mom and told her that Regan was being taken to ER and it was bad. Will said everyone needed to stay put to make sure it wasn't a trap."

Ali hadn't thought about it being a trap. She never thought this had anything to do with the kidnapping. It was probably good they weren't taking chances. Thank God her brother was always prepared for these things. She looked at Frank, her handsome sweet big brother. It was bittersweet to think that it may take a tragedy to make him see what was in front of him. She prayed it wasn't a tragedy. Walking over to Frank they hugged long without a word to each other. He finally pulled away and with a broken voice said to his sister, "I love her Al. I tried fighting it. I didn't think I was ready for all of that, but fell I did." Looking up, he stated, "God please don't take her!"

Ali comforted her brother. She told him to have faith. She watched him pace for hours. Relief came several hours after Regan arrived at the hospital.

The doctor caring for Regan came to speak to the family. Dan and Sandy were there, arriving immediately after Frank. With Dan's permission the doctor could address everyone.

The doctor said he found an extremely large dose of poison in Regan's system. He was almost positive it was eye-drop solution that was used. Two bottles of the solution in a person's system could easily cause the person to be violently ill, if not die from it.

He went on to say that she was resting now and he thought they should wait awhile before seeing her. Dan thanked the man and hugged Sandy to him. Everyone sat down to figure out what happened to Regan.

Ali called Abe and explained everything the doctor said. She asked that he let her parents know what was going on because the phone signal wasn't the greatest at the hospital. She hung up because everyone was gathering in the waiting room to discuss Regan.

Jake was the first to speak. "Any idea what is going on here?"

Before they could speak Frank stood up. "It's my fault. If I didn't treat her like shit these last few months, she wouldn't have tried to hurt herself."

Damn, Jake though, did Frank really think Regan would hurt herself over a man? He didn't think Regan was the type. He understood that suicide was something a person dealt with inside and usually all alone. But Regan, as a rule, put every thought and feeling out there. Jake wasn't a psychiatrist but he dealt with suicide victims before. There was usually some sort of mental condition that controlled it. Or in what he usually dealt with…drugs and mental or physical abuse. The Regan that was like a little sister to him was a fighter. So that put him back to square one. He had to figure out if she accidentally drank the poison or did someone give it to her?

Now Frank's outburst had Dan looking pissed. Ali was looking confused that anyone thought her friend would hurt herself and her loved ones over a guy. Then there was poor Sandy who was looking shocked at the entire picture.

Dan was the first to speak up. "What in the hell do you mean 'hurt her'?" Dan wasn't a big guy but he was tough. You don't become head of security and a large Casino and Resort by being a wimp. And the look Dan was shooting at Frank wasn't good.

Frank turned to the older man and ran his hand through his hair. "I hurt her Dan. I'm sorry. I just didn't know I loved her then…I mean I knew I just didn't want to admit it."

Jake decided to help his brother out and get back on track. "I don't believe Regan did this to herself." When everyone turned to him, he continued. "I never once thought she did this to herself. I'm just wondering how the eyedrops got down her throat?"

197

Ali spoke. "I was with her for lunch and she was fine. She was working." She got up and started pacing again. "We made plans for supper and that was it. She was finishing up and heading home." Looking frustrated she stated, "I'm going to make some coffee." Nodding to the coffee bar across the room. "Does anyone want any? I think it's going to be a long night."

After their declines, Jake continued. "Okay, so where was she between finishing work and heading home? That's what we need to figure out." Jake was interrupted by a nurse letting them know that Regan was awake and if they wanted to see her, they could go in pairs and only for a few minutes at a time.

Ali walked back to join the group when they informed her Regan was able to have a few minutes with family but it needed to be on the downlow. Jake asked the others if they minded if he went in first? He wanted to see if she could give him a clue to what was going on before he headed to Regan's house to get her phone. No one objected. Dan even suggested Frank go with him. Ali knew it was in the form of a truce. Ali assured them she was here for the night, so she was fine if they went first. Both brothers hugged her and Jake explained he was leaving after his visit and would be back later. He saw the worry in his sister's eyes and reassured her there were agents downstairs and keeping cover.

***

After the boys retreated, Dan and Sandy decided to try and find something to eat. Ali looked as her phone to view the text she received from Abe earlier. He was heading to the hospital because he got the okay to take Ana to her parents. Looking at the time, she knew he should be arriving at any minute. She smiled because he asked if he could grab her something. She replied 'that she just got his message and she'd talk to him when he arrived.' She was sure she looked a fright. Now was the perfect time to go to the bathroom to freshen up before he arrived.

Visiting hours were technically over unless there was a life-threatening emergency. So Ali was happy to see she had the bathroom all to herself. While reapplying her lipstick, she spotted Regan's client from earlier today, Sue, enter the bathroom. Ali forgot Sue now worked at this hospital. She was apparently on duty because she was in scrubs and had a sweater draped over her hands.

Looking at the lady through the mirror, Ali greeted her. As the lady returned the greeting. Ali, remembered why she was at the hospital, spun around to look directly at her. "Oh my gosh, did you know they brought Regan in earlier?" Ali put her hands to her chest. "Apparently she has poison in her system."

Sue smiled. "Well of course she does…I put it in the coffee you brought her today."

After several seconds to digest what the woman just said, Ali looked shocked. "What do you mean?"

Sue knew there was no time to waste. She couldn't believe her luck at finding Ali alone. She had been sure she would have to trick her into coming with her. But the bitch made it easy by going to the bathroom.

She moved back the sweater and showed Ali the handgun in her hand. "Listen Miss High and Mighty…one sudden move and a bullet goes through your heart. Try something funny and I'll signal my crew to make sure your little girl had a horrific tragedy. No shoutouts for those big brothers of yours…they are planning to pay your friend a visit and head out. Good thing I heard them give you your goodbyes."

Ali knew by the look in her eyes this lady wasn't kidding. "What do you want?"

Sue smiled. "I want you! An eye for an eye!" Shoving her to the door she quietly told her to move. As they approached the door Sue grabbed her arm and held her back as she peeked out into the empty corridor. Noticing it was clear she pulled Ali along toward the door. "Right now you need to get in front of me and when we exit you go left to the elevators down the hall. Once inside I need you to hit 'B' floor." She stuck the tip of the gun to Ali's cheek. "Do you understand me?" she asked with intense hatred.

Ali nodded and led the way to the elevators. Sue smiled to herself as they entered the elevator. There's no way anyone would suspect her involvement in this dead little hospital. Nothing happened here after eight in the evenings. She put in for her lunch and no one would know she wasn't outside smoking a cigarette because none of the other RN's on duty smoked. It was amazing how everything was falling into place. She was sure it was her sister's doings.

Shutting down the cameras was smart. No one paid any attention to the camera room. Yep, who knew when she woke up this morning, she was going to have the chance to get her revenge.

***

Regan was groggy and tired, but to her relief she watched as Jake came through the door. She spotted Frank behind him and wondered why he was there? She could barely talk because she was afraid it would make her sick. Yet she had to talk to Jake. She had to warn him. Trying to sit up, she whispered for a drink of water. Jake came through with the water and Frank helped her scoot up and then push the up button on the bed.

199

"Jake, where's Ali and Ana?" she whispered.

"They're fine Regan. Ali's with your dad and Sandy in the waiting room. Ana's at my parent's house with Will."

Regan started to panic. She had to throw up. Grabbing the bowl she emptied the clear liquid the hospital put in her system to help eject the poison out. Jake gave her a bit of privacy while Frank held the bowl for her. She wiped her face with a towel and fell back on the bed.

Jake thought she was too sick to talk and decided to let her get some rest. Regan was having none of it. Grabbing his arm she stopped him from leaving. "Jake, Ali. I think I have it figured out."

She took a gulp of water to clear the burning in her throat. "When I came awake a little while ago, my client, the nurse Sue, was doing something with all these gadgets on me. I guess I looked confused." She took another drink so she could cool off the burning in her throat that was trying to prevent her from speaking. "Sue started explaining to me that I had poison in my system and that the doctor was coming in to talk to me in a little while. After she left, I got to wondering how I could have possibly been poisoned. I didn't do it to myself. So then I started thinking about what I ate and drank." She took another drink. "The only two people I was with today were Sue and Ali." She paused to cough and take another drink before continuing. "Ali grabbed the three of us some coffees from the shop next door. So after thinking this, I remembered Sue's boyfriend or husband was a shady guy. Then I remembered that Sue was always asking me questions about Ali. I don't know, Jake, I have a bad feeling…"

In the next instance…everything happened at once. Jake ran from the room, Frank quickly reached for the bowl, and Regan missed the bowl and got Frank instead.

***

Jake ran into the waiting room and asked Dan if he knew where Ali was? Dan said he had no clue. She wasn't in the room when they returned from trying to find something to eat. Jake turned to exit and ran into Abe.

"Whoa Jake…what's wrong?" Abe asked.

Jake reached down and started opening a location app on his phone. "Where's Ali?"

Abe heard and saw the panic. "I don't know I just got here…why?"

Jake panicked. "Help me find her." As he rushed out the door into the corridors.

"Can you track her?" Abe was baffled as to what was happening. He could tell by Jake's demeanor, something bad was happening and it involved Ali.

Jake was rushing in and out of every room. "It won't load."

Abe and Jake looked for several minutes before they tried the ladies' restroom. They felt instant panic when they spotted her purse and makeup bag on the sink. Leaving the room they started shouting for her as Jake called in backup.

Looking down at his phone Jake was relieved to see his tracking app was loaded and had whereabouts of Ali's location. He became stressed when the directions brought them to the elevator. Not sure if they needed to go up the two levels of the hospital or down into the basement, he sent Abe up and he went down the steps.

Chapter Twenty-Two

Ali was on the verge of tears as she led the way to the basement morgue. Sue shoved her through the door and Ali came up short when she spotted the man who tried to abduct her daughter, standing in front of her, with a gun pointed right at her face. It was the same man Jake had pictures of only he was much uglier in person which was why Ali couldn't positively identify him.

Sue shoved her further in the door and spoke to the man. "We have to hurry Mac. I don't know what kind of time we have. She was here with her two brothers but they left. The older couple took off to look for food so they won't think anything about her not being there."

The Mac guy replied. "Take her out of here in one of the bags," indicating with a nod at the row of body bags handing along a wall, "or keep her alive until later?"

Sue looked at Ali to see what she thought about Mac's words. By her stricken expression Sue knew the other girl figured out she wasn't coming out of this alive. It gave her great pleasure to see the fear in her eyes.

For the first time Ali spoke with panic in her voice. "I don't understand why you are doing this?" She looked at Sue with pleading eyes. "What did I ever do to you?"

Sue just laughed. "I'm sorry sweetie it wasn't you who did anything." At Ali's confused look, Sue continued. "You see I had a sister once. I loved her as much as your brother loves you. She took care of me when our parents died." As she spoke, she flung her hands and gun around. To Ali the lady didn't look like she was in her right mind. "My sister had to make sacrifices. She did that so she could put me through nursing school." She glared at Ali. "Do you know how hard it is to put someone through nursing school? No you don't. Life was handed to you on a platter." She nearly shouted.

Ali was more confused than ever. "Sue, I still don't understand this hatred you have for me. What did I ever do to you?"

"You did nothing!" Her voice got higher as she went on. "You are a victim of circumstance." She rubbed the gun across Ali's face. "You see my sister had to make money and in order to do that she had to make choices. Her destiny was to help other girls with their choices." Her eyes flared again. "They didn't realize at the time that she was helping them by making the choices for them. She was paid well to convince them they needed to do as she said. She even gave them what made them feel good."

She moved closer to Ali making her back up as far as she could go. "She kept me from the men though. She didn't want me to have that life. I was to have better choices. A respectable job. One that she benefited from when she needed the meds to make the girls feel good and listen to her!"

"She always kept me close by to protect me. She'd rent me my own rooms so the men didn't know I was there." She smirked before continuing. "I wouldn't have known he killed her if she hadn't rented a room across the hall from where she kept her girls. I was across the hall the day he took her life. She didn't want to die…just like you don't want to die." Getting close to Ali's face she whispered, "But an eye for an eye!"

As she raised her gun Ali pleaded for her to explain. "Why me…I don't understand!"

Sue backed away as she held the gun to Ali's face. "I want to kill you because your brother Jake took my sister from me!" At Ali's confused look she continued. "Yes Princess, he's the bastard who took her life. And I promised myself I would take from him." Now openly crying she shouted, "Sally was all I truly ever had and he killed her. I want to get even." She laughed and backed up a few steps with the gun still trained on Ali. "I moved to this backwards town just to find you and make you pay." Her eyes were pure evil. "I even went to all the trouble of having your buddy do my hair." She gave Ali a look of disgust. "The first time we came face to face was while I was getting my hair done. You were talking about going to that bar in downtown Nashville. Do you know I was there that night? I was going to kill you then…but you never showed up!" she yelled.

Ali was too distraught to understand what she was talking about. Then it dawned on her it was the night she met Abe. She remembered telling Regan she was hoping to go out with Kris that Thursday night, but Kris went home and Ali met Abe.

"I see you remember what I'm talking about." Sue put the gun next to her mouth. "You didn't freaking show up. No you got knocked up by your rich baby daddy instead. So then I caught my first break because you were delivering your brat at my hospital. Of course it wasn't much of a break because most everyone delivers there. I pulled some serious hours around your due date." She pulled the gun away and stepped back a few steps. Ali noticed the guy wasn't doing anything but watching the confrontation.

Sue started laughing. "I was going to take her from you that night…your little girl! But then I heard you talking about the daddy." She laughed. "What a lucky break. I was waiting in the hall for Anita to come in and fill out the baby's birth certificate and I hear you freak out when Regan was flipping through the channels." She flung her hands, gun and all, in the air. "I couldn't believe my luck listening to you announce that Abraham Parker was your kid's daddy! I knew the gods were shining down on me!" She walked to the door and peeked out making sure no one was in the corridor. Turning back to Ali, she continued, "I decided to wait for the right time to snag her. It was going to be easier that way then getting her from the hospital…plus I figured I'd cash in with the daddy for all my troubles. The timing had to be perfect. So waiting a few years was much easier."

"Sue." Ali begged. "Please don't do this. I don't know the circumstances between you and Jake, but know he would never hurt anyone unless he had no other choice!" Tears were falling down her face.

"HE KILLED MY SISTER!" she screeched.

Before Ali could reply she heard Jake's voice coming from the doorway. "Sue, I didn't kill your sister…she took her own life."

Sue spun around with her gun and screamed at Jake. "LIAR, you made her want to take her life! She knew you were going to lock her up and for no reason. Those girls wanted the candy and they loved spreading their legs."

"No they didn't, Sue," Jake stated calmly. "Your sister stole them from their families. They didn't want to be drugged and sold that way." He looked at her calmly. "Besides, your beef is with me Sue. Kill me. Leave Ali out of it."

Her eyes became even more evil if that was possible. "You're a fucking liar…they wanted it and I'm avenging my sister. I watched from the keyhole across the hall. She begged you not to shoot her, but she knew you were going to so she jumped from the window," she screamed.

Before he could reply she held the gun up and took aim for him and shot. Jake hit the ground and leaped inside the room just as Abe came rushing up behind him and taking the bullet to his chest. Ali screamed and tossed a metal cart toward Mac causing him to shoot toward the ceiling. Jake shot twice taking out both Sue and Mac.

Ali rushed to the outside corridor to where Abe fell and was lying in a pool of blood. Ali, crying, kept begging Abe to talk to her. She was pressing her hand over his wound to stop the blood from flowing. Around her agents were swarming everywhere.

Thank the Good Lord the doctor who was caring for Regan heard the commotion and was by her side barking orders in no time. Jake ushered her away from Abe as the staff took over. She didn't want to leave him but she was smart enough to know his only chance was in the doctor's hands.

Time seemed to stand still as the doctor worked. Several long minutes Ali watched as they lifted him onto a gurney and rushed him through the elevator doors. Her legs wouldn't move as she cried into Jake's shirt. "He's not going to make it, is he, Jake? I mean you see this crap all the time."

"Al, you have to have faith that God will bring him back to you." He replied even though he didn't want to speak. It was his fault his sister was almost killed. He always knew his family was in danger when he took on working for the Bureau. That was why he didn't work too closely to where his family lived. But apparently that didn't matter. They still found a way for their revenge. Now it looked like Abe may be the one to pay.

Jake finally talked her into going to the surgery waiting room. On the way there they passed the chapel and she asked him to wait a few minutes while she lit a candle and said a prayer for Abe.

Waiting outside, with shaking hands, he called Will out at the farm and filled him in on what happened. Will reassured him everything was okay there but he would wake the parents and explain what was going on. Jake asked if he'd head to town and help out at the hospital.

Next, Jake informed one of the agents to have the staff keep everything on the low key because he was sure paparazzi was still hanging out. Tyler replied they were already there since Abe showed up at the hospital earlier. The good thing was they were kept at bay because the hospital visitor hours were over when Abe arrived and the agents and staff only allowed him through the door…unless there was an emergency from the outside which there wasn't. Since then they heard and saw a commotion with agents running inside the building. Many were trying to figure out a way to get in…but the feds weren't budging and the paparazzi was cooperating as far as they could tell. Jake told him to tell the reporters there would be a press conference soon if they promised to be good.

When Ali was finished at the chapel Jake escorted her to the waiting room where Sandy rushed to Ali and embraced her with a crying hug. Jake couldn't look at Sandy knowing it was his fault that her son was in surgery and not sure if he was going to live or not.

He was glad for the distraction when Will arrived at the hospital waiting room. He informed Jake that Ali's parents were staying put with Ana but send their love and prayers. Will left two agents at the farm to make sure there was no more trouble.

Jake pulled Will aside. "I need a favor?"

Will was worried about his partner and friend. He knew Jake was beating himself up inside about the entire ordeal. Jake was blaming himself and Will needed to make him see the light. "Anything…as long as you get it out of that stubborn-ass head of yours that you had nothing to do with this."

Jake gave him somber eyes. "How can I not? That psycho broad wouldn't have targeted my family had it not been for me."

Will was becoming angry. "Are you fucking kidding me? Her sister was ahead of a sex trafficking bust that caused four girls to be murdered by their rapist and three girls take their own lives. Not counting all the girls hooked on heroin and God only knows what else from that bitch shooting the shit in their arms."

Will could tell he wasn't getting anywhere but he kept trying. "You knew when we signed up for this job that we put everyone we care about in jeopardy. But we also save thousands of lives by risking ours. Jake don't do this to yourself."

Jake didn't want to listen. He just needed Abe to come through surgery and then he wanted to meet up with the agents sweeping the nurse's house. "About that favor…can you speak at a press conference? Abe is famous so someone has to and since I'm ahead of the case it should be me, but I want to meet up with the others as they go through their house?" Before Will replied he added, "I got ahold of Abe's agent Max and he just text back that he would be here ASAP. I don't want the conference until we know what happens in surgery."

Will nodded and told his friend he had it covered. Jake turned and spotted Amanda rushing through the waiting room doors and hug her mother. Jake mumbled that they needed to keep each other informed and he would send Frank out to check on Ali. Before Will could reply, Jake was already heading through the door.

The next several hours were full of stress and pacing for Ali. Everything seemed surreal. She refused to believe she was going to lose Abe after just finding him again. She cried every time she thought about how she would have to explain to her daughter that her daddy was gone.

Walking over to the window she looked out at the starry sky and begged God to keep Abe alive. She made all kinds of promises. She would pray more and go to church more. She would go on the road with Abe if he wanted her to. She pleaded for her daughter's sake as well.

Looking up she watched the stars twinkle and thought about how this situation reminded her of a country song.

***

What seemed like days, but was only hours, the doctor finally arrived to speak with the crowd of family and friends that gathered in the waiting room. He explained that Abe was in critical condition. The bullet went through his lung, causing lack of oxygen, which in turn caused a lung to collapse. Between the loss of blood and the surgery to remove the bullet, it was up to the Good Lord and Abe to pull through.

Sandy asked if they could sit with him? The doctor explained that he was only allowing two at a time. Abe's mother stated to everyone that Ali be allowed to sit with her son the entire time and everyone else could take turns seeing him. Ali was so grateful to the older lady, she hugged her before heading back to be with Abe.

Max and Will were discussing the press conference, that was scheduled in a few hours, and exactly how they were going to address Abe's fans. It was decided they would give the truth…just not all of it. In a nutshell they were going to explain that a hardened criminal was shooting up the hospital and Abe got in the way while he was there visiting a friend. Max was sure the people were going to be more interested in Abe's condition than with every little detail of the shooting.

Over the next twenty-four hours, with the exception of using the bathroom, Ali never left Abe's side. The first hour was the hardest as she stared at all the tubes extracting from his body. His handsome face was such a deadly white, that Ali was sure he wasn't going to pull through.

After she got over the shock, she got tough. Between family members coming in to see Abe, she whispered all the reasons for him to fight. She repeatedly explained how badly she and Ana needed him. She made promise after promise. She described in details all the beautiful ways she planned to make love to him if he got better.

After several hours of no response, the doctor decided Abe his entire family could come in to say goodbye. Ali was angry this decision was made because the staff felt this was the end for Abe. The thought of everyone giving up put her over the edge. Determined she wasn't giving up and making sure Abe wasn't giving up, she decided to threaten him to get better.

She explained how she would never let their daughter listen to 'sappy country music' again. She went on to tell him that if he didn't get better, she would just have to marry Todd and have Ana call him daddy. To her delight, Abe showed his first sign that he could hear her…he squeezed her hand. Ali smiled because she knew he was telling her he didn't want Todd anywhere near her and Ana.

A few minutes later, Sandy came in crying and asked Ali to walk over to the window. Ali was stunned when she looked out at the thousands of candles burning in the hands of Abe's fans. It was a never-ending sight.

She turned to Sandy. "How did they find out Abe was injured?"

Sandy put her arm around Ali's waist. "There was a press conference yesterday."

Ali remembered there was talk about a press conference in the waiting room the day before but was too worried about Abe to pay attention. Looking out at all the people, she smiled as she wiped at her tears. "There are so many that truly love him." She sniffled. "It's just like in the movies. I just never knew that people really came together with candles to pray for someone."

Sandy smiled. "They are from all over. According to Dan, the town was wall to wall with people coming in today."

Ali turned back and sat on the chair she was occupying before Sandy came in. Taking Abe's hand she smiled at Sandy as she took the seat on Abe's other side. "I think he squeezed my hand a few minutes ago."

Sandy smiled, dabbed at her eyes with a tissue, and took Abe's other hand. "I know he's going to pull through. He loves you and Ana too much to leave!"

"And he loves his momma and sister too much to leave." Ali stated.

Just then they both felt his fingers softly squeeze into their hands. Each one looked at Abe's sleeping face and then at each other. Ali was the first to speak. "He just did it again!" Her voice was raw and full of shock.

"I felt it too!" Abe's mother replied as she brushed his hair off of his forehead.

Both ladies were looking at his face when they noticed his mouth moving. Ali and Sandy quickly moved closer to hear what he was saying. Ali couldn't understand what he was saying. Sandy gave Ali a confused look. "I think he said something like...my baby calls no one daddy but me."

Ali softly laughed and kissed his forehead. "I promise you Abe, Ana will only ever call you dad!" She covered her hand over her mouth to stop the tears and she looked at the smile that came across his face.

After a night of Abe in and out of sleep, the doctor declared Abe was going to make a full recovery. His vitals looked good, but it would be a few months before he would be singing for his fans. Abe was fine with that. He just wanted to hold Ali's hand and stare at her beautiful face.

He remembered the fear he had when he and Jake went looking for her. He heard the shouting coming from the morgue and knew the crazy lady was going to kill her. He remembered Jake in the morgue entrance doorway and his plan was to sneak past him to the next set of doors that read morgue exit. He was hoping to be the distraction Jake needed. But who would have guessed the crazy broad would shoot the second Abe tried to sneak past?

***

Family came and went throughout the day. There were guards posted outside his door to keep out the paparazzi and fans. Everyone cleared out when Abe started to fall asleep later that afternoon. Just as he started drifting, he woke up to Jake standing over his bed.

Abe smiled at his friend. "I guess I don't make a good Hutch to your Starsky?"

Jake grinned, but Abe noticed it didn't reach his eyes. "You did good. The timing just wasn't so good."

"Bad luck on my end." He smiled. "It's not so bad, I got your sister to declare her love for me." He rolled his eyes. "Well she did when she thought I was unconscious." He gave Jake a perplexed look. "Come to think of it, she hasn't said it since I woke up."

"I think you're good buddy," Jake walked over to the window before looking back at Abe. "Listen Abe, I came here to apologize."

"What do you have to apologize for? You caught the kidnappers and saved your sister all in one whack!"

Jake shook his head slowly. "It was my fault from the beginning. That crazy lady was after me. And the way she was going to get to me was by taking my sister out. She had been hunting Ali for almost five years." He looked back out the window. "Her house was a shrine of pics of Ali and Ana. She lived her last five years seeking revenge because she wanted to hurt me!"

"Jake, I know what happened. Will filled us in. But listen man…this wasn't your fault. You saved so many lives by busting her sister and her pals. I can't imagine what those girls went through."

Jake shook his head. "I should have gone undercover. I shouldn't have charged in as myself when I busted them. By doing that I put everyone in my family at risk."

"Don't you realize that you save hundreds of lives all the time? Everyone you save in turn saves more. Every criminal you bust, makes the next criminal with a sick mind think twice about pulling the same crap." He looked Jake hard in the eyes. "Do you realize that could be Ana one day being lured into their sick world? So we need people like you to come in and rescue the helpless. So you have to quit beating yourself up about this!"

Jake walked and stood at the end on his bed. "Listen…I just wanted to stop by and say I'm sorry…" He held his hand up when Abe was about to argue that he didn't have to apologize about. "And ask that you watch out for my two girls." He grinned. "You actually make a good Hutch. But anyhow I'm needed in Memphis and everything is pretty much wrapped up here."

"Did you tell your sister goodbye?"

He shook his head. "No, but she knows how to find me." For the first time since entering the room, his grin actually reached his eyes. "Tell her that she will be happy to know that Jena had retracted everything in the gossip rag and as of this morning she had been sentenced to two hundred hours of community service…aka street and highway cleanup."

"I wish you would stick around and tell her yourself. She's coming back with Ana. She's going to be bummed she didn't get to see you!"

"I'll be back soon. Because I'm betting I'm going to be in a wedding sometime soon?" he asked with his eyebrows lifted.

Abe grinned. "I have to first get her to admit she loves me when I'm conscious."

Jake chuckled and said his goodbye.

***

Abe loved the sound of his little girl rushing into the room saying daddy, daddy. Because he couldn't hug her, he held one of her hands. At first, she was eyeing up all the contraptions that were hooked up to him. Yet it didn't take long for her to ask about every wire and hose. He was clueless to what each one did so he made up things as he went along. He explained that the tube going into his nose was there to shoot scents of chocolate up his nose. And the one to his chest was to give his insides a bath. Of course the bag of water dripping into his arm was because his fingers were thirsty.

Ali smiled as Ana giggled at Abe's crazy explanations. She loved that he was so good with his daughter. Heck, she loved everything about him.

Abe looked up and smiled at Ali as he spoke to Ana. "So guess what Ana?"

"What Daddy?"

"Well it would seem that your mommy loves me!" he grinned.

"Duh!" stated the little girl.

Ali didn't understand what Abe was up to? Her only guess was he was letting her know he heard every little thing she told him when he was "unconscious!" Then it suddenly dawned on her everything she whispered to him…including every way she planned to have her way with him.

Abe laughed at her blush and knew she was remembering the things she promised him. He winked at her and turned to Ana and said, "I bet you didn't know this…but I love your momma as much as I love you!"

His little girl's face lit up. "You love me too?"

He rubbed his hand down her hair. "More than you know baby girl!"

"I love you too, Daddy!" She smiled, Abe choked back tears and Ali rubbed at the tears running down her face!

Abe reached his hand to Ali. She walked over and took it before reaching into him. "I love you, Abe Parker." She kissed him softly.

***

Regan and Frank came to see Abe after Regan received her discharge papers. Sandy, guessing the group wanted to discuss the events from the past few days, decided to walk Ana to the cafeteria. After they left, Abe filled them in on what he knew as fact and what was speculated about Sue and the kidnapping.

Regan, in hindsight, put together many things about Sue's obsession with Ali. Ali explained everything Sue said to her in the morgue. It still gave her chills to talk about it.

Talk jumped from one subject to the next. Yet it didn't take long for Regan to bring up Jake. "Will explained that Jake was beating himself up over the entire incident."

Ali was surprised to hear this. She had rarely left Abe's side so she was clueless to what Jake was putting himself through. "Why would he be beating himself up?"

Frank replied. "Because Sue retaliated against him with you as her target, he feels like he put you and Ana in the line of fire!" Before Ali could reply, Frank continued. "Al, I know and everyone here knows that's not the case. We also know that what Jake and the boys do is so important that without it this country would go to hell." He paused, before continuing. "He always was far enough away so he could separate his work from his family, yet close enough to be here when we need him. The 'never marry and settle down because I'd put my wife and kids in jeopardy' attitude he could control, but he already had a family so he couldn't stop the psychotic criminals from coming after his family. His biggest fear became his reality the day Sue came looking for you."

Ali was genuinely upset. "I never once blamed him. Sue was the crazy, strung out, psychopath."

"I get it." Frank stated and hugged his sister. "Just give him a little time to work through the fear he felt of you and Ana in danger out of his system."

Abe watched as Ali nodded before staring at his sister's hurt look while she stared out the window. He was sure something intense happened between

and Jake. He just hoped they'd figure it out before things got awkward
en the two families!

Chapter Twenty-Three

The recuperating process took a few weeks. Yet in no time Abe was up and ready to go. Ali thought he was pushing it but he reassured her he was doing fine.

Abe had plans and he was in a hurry to see them through. His first item up was canceling his tour. It wasn't by choice, even though he wasn't bummed about it. His doctor explained that his lung would take a while to completely repair itself so no singing for months.

Max agreed this was the out Abe needed. So Abe took it and ran. It was crazy, but he was ecstatic to be walking away from all the craziness that came with the music industry. His time in the hospital gave him time to think about the important things in life…Ali and Ana.

In no time Abe fell in love with the town of Ramona and its corky people. He laughed because the town was notorious for having fundraisers. There was one for everything.

Abe smiled as he adjusted the bow tie, that went perfectly with his tux, as he got ready for the father/daughter dance fundraiser. The event was scheduled for the evening at the town social house.

The rule was little girls four through eighteen could attend with their fathers, grandfathers, uncles, or any close males in their lives. So of course his Ana wanted her daddy, grandfather, and all her uncles, minus Jake because he was undercover somewhere.

Ali, determined she wasn't missing out on the evening, volunteered herself and Regan to help with refreshments. Of course Sandy and Lana refused to sit at home in either, so they volunteered at the dessert table. Abe had to chuckle as he thought about how the town was going to feel like Mason and company took over the event.

The dance was in full circle. Girls of all ages danced with the special men in their lives. Ali was dancing with Frank Sr. and Regan was twirling around the dance floor with her father Dan.

Abe was having a great time spinning his daughter in his arms as the band, the same one from New Year's Eve, played one of his upbeat songs. Ana was 't word for word. Abe knew tonight was the best night of his life, with ِtion on the night he and Ali met.

Throughout the evening Ali and Abe would make eye contact and smile. Every time he looked at her, she took his breath away. He wondered how he ever got so lucky…but then the thought of his father popped in his head and then he knew.

Looking up, he noticed Dean nodding at him that it was time. He walked Ana over to her mother and explained he'd be right back before taking off. Mother and daughter didn't give his retreat a second thought.

Suddenly they looked up to see Abe on the stage with a microphone in his hand asking everyone to give him their attention. Ali was immediately worried that it was too soon for Abe to be singing. The doctor said it would be months.

Abe smiled as the crowd quieted. "Thank you, ladies and gentlemen." He gave everyone that smile that seemed to mesmerize people. "I'm sorry to interrupt your evening but this will only take a minute."

Ali was confused to what Abe was up to. She caught Regan's asking eyes, but shrugged because she was clueless.

Abe continued, "I want to start by saying thank you Ramona for taking care of us again and again. I was blessed to have you pray for me. I also know that you will always look out for my loved ones." He paused because many people started applauding. He waited until it died down before continuing. "I'd like to take a moment to ask Ali and my daughter to come join me on the stage." He grinned as he looked at Ali's stricken face through the crowd.

She was ready to bolt. The only thing that saved her was Ana pulling on her arm and rushing through the crowd to get to her daddy. Ali almost tripped up the steps to get to the stage.

Ali reached Abe and whispered under her breath. "What are you doing?"

Abe gave her a big hug and whispered, "I love you!" into her ear. She was sure her mouth dropped open when Abe got down on one knee. "Ali Mason and Ana Mason-Parker, my life and my loves, will you both marry me so we can become a family?"

Ali put her hands to her open mouth and could feel the tears fall. Ana jumped up and down and was shouting. "Yes, Yes, Yes!" Abe stood and opened a necklace box for his daughter and put the locket around her little neck!

Abe grabbed the little girl and gave her a hug before putting her down. He kneeled and took out a ring box and looked up at Ali and continued. "Ali, you have made my life complete. From the moment I met you, you've grabbed my heart and have taken possession of it. And in turn you've giving me two of the most valuable things I could ever want..." He smiled at her tears. "My daughter and your love! Will you marry me?"

Ali smiled through the tears. "Yes! Of course yes…I'll marry you!" She hugged him. "I love you so much!"

Abe was so excited, he slipped the ring on her finger and twirled her around and kissed her hard on the mouth! Grinning he stated, "I love you, and this is one country song that doesn't end sadly!!!"

The End

CPSIA information can be obtained
at www.ICGtesting.com
Printed in the USA
LVHW010854070121
675854LV00009B/633

9 781643 781457